The Desert Siren

Also by Kim Antieau

Novels
The Blue Tail • *Broken Moon* • *Butch*
Church of the Old Mermaids • *Coyote Cowgirl*
Deathmark • *The Fish Wife* • *The Gaia Websters*
Her Frozen Wild • *Jewelweed Station*
The Jigsaw Woman • *Maternal Instincts* • *Mercy, Unbound*
Queendom: Feast of the Saints • *The Rift* • *Ruby's Imagine*
Swans in Winter • *Whackadoodle Times* • *Whackadoodle Times Two*

Nonfiction
Answering the Creative Call
*Certified: Learning to Repair Myself and the World
in the Emerald City*
Counting on Wildflowers: An Entanglement
Old Mermaids Book of Days and Nights
The Old Mermaids Oracle
*The Salmon Mysteries:
a Reimagining of the Eleusinian Mysteries*
*The Salmon Mysteries Workbook:
Reimagining the Eleusinian Mysteries*
Under the Tucson Moon

Collections
Entangled Realities (with Mario Milosevic)
The First Book of Old Mermaids Tales
Tales Fabulous and Fairy • *Trudging to Eden*

Chapbook
Blossoms

Blog
www.kimantieau.com

Photography
www.kimantieau.smugmug.com

The Desert Siren

Kim Antieau

Green Snake PUBLISHING

The Desert Siren
by Kim Antieau

Copyright © 2012 by Kim Antieau

ISBN: 978-1-949644-35-7

All Rights Reserved.

Cover illustration copyright © by Elena Duvernay | Dreamstime.com
Book design by Mario Milosevic and Kim Antieau
Special thanks to Nancy Milosevic and Ruth Ford Biersdorf

Electronic editions of this book are
available at most e-book stores.

Published by Green Snake Publishing
www.greensnakepublishing.com

www.kimantieau.com

for all those who live in the borderlands

and

in memory of

Olivia Elizabeth Luna Noguera,

who never made it home

Chapter One

Connie Johnson heard Jimmy barking in her dream. And a truck speeding away. She opened her eyes—her heart racing—and the dog still barked. For an instant, she smelled ocean. She threw off the covers and ran to the window. Jimmy chased Chuck's yellow pickup as it headed toward the open ranch gates. Dust billowed up behind the vehicle, like an instant smoke screen, enveloping the truck so that it nearly disappeared from view as it drove away.

Chuck turned the wrong way. He was supposed to go out to-day and round up strays with her brother, Philip. Instead he had turned west, toward town.

Jimmy was howling.

"Damn dog," Connie said. She sat on the bed, reached for her jeans, and pulled them on.

Was her alarm clock broken or had Chuck turned it off?

She pulled off her camisole, threw it into the closet, then grabbed another camisole from the clean clothes piled in the basket that was usually in the closet to collect dirty clothes.

She hadn't had time to fold clothes yesterday, or the day before. She was spending more and more time taking care of other people's horses. She preferred that to doing anything with cattle. That was Chuck's thing.

Thirty years ago he was the one who had wanted to come live on the ranch her aunt Delilah had left to Connie and her brother. Chuck and Phil had decided that raising cattle was the way to make their fortune. They had divided the land between the two families—Connie and Chuck taking Delilah's old house and Phil and Marilyn building a new house—but they managed the cattle part of the ranch together.

Connie didn't like cattle or cattle ranching. She had cried when they took down Aunt Delilah's sign "Sky Blue Horse Ranch" and put up "C&C Ranch."

She should have realized the new name of the ranch foretold her future: one with no imagination.

She glanced at the pile of clean clothes. She hadn't folded them and put them away and neither had Chuck. Not that he ever would. In the beginning of their marriage, they had argued about such things. She'd say, "Just because I've got ovaries that doesn't make me any more capable of doing laundry or cooking or cleaning than you!" He'd agree, but if she wasn't out on the range working the cattle, she had to do something to contribute to the household.

Yep, that was what he had said.

"You can't spend your life looking for a mythical herd of Irish horses like your aunt did," he said. "She had a dead rich husband. She didn't need income. You don't have that." He had grinned when he said that last little bit. She still remembered the conversation even though it had happened thirty plus years earlier. Maybe because they had similar conversations over the years since then—until they didn't.

Sometimes during these conversations, she'd say, "They

aren't *Irish* horses. They don't have a nationality. They're *sea* horses."

Only that hadn't done much for her argument.

Irish or not, according to Aunt Delilah, no one could see these mythical horses unless they had "the gift." Most people could see one or two hoof prints belonging to the sea horses. But if someone had "the gift" they could see more—they could actually track and find the horses. On some hot desert mornings, a person could smell them, Aunt Delilah said, and they smelled like the ocean.

No one actually believed Aunt Delilah. At least no one in Connie's family—not even Connie, even though she and Manuel had looked for the horses when she was a girl and her parents sent her and Phil to the ranch for the summers.

At least, she didn't think she believed in them.

Why was she thinking about the sea horses now?

Maybe if she threw the clean clothes on the floor, Chuck would pick them up and put them away.

No. She had tried that when they were younger, before Amy and then Matt were born.

She shook her head. She didn't have time for reminiscing. She was already late. She had to check on Alice's horse. It had eaten something it shouldn't have—probably some trash the migrants or drug runners had left behind as they tramped through the Ellis ranch. Yesterday Charlie Dunnett had called about a colt of his who had gotten spooked and clawed by a mountain lion. She needed to look at his horse today.

Jimmy was still barking.

What was wrong with that dog?

She needed to call Chuck and find out what was going on.

Connie hurried out of the bedroom and went down the stairs. A second story on a house in the Sonora Desert was a stupid idea. She should have never let Chuck build it on the end of Delilah's house—the house that had been in her family for a hundred and fifty years. But Chuck didn't think a house was a home without a staircase. Even in the summer when the upstairs was too stifling or in the winter when it was too cold.

Connie went down the hall and through the living room to the front door. She flung it open and went out and stood on the porch. The cool air smelled slightly of mesquite. Desert scrubland rolled away from the house in all directions, flat as a pancake, until it started dipping here and there, creating bigger than mole-hill hills until finally the land became mountainous in the distance. Today an early morning fog or haze turned the mountains almost blue so that if Connie hadn't lived in this place for most of her adult life, she wouldn't have known the mountains were there.

"You act like he's never coming back, you old sheep dog," Connie called to Jimmy. "I think you've gone crazy spending too much time with the cattle. I can relate." The black and white Australian sheep dog ran into the house past her.

Connie followed him into the kitchen.

She saw a note on the table. The paper looked too white against the yellow tablecloth, almost like a flat bleached bone, with black markings on it where a coyote had gnawed on it.

Connie realized her heart was still beating in her ears, as though her heart knew something she did not.

Her left hand shook as she reached for the paper.

She heard Jimmy's nails on the stone floor. She needed to trim them soon: The sound was becoming maddening.

She recognized her husband's elegant handwriting immediately. Her left-hand scrawl was barely legible, while Chuck's looked like calligraphy. Or something. Something beautiful.

She wanted to keep thinking about how it looked so she wouldn't have to see what it said.

What Chuck had written.

Chuck rarely wrote her a note. He rarely wrote anything, except maybe a list for the hardware or feed store.

She read the first sentence.

"I can't do this anymore."

She blinked and kept reading. "I want to find someplace with water. I took a little money to get started. The combination to the lock is Amy's birthday left, Matt's birthday right, your birthday left."

Connie pulled out a kitchen chair and sat in it.

"What lock?" She didn't remember any lock.

Her hands began to shake.

"He took money?" What money? They hardly had any money.

She felt like she was going to throw up.

Chuck had left her?

He left her?

After thirty years.

After thirty years, he left her.

Without having the guts to face her?

What about the kids? Had he called them? Sent them letters?

Had he written, "I can't be your father anymore. I want to find someplace with water."

What didn't he want to do anymore? Her? The ranch? What?

She tried to remember what had happened yesterday. What had been the last straw? He had said that in the letter, right? Yesterday was the last straw.

She picked up the letter again.

No, nothing about a straw.

Had he been planning this for days, weeks, years?

She got up from the table and began to pace. Jimmy watched her and whimpered.

"Yesterday, yesterday." He had been out with Phil all day, buying cattle or looking for strays.

She and Chuck had gotten home about the same time.

The sun had been going down and everything was golden. Golden tinged with red. They had stood on the porch together, looking around.

He had said, "It looks like Midas himself was here, touching each piece of our world with gold."

She had smiled and reached for his hand.

Connie laughed and shook her head as she walked back and forth in her living room. Chuck had said no such thing.

He had actually said, "It's gonna be a cold one tonight."

And then they had gone into the house together. Connie had heated up leftover spaghetti, and they had eaten in silence.

He hadn't talked about cows, and she hadn't talked about horses. Or the children, who were now both grown.

Connie had thought their silence was companionable.

They had been together for so long that they didn't need to talk.

He went to bed before she did. Had to get up early, he said. Manuel had told him about some winter strays up in Black Canyon.

Had they kissed each other good night? Said "I love you?"

Maybe he had bussed her on the cheek.

She hadn't looked up from her crossword puzzle.

Had she?

She must have said, "Love you." Or "good night, sweetie." Something.

She wanted to call Phil now and see if something had happened yesterday between Chuck and Phil. Or Manuel.

Manuel would know what was going on. He would help. He was always there for her, always had been since they were kids.

Or maybe she should call her children.

No. She wanted to talk to Chuck. Find out what the hell he was thinking.

She went to the kitchen, picked up the phone, and called Chuck's cell phone.

She heard the phone ring in the house. She followed the sound to the coffee table in the living room. There on top of Sunday's newspaper were Chuck's keys, cell phone, and a closed combination lock, like the one she'd had in high school for her gym locker.

She hung up her phone and picked up the lock. On the back of it was a tiny red sticker of a heart.

"Aw, the key to your heart, eh?" she said.

Only it wasn't locking or unlocking anything except itself.

Chuck had left her a lock that didn't lock anything?

She twirled the dial on the lock, then turned it to the left to ten. Amy's Birthday was September 10th. Then she turned it right to twenty-four. Matt's birthday was May 24th. She turned it left to twenty-one. Her birthday was June 21st.

She pulled on the metal bar, but it did not click and it did not come out of the lock.

She twirled the dial again and started all over. Left, right, left. Same numbers. Same result. She tried three or four times, but nothing happened. She looked over at Jimmy.

"I wonder if it's too late to chase him down," Connie said. "Before he gets too far away." She laughed grimly. Jimmy stared at her.

She wondered why Chuck had used her birthday anyway. He never remembered it.

When they first got together, he said, "As far as I'm concerned, you were born when I was born. We were just separated at birth."

"That's creepy," Connie had told him. "That would make you my brother."

"I thought I was the literal one," he said. "I meant I can't imagine we were ever separate, so of course we'd have to be born on the same day. Like soul mates."

Not *actually* soul mates but *like* soul mates.

She had laughed and laughed. It was probably the only sentimental thing he'd ever said to her, but it had done the trick: She fell in love with him in that moment.

Connie turned the lock to the left and stopped at ten. Then to the right to twenty-four. Then to the left to five. Chuck's birthday was November 5th.

The lock clicked. Connie pulled on the bar and the lock opened.

"I was not born on the day you were born," Connie said. "And we obviously were not even like soul mates."

She closed the lock and wrapped her fingers around it. She was going to throw it long and hard. She aimed it at the kitchen window, the one over the sink. She was in the living room, but she could throw it that far. She had a straight shot.

She reached back—her idea of a windup.

Then she stopped.

Glass would go everywhere.

She'd be cleaning it up forever. Jimmy would probably get some in his paws. Or he'd eat a shard or two on mistake.

She walked into the kitchen, opened the junk drawer, and dropped the lock inside. Then she kicked the drawer shut.

Chapter Two

Connie stood in the kitchen for a time. She wasn't sure for how long. She meant to be there for a minute. It was so quiet. Just the ticking of the small red clock over the stove. She wanted to be in the quiet before it all broke loose. And it was going to break loose. Wasn't anything she could do to stop it unless Chuck changed his mind and came back. Otherwise, she was left to answer questions. To make it all right.

After a while, she realized she had been still for a long time. She went outside to her car. She didn't stop to lock the house. For years—decades?—they hadn't locked the house during the day, in case one of their neighbors happened by and needed something, like shelter from the sun or a monsoon rain. Now, strangers were more likely to stop by than neighbors.

She didn't mind strangers. None of them did. At least, that was the way it used to be. People had wandered over the border between Mexico and the United States since that particular political line in the sand had been drawn. But something had shifted in the last few years. Lately, too many of the wanderers weren't looking for work or a better life: They were putting down trails to traffic drugs into the United States and guns into Mexico.

Last winter, someone shot and killed her friend and neighbor, David Emmett, while he was out on his ranch. Killed his dog, too. He lived long enough to drive his truck away from the scene. Everyone figured he had seen a stranger on his land and had gone to ask if he needed help.

Whoever it was, they had shot David dead. Left his family and friends bereft.

Connie unlocked her truck, let Jimmy in next to her, and drove off in a cloud of dust. Her red pickup sped beneath the metal archway over their drive where the "C&C Ranch" sign hung.

She wasn't sure where she would go. She couldn't tell anyone. Not yet. Maybe something was wrong with Chuck. Maybe he was sick and didn't want to burden her.

No, that couldn't be it. When he was sick he wanted her to wait on him hand and foot.

She turned right, onto the road that went west into town. The road was rutted because of the increase in traffic from the Border Patrol; she had to slow almost immediately. It used to take her about twenty minutes to get into town. Now it took her twice as long, and she had to replace her windshield at least twice a year because of cracks caused by flying rocks. Plus they broke axles on the road, ruined tires. And hardly any of their suppliers would come down the road any more. Whatever supplies they needed, the ranchers had to go into town and get them.

Connie slowed the truck even more so she wasn't throwing up dust on everyone who went by. Not that she was passing anyone. She hardly noticed the majestic countryside all around her: barren and big and beautiful all at the same time. She had tried to describe it to relatives and friends who had never been to the

Southwest.

"It is deep," she'd say. "And present. You have to pay attention every moment. You can't be swept away by it or you will be swept away."

"But what does it look like?"

"It depends upon the time of the day and year and how you feel. And where you are. There's grasslands. Desert scrub. Mountains. Some days the mountains seems like ancient beings watching and protecting me from far away. Other days I see only desert scrub and I feel like I'm living in a wasteland."

"But what does it look like?"

"Like a poet's soul."

No one she knew had a poet's soul, except maybe for Manuel, so no one knew what she was talking about.

Maybe Samantha, too. Amy's daughter. Her grandchild. Sometimes a five-year-old was much more articulate than a fifty-year-old.

Now a bank of clouds shadowed the mountains so that they looked sharper, more visible. So silent and far away.

No help to her now.

How would she explain Chuck leaving to her children? They would blame her, no doubt. They always did. Dad was the quiet saint. Mom was the—Mom was what?

She had no idea what they thought of her.

If she and Chuck got a divorce, what would happen to the ranch? Would he get half, even though the land had been in her family for generations? Or would she have to sell it to pay him off?

Or would he try to kick her off? He had been the one who wanted to live on the ranch after Aunt Delilah died. Neither one of them had known anything about ranching. Well, not much. She and her brother Phil had at least spent nearly every summer on the ranch because their parents wanted them out of Phoenix when they weren't in school.

Connie had wanted to move to the coast when she and Chuck married. Wanted to live by the sea.

He was the one who wanted to live in this water-starved desert.

He was the one.

What couldn't he do any longer?

The marriage or the ranch?

She would have given up the ranch for him. She snapped her fingers. Just like that.

He could have asked.

Maybe he was having a mid-life crisis? Why hadn't he bought a sports car and had an affair like other men?

Maybe he was having an affair.

No. She had known where he was every minute of the day.

Connie reached town—and pavement. She drove around, looking for Chuck's pickup. She went by The Grill. The sign "cowboys welcome" hung crookedly in the corner of the big picture window. Someone waved to her. She waved back. No Chuck.

She went by the bank. The post office. Hardware store. No pickup.

She parked the truck, told Jimmy to stay, then walked to the bank. She ran her fingers through her short hair, suddenly realizing she hadn't washed her face or brushed her teeth or hair. Someone might notice something was wrong.

She shrugged. Naw. She was no fashion plate, never had been. No one would notice anything.

She ran up the concrete steps and went into the bank. Three bank tellers looked up as she came in. The women all smiled and said, "Hello, Connie." Then their smiles disappeared and they looked down at whatever was in front of them.

Connie walked over to Patricia, one of the tellers. They didn't know each other well, so she wouldn't ask many questions.

"I need to see the balance on our accounts," Connie said. "Our checking and savings."

"Do you have the account numbers?" Patricia asked.

Connie shook her head. "I forgot my wallet."

"That's all right," Patricia said. She typed something and looked at her computer screen. Then she wrote two figures on a blue strip of paper and pushed it across the marble toward Connie.

Connie took the paper and put it in her back pocket. She wasn't going to look at it now. Not in front of these women.

"Good lord, Connie."

Connie looked over and saw Jamie Collins, the bank manager.

"What?" Connie said.

"Did you walk out of the house this morning and forget something?" Jamie pointed to Connie's feet.

Connie looked down.

She was barefoot.

She had walked barefoot across the desert out to her car and hadn't noticed. She had driven all this way, walked up the concrete steps, across the hardwood floor. And she hadn't noticed.

Tears filled Connie's eyes. She batted them away.

"I guess I was preoccupied and forgot," Connie said.

All the tellers were staring at her now.

Jamie stood on the other side of a gate that prevented people from walking back to her desk willy-nilly. She opened the gate and walked over to Connie.

"You've always been such a jokester," Jamie said loudly. She put her hand on Connie's elbow and led her toward the door and said quietly, "Do you have some shoes in the car? These girls are gonna think you've lost your mind. What can I do? What's going on?"

Connie pushed open the bank door and went outside with Jamie close beside her. Over the years, they had become friends, of a sort. They saw each other at all the same events and sometimes sat together at them. They'd joke around with one another. Jamie called her a skinny wretch and Connie called her a money mogul. Not exactly scintillating put-downs, but then Connie had never been good at teasing.

Now Connie could feel the cold on her soles as she hurried to the truck. Jimmy looked out at them. Connie opened the door and reached into the back seat and dug around. She came up with a pair of boots. She sat on the driver's seat and pulled them on. They felt a little loose. Jamie watched her.

"Chuck left me," Connie finally said.

"What?"

"Just disappeared this morning," she said. "Left a note that said he couldn't take it any more. Or something like that. He didn't say what he couldn't take. I guess it was me because he didn't take me with him."

"I'm so sorry, Connie. What can I do?"

Connie stood and pulled out the piece of paper from her pocket. She looked at the totals in her savings and checking accounts. Thousands of dollars were missing.

Connie sighed. "I guess I should close my accounts and move them to another account, or at least take his name off our accounts. Maybe if he doesn't have access to any money he'll be forced to come back and at least tell me what this is all about."

Jamie nodded. "And the credit cards. If you have any joint credit cards you better change those."

"Everything we have is joint," Connie said. "We've been joined at the hips for thirty years. I guess he decided he needed a hip replacement."

"Dickey left me once," Jamie said.

Connie closed the door to the truck and walked slowly back

to the bank with Jamie.

"I didn't know that."

Jamie nodded, then shrugged. "Thought he'd shack up with some barmaid from the Crossroads. That lasted about a week and he came back."

"You took him back?"

"Sure, after thirty plus years, he knows where all the bodies are buried," she said. "And I need that info should I decide to dig any of them up. But I did wish we had a pool so I could have had a fling with a pool boy or something. Although, honey, he'd have to be a pool *man.*"

Connie knew she should laugh, but it didn't seem funny. Nothing seemed funny.

They went back into the bank. The tellers were busy with customers so no one noticed Connie this time—now that she had on boots. Jamie opened the gate, and the two of them walked through it. Connie heard it click closed as they walked away. Connie sat on the other side of Jamie's fake wooden desk while she closed accounts and opened new ones. She tried to pay attention and not twiddle her thumbs or count things. She counted things when she was stressed or nervous. An old habit. Tiles on the floor or ceiling. Bullet holes in road signs. Stars in the sky. This was an old bank in one of those big old majestic bank buildings with a marble floor and a row of wooden teller stalls with metal filigree around the boxes almost like a picture frame around each teller. And the ceiling went up high, way above the second story. Connie had never been on the second floor. She suspected that was where the real bank manager resided. The one who made all the decisions. The one who had all the money?

Yep, this bank had been built on all the money ranchers had borrowed over the last couple hundred years.

Connie was glad she and Chuck had never had to borrow any money, at least not to help keep the ranch going. They had taken out loans to help with college tuition, but they had paid them all back.

No, not much to count here except money that didn't belong to her. She stared at the painting of some old bank manager or bank owner. His brown mustache twirled up at the ends and his cheeks were rosy. His smile brought out a gleam in his eyes. He seemed like a jolly guy.

Must come from all that money he had.

"Do you have outstanding checks on your account?" Jamie asked.

Connie looked over at her. "I don't know," she said. "I didn't bring anything with me."

"It's all right," she said. "If any checks come through, we'll call you so that they're not bounced or sent back. But the old debit card won't work any more. So throw that one out."

Connie rubbed her stomach. "It feels too soon. Like after someone dies. Like I'm robbing the grave. Chuck was—is— a good man. Maybe something's going on that I don't under-stand."

"Well, this might get him home so you can understand."

When they were finished, Jamie said, "Now take care of those credit cards when you get home. If your name is on them, you're responsible. I know you're not one of those women who let her husband take care of all the business stuff. Go home now and protect yourself. Call me if you need anything."

Chapter Three

Connie went back outside. The sun was all the way up now—and already too bright. It was going to be a warm day. She opened the truck door and let Jimmy out. She watched him walk around in a circle for a bit. Then he lay down.

She heard her name and turned around.

"Oh crap," she murmured. Her brother and her son, Matt, strode down the street toward her.

Matt waved and smiled.

She grimaced. It was the closest thing to a smile she could muster.

"What are you doing in town?" Matt asked. He hugged her waist and kissed the top of her head. "Where's Dad?"

"I've been trying to track him down for days," Phil said. "I keep leaving him messages."

"You never called the house," Connie said.

"He's never there," Phil said.

"I had some banking to do," Connie said. "Now I need to get home."

She turned to get into the truck, but her son said, "What's going on, Mom? Dad's been AWOL for days. And you're in town wearing a pair of my old boots."

That was why they were so big.

She sighed and turned around to face her brother and son. They both looked like cowboys, standing across from her in their jeans, dark shirts, and cowboy hats. Their skin was dark and ruddy from so many years out in the sun. Because of that, Matt looked much older than his twenty-five years. Phil and Matt looked alike, too, more like son and father than uncle and nephew. Must be because Matt took after her, not Chuck. Matt and Phil both had bright blue eyes and all their eyes were on her.

"Your father has left me," Connie said. "He wrote me a note saying he couldn't do it any more."

Matt stared at her, swallowed, blinked. Then he said, "Couldn't do what?"

Connie shrugged. "I don't know. That was all he said, essentially. He left without speaking with me. Must have turned off the alarm, and then he snuck out. Took some money and the truck with him."

Matt looked at Phil. "Did he say anything to you?"

Phil's face looked slightly gray now. "No. He's been upset since David was killed."

They had all been upset since David Emmett was murdered.

"He hasn't been with you the last few days?" Connie asked.

Phil shook his head.

"He said he was working with you," Connie said, "buying new cattle, checking some fences."

"No, he never showed up," Phil said.

"I don't understand why you didn't call."

"I did. I called him."

"Why the hell didn't you call me?" Connie asked. "You must

have suspected something was wrong. Or were you covering for him? Does he have some chickie on the side?"

"What side?" Phil asked. "All we do is work. I'd love to have time for a chickie on the side."

"I'll tell Marilyn that," Connie said. "She'll be happy to hear it."

"What do we do now?" Matt asked.

"I'm going home," Connie said.

"You can't stay there by yourself," Matt said.

"I need to go home," Connie said. "I need to figure things out."

"You want me to call Marilyn and have her come over?" Phil asked.

"I'm not sick," Connie said. "No one fucking died. My husband just left. I'm going back to the ranch."

"We'll follow you," Matt said.

"Maybe he'll come back," Phil said.

"What were you two doing in town anyway?" Connie said. Not that she actually cared.

"It's Tuesday first of the month," Phil said. "Remember? You used to come every month."

Oh, yes. The Borderlands Ranchers Association monthly business meetings.

"You think because I didn't come to this monthly meeting Chuck decided to leave me?"

"Well, you haven't taken an interest in the ranch for a while," Phil said. "I'm just saying—"

"What? What are you saying?" Connie moved closer to him. "I work my ass off on that stupid ranch."

"Taking care of your horses, chickens, and gardens," Phil said. "That ain't a fucking cattle ranch. That's gentleman farming."

Connie wanted to punch her brother. He must have seen

it, sensed it, something, because he stepped back just as Matt grabbed both of her arms.

"Uncle Phil, don't be such an asshole," Matt said. "Jesus. Mom, come on. We need to get home and tell Amy."

"Yeah," she said, shaking off her son. "Let's go home and ruin her day, too." She pushed her brother in the chest. "If I never see you again, it'll be too damn soon."

"Let me drive, Mom," Matt said.

"No."

"Mom." He held out his hand for the keys.

She glared at him and then dropped the keys into his palm. She went to the other side of the truck and opened the door. Jimmy whimpered. Connie got in the passenger seat. A moment later, Matt started the truck and drove them away.

Connie stared out the window as they headed home, seeing nothing. An occasional tear rolled down her cheek and she wiped it quickly away. Matt didn't say anything. He was a good kid. He wouldn't ask too many questions. He wouldn't accuse her.

Amy might.

As they came down the drive toward the house, Connie hoped she would find Chuck there, ready to apologize for his ludicrous behavior. She was disappointed: His yellow truck was not there.

"Wish he'd taken the green truck," Connie said. "Because it's a piece of junk. And I wish he hadn't taken thousands of dollars from our savings account."

They got out of the truck and started toward the house.

"Did he take a lot?" Matt asked.

"It was for us," she said. "Didn't leave me with much."

"Bastard," he said.

"I can only concur," she said. "You call Amy if you can stand to. I need to feed and water the horses."

Connie went to the barn. She heard whistling and hurried toward it. She knew that whistle, recognized it, had heard it her whole life. Chuck must have returned.

She followed the sound to the back stall. She went through the open door.

Manuel was pitching out horse manure

He looked up at Connie, started to smile, then stopped.

"You all right?" he asked.

"I thought you were Chuck," she said.

"No, I haven't seen him," he said. "I was meeting him here. We were supposed to ride up to Black Canyon. He never showed. And the horses seemed restless, so I fed them. Chickens, too."

"Thanks." She walked through the stall to the corral. The horses were just beyond, in the pasture. Chuck rarely rode any more, so they only had four mounts: Gracie, a piebald Matt and Connie sometimes rode; Leo, Chuck's Appaloosa mule; Poppie, Amy's old quarter horse; and Loosey, Connie's black mare.

Connie whistled, and the horses all looked up. She waved. They watched her for a moment, ears forward, then dropped their heads and began to graze again.

"I wish they got ridden more," Connie said. "I don't go out as much as I should. They're all getting too wild."

"They're fine," Manuel said. "What are you worried about?"

Connie didn't answer him.

Manuel's parents had owned a ranch in Sonora and had been friends with Aunt Delilah when Connie and Manuel were kids. They had spent many weeks of many summers together: Connie, Manuel, and Philip.

After his parents retired, Manuel had managed their failing ranch for a few years, trying to save it. When that didn't work, Chuck hired him to work on their ranch. That had been ten years ago. Phil and Chuck had toyed with the idea of hiring him as manager, but they kept toying and never deciding.

Connie glanced at Manuel. He had been her closest friend

for almost as long as she could remember. But she did not talk to him about her life with Chuck. Neither of them talked about their respective marriages.

"If Chuck isn't coming," Manuel said, "we could saddle up and go look for the sea horses. It's been a long while since we did that."

Connie looked at him. What a strange thing for him to say on this particular morning. They hadn't gone looking for the sea horses for a long time.

"Why would you mention them today?" she asked.

He shrugged. "I dreamed about them last night. Or something. I woke up thinking I smelled the ocean."

"Me, too," Connie said.

Manuel smiled. "Ah, so we are still connected."

Connie bit her lip. She felt an urge to burst into tears and fall into Manuel's arms. Only she wasn't that kind of woman. She didn't fall into anyone's arms. And she didn't fall apart.

"You never really believed the horses existed, did you?" Manuel asked.

"Did you?" she asked. "Delilah said our family was supposed to be caretakers for a mystical band of sea horses. Seemed like a fairy tale to me."

Even so she had liked the idea of a herd of horses roaming these lands, a herd of horses that could never be found, could never be tamed, could only be seen—sometimes—in the reflection of rainwater or in the shadows when a cloud moved overhead. Or smelled when the wind brought the scent of the sea to the desert.

Aunt Delilah had said they were "grand horses made of foam, water, and light that our mer ancestors rode to their cities below."

Whenever Aunt Delilah had talked about the horses—especially when she called them sea horses—Connie's mother would roll her eyes. Later she'd tell Connie that those stories had come from their grandmother who had been a little batty in the last years of her life.

"This is the desert," her mother said. "We don't have sea horses or fairy dust or leprechauns or anything else even close to that. We do have scorpions, rattlesnakes, and sun that could peel the skin right off your back."

Which was why they lived in Phoenix, where the weather was a bit mellower.

Connie had never seen any sign of a herd of horses. Neither had her brother or Manuel. And as the summers went by, Connie had decided her mother was probably right: The story of the sea horses was just a crazy tale invented by a crazy grandmother.

Aunt Delilah believed to her dying day in the existence of the sea horses.

Delilah was sure if she ever found the sea horses, all her dreams would come true.

Connie never asked what Aunt Delilah's dreams were.

She glanced over at Manuel. He rented a house down the road from theirs, on the same property, where he lived with his wife and their little girl, Gabriela. His wife, Isabella, was much younger than Manuel. When he first brought her home, Connie had teased him about it—until she saw that the age difference did worry him. Then she let him alone.

Manuel came and stood next to her.

"I liked it when we used to go out and look for the sea horses," Connie said.

"The *magic* sea horses," he said.

Connie smiled. She liked his English, tinged with that sing-song rhythm that often accompanied Native American and Mexican speakers when English was not their first language. Even though Connie knew Spanish—her grandfather and great grandfather were Mexican, after all—she spoke it like someone who had learned it as an adult. And she had no gift for it. Her English never sounded like she was singing a song.

She smiled.

"What?" Manuel asked.

She shook her head. "I was just thinking how ridiculous Chuck would think I was if I said out loud what I was thinking, about how when you talk, it always sounds like a song."

Manuel shrugged. "Chuck does have a limited imagination."

Connie laughed loudly, tipping her head back.

Manuel smiled.

"By the way," he said, "I was up in Box Canyon the other day and I saw some horse tracks. I tried to follow them." He shrugged. "But they went nowhere."

Connie nodded. How many times over the years had Manuel told her about horse prints he had tried to follow? How many times had he urged her to come out with him to try to find the horses?

It had been many years since she had looked for the sea horses.

"Aunt Delilah had many fairy tales to share about those horses," Manuel said. "She thought they could save the world—at least this world."

"I wonder why," Connie said. "How could a non-indigenous creature save this world?"

"Creatures from the other world are indigenous anywhere they live."

Connie sighed. "Manuel, Chuck has left me," she said.

He didn't say anything for a moment. Then he asked, "For good?"

He tried to look at Connie's face, but she turned away. She didn't want him to know about her personal life with Chuck.

Maybe because her life with Chuck was not that personal.

She had no deep dark secrets. At least she didn't think so. She didn't long for something or someone other than her husband.

Not really.

Maybe she had at one time.

She hadn't had any affairs. She hadn't embezzled money from anyone. Or ever stolen anything. She had never committed any crime of any kind.

She had come out to this land to live with her husband because that was what he had wanted.

She couldn't remember what she had wanted.

Crap.

How could she have let herself become one of those women?

She glanced at Manuel. He watched her. His eyes were so brown. As brown as her son's eyes were blue. What color were Chuck's eyes? She squinted as she looked at Manuel. His black hair was just beginning to gray, unlike hers which had turned white many years ago.

What color were Chuck's eyes?

"My guess is that he is never coming back," she said.

"I'm sorry," he said.

"I am, too," she said.

"Is there anything I can do?"

"You already did it," she said. "Thanks for taking care of the animals. I'm afraid this has thrown me off my stride. I better get back to the house."

She walked by him, out of the stall, and headed out of the barn.

"Hazel," she said to the air.

"Were you talking to me?" Manuel called.

"No, I was just saying Chuck's eyes were hazel."

"I think they're blue," he said.

Connie stopped and turned around. Manuel was leaning out of the stall looking at her.

"Blue? Really?"

Manuel grinned.

Connie groaned. "You have no idea."

"No idea," he said.

Connie laughed. "Bastard."

He shrugged. "At least I got to hear you laugh."

"Might be the last time for a while," she said.

She turned around to leave again. When she was almost out of the barn, she heard Manuel say, "Sky blue."

"His eyes are not sky blue," Connie shouted.

"Not his," he called.

Connie shook her head. She turned around again, but Manuel had gone back into the stall. "Don't flirt with me on the day my husband leaves me. It's not fair. I'll tell your wife."

"If she saw your eyes, she'd say they were sky blue, too," he said.

"She would not," Connie said.

"No, she would not," he said.

Chapter Four

Matt was on the phone to Amy when Connie came into the house. He rolled his eyes at her and held the phone a few inches from his ears. She could hear her daughter's frantic voice.

"What are you going to do if you come out here?" Matt asked the phone.

Connie put her hand up and waved and mouthed, "No, no."

"Mom's got enough to deal with," he said.

Jimmy whimpered. Connie looked down at him. "Get some spine, you old sheep dog. You can't walk around crying all day. There's food in your bowl, water in your dish, sunshine out the door."

The dog looked at her. She patted the top of his head.

"She doesn't need you," Matt said. He walked out of the room so she couldn't hear him.

"I need to do something," Connie murmured.

She called the credit card companies and canceled the cards she and Chuck shared. They only had a couple credit cards together, so it wasn't as difficult as she thought it would be. She had her own credit cards, and he had his own. She wondered if she would be responsible for paying his bills if he used his cards? She decided she needed to call their lawyer, Bennett Shaw, which she did. He promised to get back to her, but he suggested she get a divorce lawyer.

"A divorce lawyer?" Connie said. "He just left a few hours ago. He could come back any minute."

"My experience is that when a man walks out like that," Shaw said. "He ain't coming back."

"I thought men never left unless they had some chickie waiting in the wings," Connie said. She sat at the kitchen table rubbing her face, with the phone up against her left ear.

Shaw didn't say anything for a moment.

"What?" she asked. "Do you know something I don't?"

"No," he said. "I don't know anything."

"Christ on a crutch," Connie said. "I can't believe this is happening."

"You did the right thing in calling," he said. "Most women wait until it's too late, and they're wiped out financially."

"We don't have any money," she said. "Although he did take several thousand from our savings account. I closed the account and put it all in my name so he can't do it again."

"There's the ranch," he said. "His name is on the deed, along with yours and Philip's."

"I don't think he wants the ranch," she said. *Any more than he wants me.*

"He might want his share of the value of the ranch."

"There is no fucking way."

"Mom, language, the dog is present."

Connie looked up. Matt put his hand on her shoulder and smiled. Then he pulled out a chair and sat next to her.

"He's legally entitled," Shaw told her.

"Even if he abandoned the marriage?" she said. "Even though

the land has been in my family for generations?"

She knew the answer to that.

"Never mind, Bennett. I vaguely remember you advising me against adding his name to the deed twenty years ago when we did it. Guess you were right."

"I don't know," Bennett said. "Chuck's a good man. Maybe he won't want anything. Maybe he just wanted to leave."

"Yup," Connie said. "I guess I should hope he was so sick of me he'll never come back."

"There's always hope," Bennett said dryly. "I'll talk to you later."

She put the phone down and looked at her son.

"Did you have any idea?" she asked.

He shook his head. "Dad never talked about anything with me, except the ranch," he said. "Cattle. I guess still waters run deep."

"What's that mean?" Connie asked. "He's deep because he left me?"

"Hey, Mom, don't take it so personally."

"The man I'm married to for thirty years leaves me and I'm not supposed to take that personally? Good lord, Matt. That's very personal."

"He left me, too," Matt said. "And Amy. Who is coming, by the way. Bringing Samantha. Julian is staying behind."

"She thinks she knows everything and can fix anything," Connie said. "Maybe she can fix this."

"Phil called," Matt said.

Connie groaned.

"You're gonna have to talk to him," he said. "We need to look at the books. See what kind of shape the ranch is in."

"He can come," Connie said. "But tell him not to say any more stupid ass things. I've got a gun in the front closet, and I know how to use it."

Matt patted her hand. Then he got up and left the room, probably to talk to Philip alone.

Connie got up from the table and went back to the office. She hardly ever used the office any more, but she knew where the books were. She usually was the one who got them ready for the accountant at the end of the year, but Chuck did them month by month. This year Chuck had done the tax preparation himself. She hadn't minded.

She looked around the small room. It was remarkably tidy. She wondered when Chuck had done that.

She grabbed the books from the shelf across from the desk. Every year Chuck swore he was going to do all the bookkeeping on the computer, and every year went by without him doing anything on the computer, except sending the occasional joke to Amy. He still considered Amy his little girl. Anything she said or did was interesting and amazing to him. He cared about Matt, she knew—at least she thought she knew—but Amy was the apple of his eye, the shine on his shoe, the step in his boot, and whatever other cliché she could think of. If he told anyone about his plans to leave, he would have told Amy.

Connie brought the accounting books into the kitchen.

"Phil's on his way," Matt said as he came back into the room.

"Did your sister know anything about this?" Connie asked as she dropped the books onto the table.

Matt shrugged. "I asked her. She said he hadn't called her in a couple of weeks. She sounded quite perturbed that he'd left her in the dark. Daddy's little girl out of the loop."

"Please don't fight when she gets here," Connie said. "I can't act as referee any more."

"I don't fight with her," he said. "She's just such a know-it-all that she gets on my nerves. She pokes at me until I poke back."

Connie held up her hand. "I don't want to hear about it."

She sorted through the books until she found one that contained the accounts for the previous year and the current year. She opened it. It was a simple set up: He recorded what money came in and what money went out. Pluses and minuses.

She started with January of last year. She found the usual expenses: feed, tools, lumber, fencing, vet bills. Bimonthly checks to the help: Matt, Manuel, the other hands. And the monthly salary checks: one to Chuck and one to Phil, for the same amount. That was normal. Each family took a stipend every month unless the balances were running very low.

In June, Chuck wrote out one check to Phil and two to himself.

Must be an error, Connie thought. He just mistakenly wrote down the same amount twice.

She flipped to July.

Same thing. One check to Phil. Two to himself.

August.

September.

October.

November.

December.

January.

February.

He wrote it down in black and white.

Hadn't even tried to cover it up.

Why hadn't the accountant said anything to her or to Phil?

Why would he? Chuck had written it all down.

He was paying himself double each month. And pocketing the money for himself.

He had embezzled money from the ranch.

Thousands of dollars.

No wonder they were in so much trouble.

She wondered if he had been doing it for years. She would

have noticed. Wouldn't she have? She had gotten everything ready for the accountant two years earlier.

She would have noticed.

Of course, she had not noticed Chuck was unhappy.

Had not noticed he was stealing.

Had not noticed he was about to leave her.

"Mom, what did you find?"

Connie pointed to the ledger. Matt got up and looked over her shoulder.

"What am I looking at?" he asked. "That's how much you guys make a month? I guess I shouldn't complain about my paycheck. Sheesh. But you get paid twice."

"No, we didn't get paid twice," Connie said. "Your father has been stealing from the ranch. From me. From you and your sister. From my brother." She groaned. "From my brother. We're never going to hear the end of it."

"I can tell him," Matt said.

"No, I'll do it," she said. "I'm sure he'll be on the phone to a lawyer in about five minutes, trying to figure out a way to sue me. Sometimes I can't believe we're related."

"He's not that bad," Matt said. "He's really a good guy. You'll see."

"I can't do this right now," Connie said. "I just need a moment to breathe, to think. I'm going upstairs for a minute. I'll be back down soon, when your uncle gets here."

She pushed away from the table, walked down the hall, and went up the stairs. Jimmy followed her.

She was too tired to tell him to go away. She dropped down onto the bed and curled into a ball. Jimmy got on the bed with her and pressed his back against hers.

"Thank you, old friend," she whispered.

She closed her eyes. How was she going to do this? She had never been alone in her life. She didn't know how to run a cattle ranch. Not really. And more importantly, she did not want to run a cattle ranch.

She didn't know what she wanted to do.

Sleep.

Yes, she wanted to sleep.

She didn't know if she had ever been this tired in her life.

She sighed and fell to sleep.

Chapter Five

Connie opened her eyes.

It was dark. She quickly sat up.

Where was she? What was going on?

Where was Chuck?

She glanced at the clock. It was nearly 7:00 p.m.

Jimmy hopped off the bed and left the room.

It suddenly all came back to her.

Her lying thieving cowardly husband had left her and run off with thousands of dollars that didn't belong to him.

She got up and ran her fingers through her hair. She didn't want to think about him that way. She had loved him twelve hours ago. Had planned to spend the rest of her life with him.

Something must have happened for him to change this way so suddenly.

Maybe he was sick.

Maybe he had lost his way and hadn't known how to tell her.

Connie went down the stairs. She heard voices. She walked

toward the light and the sound. She turned the corner and saw Matt, Marilyn, and Philip sitting around the kitchen table.

They all looked over at her. Marilyn got up from the table and went to Connie and put her arms around her.

"I'm so, so sorry," she said.

Connie embraced her sister-in-law.

"Thanks, Marilyn."

Marilyn let her go and looked at her.

"And I'm sorry my husband was such an asshole when you first told him," she said.

Phil got up and came over to Connie. Marilyn moved out of the way, and he hugged Connie quickly and then let her go.

"I am sorry," he said. "I was just pissed, and you were there."

"You might not be feeling so generous once I tell you what Chuck did," Connie said. She leaned against the counter.

"They know," Matt said. "You were dead to the world, so I told them."

"I made dinner," Marilyn said. "Sit. I'll bring you some."

Connie sat at the table. A moment later, Marilyn put a plate of food in front of her. She couldn't focus on what it was. Potatoes? Steak?

"We've been trying to figure out what to do," Matt said. "Do we call the police? Do we hire someone to track him down?"

"I don't know that it's against the law to steal from yourself," Connie said.

"It is against the law to steal from me," Phil said. "But since we never incorporated or anything, I'm not sure he did anything illegal. We'll have to talk to a lawyer tomorrow."

"If he comes back and wants a divorce," Connie said, "he could get half of the ranch or else we'd have to pay him. Which may come out to what he stole."

"The ranch is worth more than that, isn't it?" Matt asked.

"It depends," Phil said. "As a ranch or as a subdivision?"

"Who would want to subdivide so close to the border?" Marilyn asked, "especially with all the trouble we've been having with undocumented workers and drug runners. I wouldn't want to live here and I live here."

"I'd still like him to come back," Matt said, "just to see what's going on."

Connie nodded. "I was wondering if maybe he's sick. Maybe something happened."

They were all quiet.

"In any case," Phil said, "we are really strapped for cash because of what he did. We've got to figure out something. We've got expenses coming up, salaries to pay."

"Don't we need to figure out even more basic stuff?" Marilyn asked. "Maybe Connie doesn't even want to stay here."

"What do you mean?" Connie asked.

Silence again.

Phil cleared his throat. "Well, you haven't been interested in ranching for a long time now."

"That's true," Connie said. "I love this land, but I don't like cattle ranching."

"We can't afford to just ride the range all day like you do," Phil said. "We've got to make a living off the land."

"Don't start that shit again," Connie said.

"Hey, Phil, stop it," Marilyn said. She sat next to Connie. "It's been no secret that you've been unhappy here for a while. You used to work the ranch with Chuck and then you stopped. You were going to wrangle horses, but you decided not to do that. The community has had the benefit of your horse doctoring services over the past few years, and that has been great. You can cure any filly, colt, mare, or stallion of whatever ails them. It is a gift. That's enough if you're happy with that. But with Chuck gone, is that still how you want to spend your days?"

"I don't know what you're all talking about," Connie said. "I help bring the cattle in. I talk to the brokers. I do the books. I order the supplies. I do what needs to be done. Sure, I've taken a few months off." She squinted. "I don't even know why. I was tired, I guess."

"Mom, it hasn't been a few months," Matt said. "It's been since I got back from college. Pretty much."

"That long?"

No one said anything.

"Since you found that girl—" Phil started. Marilyn shushed him.

Connie took a bite of food. Beans. It was beans and rice. Marilyn remembered she didn't eat beef. Not even their own beef.

She put the fork down again. She felt like she was going to cry, and she did not want to cry in front of them. She did not want to cry in front of anyone.

She hadn't cried when she found the girl.

Had she?

Maybe. Maybe she had wailed.

She didn't remember.

She remembered being angry.

She remembered she was riding Loosey in the scrub near Box Canyon, looking for strays. Jimmy started barking. Loosey took Connie to where Jimmy was. She figured he had spotted someone who was trying to sneak across the border. Since stricter border enforcement had made it more difficult to cross illegally via towns and main roads, more and more human traffic came across their ranches, leaving more and more garbage, running off more and more of their cattle, damaging more and more of their property.

Too often the walkers—which was what Connie called the people crossing the border—would get this far and realize they were lost or their *coyote* had deserted them. When Connie or Chuck ran across any migrants, they usually gave them water and then called Border Patrol.

Lately Border Patrol had advised against giving aid. Stay away, far away, and call the Border Patrol. If the walkers were drug runners and saw them reach for a cell phone, they might shoot them. That was what everyone believed had happened to David Emmett.

Connie hadn't had her cell phone that day. She had been happy to be far from home, far from anything except her horse, the mountains, and the scrub. Manuel was somewhere not too far behind her. She let Loosey take her to where Jimmy stood barking.

Then she saw a young girl lying on her side on the hard dirt. Near her was a sand bar, as though a tiny lake or river had once spilled out here. The girl was naked except for her underwear and one blue shoe.

Connie got off Loosey and hurried to the girl's side. She touched her arm, but it was cold and hot at the same time.

"Hello, hello," she said.

She gently turned the girl over. Her black hair was matted against her forehead. Her eyes were closed. Connie tried to find her pulse. She pressed her fingers against her wrist and then her throat. She thought she felt something in her neck.

She jumped up, went back to Loosey, and pulled the water bottle out of the saddle. Ran back to the girl. Poured water into her hand and then dribbled some on the girl's lips.

Did the girl moan?

No. She couldn't have.

Did she breathe in and then out?

Connie thought she felt her breath.

"Come on, darlin', come on."

A vulture circled overhead.

Connie felt for the girl's pulse again. Pressed her ear against her chest.

Nothing.

She heard another horse. Looked up. Manuel was there. Was at her side.

"She's been dead for a while," he said.

"No, I just heard her breathe," Connie said.

"Consuelo," he said softly, "look at her leg. It is stiff where you turned her over. She is either coming out of or going into rigor mortis."

Connie groaned. She unbuttoned her shirt and took it off, then gently spread it over the girl.

Was she nine? Ten?

"They just left her like this?" Connie said. "How could they?"

"Maybe they all died, too," Manuel said. "Maybe they were being chased. Who knows? Does it matter?"

"I should find her other shoe," Connie said.

Something about her little bare foot out in the sun, out in the wild, so vulnerable and susceptible to predators—something about it made Connie feel desperate, as if the finding of that shoe would make everything better.

But she didn't get up, she didn't leave the girl's side. She sat under the wicked hot sun, her shoulders bare to the sky blue sky, her hand resting on the part of her shirt that covered the child's arm.

Manuel called Border Patrol.

Loosey stood next to Connie and the girl, providing a bit of shade. Jimmy wouldn't come near. A breeze blew through the area for a few minutes. It smelled strange. Like water. Or the sea. Connie thought of her aunt's sea horses then and wondered how anyone could believe in anything magical during times like these.

A bird flew overhead once, and Connie thought it sang out, "Sweet sister, sweet sister." Those words became a refrain in her head.

But that had all happened four years ago, give or take a few months.

Border Patrol had come and gotten the dead girl. Took her away. Connie and Manuel had continued looking for stray calves.

They never learned the girl's name. Never knew her story. She was an unknown being, dead on the desert floor, just like a dead rabbit, coyote, or javelina.

Had the girl been dreaming of coming to the United States where her mother lived and worked? Or had she been kidnapped to be sold into sexual slavery? Was she a young drug mule? Had she begged her parents not to leave without her? No, her parents would not have left her side, Connie was certain of that, even if her parents had dreamed of a better life.

Dreams died in this desert.

Connie almost smiled at the thought. What a cliché. She was now thinking in clichés.

Would that girl have lived if she had had enough water? Had she died of thirst or of exposure?

Connie had hated thinking of her as "that girl," so after a while she had started calling her Rosalia.

"Forgive me if it's the wrong name," Connie had said to the girl she kept seeing in her mind's eyes. "Which I'm sure it is. But it's a name."

Connie hadn't been able to sleep for weeks after it happened.

Months?

She'd lay in bed and wonder what Rosalia's life had been like in Mexico.

If that was where she had come from.

No one knew.

Every time Connie went out onto the ranch after that, she looked for the little girl's blue shoe.

They found tracks of walkers on the ranch every day. They found their garbage, their feces, vomit, empty plastic water bottles, clothes.

But she never found the blue shoe.

Now Connie looked up from her plate. Everyone at the table was watching her.

"What?" she asked.

"You haven't said a word for about fifteen minutes," Matt said.

"Sorry," Connie said. "Look, I don't know what we should do. I know we owe you that money, Phil. Or we owe the business. I'll call Shaw again tomorrow and see if he can try to find Chuck so we can get the money back."

"Have you looked through his mail?" Marilyn asked. "There might be something more going on."

"What do you mean?" Connie asked.

"We should find out everything we can," Marilyn said.

Connie got up from the table and went into the office. She sat at the desk and started flipping through papers. She found bills, correspondence with the Borderlands Ranchers Association, and a pile of unopened mail. She began opening envelopes. She found overdue bills from the hardware and feed stores, but they weren't for much.

Three envelopes from the bank were unopened—not from their bank, but from the Other Bank in town. That's what they had always called it: The Other Bank, the one that held most of the notes on most of the ranches in the area. Most, but not all: C&C Ranch had been free and clear when they took it over from Aunt Delilah and it had remained so over the ensuing thirty years.

Connie's fingers shook as she opened the first envelope from the bank.

It was a notice of payment due on their bank loan.

They did not have a bank loan.

Chuck Johnson's and Philip Mahoney's bank loan.

Connie opened the second envelope.

It was an overdue notice for the loan.

The third envelope.

Notice of intent to call in the note. "Please contact us immediately."

Connie got up and hurried into the living room. She picked up Chuck's phone from the table, turned it on, and checked the messages on his voice mail. He had several messages from Martin Irving at The Other Bank.

Marked urgent.

Urgent.

Urgent.

Connie put the phone down and turned around and faced the kitchen. Her brother looked at her.

"Why didn't you tell me?" Connie asked. "Does Marilyn know? Matt? The payment is overdue. They want to call in the loan."

Phil cleared his throat and looked away from her. She hated when he did that. It was his tell that he was nervous and she felt like a predator must feel when their prey hesitates. She wanted to pounce on him.

Wanted to rip his heart out.

Or the equivalent.

"What's she talking about, Philip?" Marilyn asked.

"We had some capital expenses," Philip said. "You know, none of these ranches can keep going without some kind of loan. We were falling further and further behind. Didn't you wonder how we were able to buy the equipment to put in those watering holes, or how we were able to buy more cattle?"

"We were doing all right without them," Connie said.

"No, we weren't," he said. "If you haven't noticed, we're in the middle of a drought that might last until the end of time."

"Then we should have had a family meeting," Connie said. "We should have talked about it. It wasn't me who drove off Chuck. It was the pressure of trying to make these payments! Chuck's never been good with that kind of stress. You should have come to me."

"Philip, what is going on?" Marilyn asked

"They took out a loan on the ranch," Connie said. "The payments are overdue and the bank wants to call in the loan."

"We were going to go talk to them today," Philip said. "That was one of the reasons I was in town. I was supposed to meet Chuck."

Connie rubbed her face.

"And what were you going to tell them?" Connie asked. "As far as I can tell, we've got no money in the accounts because Chuck ran off with it all."

"I wasn't going to tell them that," Philip said, "because I didn't know."

"You did this behind my back?" Marilyn asked. "We've got two kids in college. We've got a home."

"I know," he said. "We got enough for the kids. We got enough for the mortgage."

"You mean you've got money in savings for college tuition?" Connie asked.

"Yes. I'm not an idiot."

"I wouldn't bet on that," Marilyn said. "If they call in the loan, can you pay it?"

Philip shook his head. "Maybe if we all cash in our retirement funds and empty the kids' tuition accounts."

"What about making payments on the loan?" Connie asked.

"I thought we were making payments," he said. "Until a couple of days ago. Then Chuck told me we were in trouble. That's when he made the appointment with the banker."

"You need to go back to the bank and figure it out," Marilyn said. "Can you stall the bank, at least until we can take the cattle to market?"

"I don't know," Phil said.

"My head hurts," Connie said. "I don't think I can talk about this any more. Phil, can you go to the bank tomorrow? Matt, go with him. Unless you want to go, Marilyn."

"I've got to work," she said. "But you better tell me everything."

"I'll go through Chuck's papers tomorrow and see if there are any other surprises," Connie said. "Now, can you all leave? I'm tired."

"Let me stay, Mom," Matt said. He rented the bunkhouse apartment at Phil and Marilyn's house.

"No," Connie said. "I'm all right."

Marilyn and Matt hugged Connie and kissed her good-bye. Phil held his hat between his hands and mumbled a good night. Then they all went out into the dark.

Connie stood on the porch and listened to the coyotes yip in the distance. Above, the stars twinkled brightly. It was too cold.

She went inside and shut and locked the door before they all drove off. She turned off all the lights—except the one over the kitchen sink—and then she and Jimmy went upstairs to her bedroom.

Chapter Six

Connie kept waking up. Once she thought she heard someone coming into the house. She got the shotgun from the closet, made certain it was loaded, and then she went quietly down the stairs. She was alert enough to avoid the step that creaked. She made it downstairs and found no one.

She stood in the kitchen, by the light over the kitchen sink, with the shotgun in her hands, listening.

She heard the refrigerator hum and the clock tick.

Then she heard Jimmy's toenails on the living room floor.

"Tomorrow we're going to clip those," she told him.

She went back upstairs and fell to sleep.

She awakened again, around 3:00 a.m., thinking she heard footsteps outside. She surreptitiously looked out the window. She saw the drive winding away under the C&C Ranch sign. Nothing stirred. No walkers trespassed. No Chuck returned home.

All was well. Or as well as it could be.

Another time she smelled an ocean breeze. She looked out the window and saw Rosalia dancing under the full moon. She wore two blue shoes and a blue crinoline dress. She looked up at Connie and waved.

Connie woke with a start.

It took her a moment to remember—to comprehend what had happened—and then she got up and took a quick shower.

Jimmy was sitting outside the bathroom door waiting for her when she finished showering. She came out fully dressed, the way she always did. She didn't walk around the house naked. She'd stopped doing that when the kids got to a certain age.

And then she had stopped being naked even on the way from her bathroom to the bedroom.

Had it been because she didn't want to give Chuck any ideas?

No. It was because he didn't have any ideas. He had lost interest in her a long time ago. She couldn't remember the last time they had made love.

Or wait. Yes, she could. She shuddered. One night he had come home after a meeting in town. He had fumbled around in the dark for her. She was tired, and he smelled like booze. But she complied. It had taken too long, and then it had been too quick. He started snoring before she could roll away from him. She had felt used and dissatisfied.

She'd gotten out of bed and taken a shower then.

Now she tried to remember what Chuck had been like when he was young.

Or what they had been like together.

"Ugh," Connie said. "I don't like these trips down miserable memory lane."

Jimmy whined.

"It'll get better, sheep dog," she said. "Either that or it'll get worse."

She let Jimmy out and made herself breakfast. She wasn't hungry, but she ate the oatmeal anyway. She had to throw half of it out: She was so accustomed to scooping up enough dry oats for two that she hadn't noticed she'd made too much until the oatmeal was ready. She was washing out her dish and the pot when she heard a car drive up. Jimmy barked once and then was quiet. Must be friend rather than foe.

She went to the front door and opened it before anyone could knock or ring the doorbell. Alice got out of her car and hurried up the walk to her.

"Brrrr, it's cold," she said. She gave Connie a quick hug and then came into the house. Jimmy followed her. Connie shut the door, and the two women went into the kitchen. Alice got herself a cup of coffee, then sat at the table, across from Connie.

"So what are you going to do?" Alice asked.

"Good morning to you, too, Alice. How is everything?" Connie smiled. The smile felt peculiar on her face.

"Good morning. I'm fine. I heard about Chuck."

"Which part?" Connie asked. "That he left me or that he stole from the ranch or that he took out a loan without telling me and now the note is due."

"Whoa," Alice said. "I didn't hear all that. Just that Chuck left. Howard is beside himself. He can't imagine what got into Chuck."

"Howard is beside himself?" Connie asked. "How could you tell? Did he blink faster?"

Alice laughed. "If we didn't like the strong silent type, we shouldn't have married cowboys."

"I didn't marry a cowboy," Connie said. "I married an accountant who decided to become a rancher. This is what he wanted and now he's the one who is gone! What am I going to do?"

"You could sell the ranch, take the money, and buy a condo somewhere, then travel for a while."

"Who's going to buy the ranch in this market?" Connie asked.

"So what do you want?"

"I want my husband back," Connie said. "But don't tell anyone I said that."

"This could be a golden opportunity for you," Alice said.

"Oh man, don't give me your glass half full speech. No New Age crap. We don't create our own reality." Connie knocked on the table. "This table is here whether I believe it is or not. My husband left me and took our money whether I believe it or not."

Alice sat back and stared at her. "I don't blame you for being defensive. But you're the one who told me you wanted something different for yourself. You told me two days ago that you weren't happy, that you had no idea how you had gotten to this point in your life."

"What a great friend you are," Connie said, "throwing my own words back in my face."

Alice smiled.

"I was just bellyaching then," Connie said. "Everything was fine. My family was healthy. I had a home and a husband. I loved Chuck. I *love* Chuck."

"Really? What do you love about him?"

"What do you love about Howard?"

"I love the way he laughs. It's a kind of chuckle, you know, like Santa Claus. I love the way he pets the dogs or reads stories to our grandkids. I love the way his pot belly presses into my belly when we make love—"

"Too much information," Connie said. "I get the idea."

"So? What did you love about Chuck?"

Connie looked around the kitchen. Then she rubbed her head with all her fingers. "I loved that he loved me," Connie said. "I loved his familiarity." She sighed. "That doesn't seem like much. But he was a good father and a good husband. He worked hard. He didn't cheat."

"And you felt like you couldn't talk to him about anything," Alice said. "He made fun of any of your aspirations. You never got to have the horses you wanted. You never got to do any of the things you wanted to do. What about your dreams?"

"This is stupid," Connie said. "I'm too old for this. I don't have any dreams. If I had really wanted to raise horses, I would have done it. I liked the idea of having the horses, but I'm not a wrangler. Phil said I was running a gentleman's farm, and he is right. I like the *idea* of lots of things, but I don't necessarily want to do the work."

"I don't believe that," Alice said. "I think you just don't know what you want."

"And right now I don't have the luxury of figuring that out," Connie said. "How do I keep the bank from taking my home and throwing me and the rest of my family out into the streets?"

"We don't have streets out here," Alice said. "When Howard had his heart attack, we looked at our whole way of life. And we changed some things."

"Yes, I know," Connie said. "You do yoga and meditation and think about the existence of God."

"Don't make fun," Alice said. "I expect that of other people, but not of you. You studied literature. You're supposed to understand story and meaning. Howard and I stopped. We were still for a while. Then things became clearer. We had insights. They are our insights. Not yours. I think you should grab this opportunity. Look at what happened to Dorothy Emmett after David was murdered. She's just had one terrible thing after another happen to her."

"So you're saying that could happen to me if I don't sit still and gaze at my navel?"

Alice gulped her coffee. "Well, let me know if you need anything." She got up from the table.

"I'm sorry, Alice," Connie said. "I know I sound bitter and

cranky and I am. I've been a part of a couple for as long as I can remember. Before that I was in college with a roommate. Before that I lived in my parents' house. I feel like I'm eighteen years old again, only I know more now, and I know it's a fucking scary place out there. I don't know how to do anything. I couldn't make a living if I tried. I'm afraid to be still or to think too long or hard because I'll be overwhelmed with terror. I've been in this part of the country too long, Alice. I've adapted to their ways: I don't know how to communicate. I don't know how to dream."

"Someone once told me that when we lose our dreams, the land dreams for us."

Connie stood and hugged her friend. "I was very young when I said that."

"I had just miscarried," Alice said, "and I thought nothing would feel good again. And that was exactly what I needed to hear. Every day for a long time I went out on the land and looked for my dreams. They were in pieces for a time and I found them in odd places: in a cloud bank over the mountains, in a glint of a pottery shard found in the middle of the desert, in the sound of the crow's wings in the dry air. But eventually, I was myself again, filled with my own interests, my own dreams."

Connie kissed Alice, and then she left the house with her. She watched Alice get into the car and drive away.

After Connie fed and watered the horses and chickens, she spent the morning going through the office. She didn't find any more surprises. Bennett Shaw called with a recommendation for a divorce lawyer. Phil and Matt hadn't phoned or stopped by, so Connie assumed they were still at the bank.

She didn't know what else to do with her day.

She had to do something besides sit and wait for the other shoe to fall.

Connie went out to the barn and whistled for Loosey. The black horse came running. Connie held out a carrot for her. Loosey ate the carrot all the way to Connie's palm and then licked her hand. Connie laughed. Loosey had been a handful from the moment she had dropped from her mother's womb. She kicked and bit and when it was time to get her used to the saddle, she wouldn't allow anything on her back for a long time.

Connie didn't know who Loosey's sire was. Her dam had gotten loose with several other mares one autumn and wasn't found until spring.

Two of the mares gave birth to stillborn foals.

Loosey's mother birthed Loosey.

To Connie, Loosey's mysterious beginnings made her extra special. Everyone else had wanted to sell her. Everyone else being Phil and Chuck.

They didn't think Loosey would ever be good for anything.

Connie liked her personality. And her color. Her coat reminded Connie of a black jaguar's coat: If you looked closely enough, you could see the spots beneath the black. Most likely that meant Loosey had Appaloosa ancestors, but Connie sometimes told people Loosey's father was one of the elusive jaguars that roamed the nearby mountains—at least she hoped they roamed the mountains. She had never actually seen one.

So Connie named her Jagaloosa and nicknamed her Loosey.

Eventually Loosey had allowed Connie to put a blanket on her back. And then a saddle.

But she would never take a bit.

Connie understood.

So she trained her without the bit.

At the time, every single horse person she knew had told her she was crazy.

Said the horse would never do what she was told.

Would never go after cattle.

Would never stop or turn on command.

Loosey and Connie proved them all wrong. It was true that

Loosey did go her own way sometimes, but if Connie didn't have anything else going on, she gave Loosey her head. That was how Connie explored her land, this place she called home.

But when she needed to cut a calf out of the herd or bring a stray home, Loosey knew what Connie wanted and the three of them—Jimmy, Connie, and Loosey—did the work.

Although, as Philip had pointed out last night, they had not done any of that kind of work for a long while.

"Come on, girl," Connie said to Loosey. "Let's look around and see if we can figure anything out about what's next for us."

Connie saddled Loosey, mounted up, and called for Jimmy. Then the three of them headed out. She usually went north, toward the mountains, but today she turned Loosey southeast. She rarely went that way any more: too close to the border, too close to where Chuck usually had the cattle graze, and too close to where she had found Rosalia.

They followed a trail through the scrub and wound through a kind of mesquite forest. These dark gnarly trees reached deep into the desert ground, and Connie knew their roots were much longer than their trunks. Many saplings had sprung up since last she had been this way. Common wisdom was that a person could follow the trail of cattle in the West by following the trail of mesquite. Cows ate the mesquite pods and then the seeds in their cowpies sprouted and took hold in the harsh desert.

Connie stared into the distance. The mountains were hazy again today. A red-tailed hawk circled overhead. Two smaller dark birds tried to drive the hawk off, but it kept circling.

"Wonder what the hawk sees," she said out loud.

She looked down.

The desert ground appeared hard, dried out. They were walking over a wasteland. Hardly anything grew here on the blond desert floor. Piles of cow flop dotted the landscape, like giant squashed chocolate kisses.

In the distance, she saw a few dozen cows by the watering trough.

"What's happening here?" she said. Years ago, they had gotten help from government agencies to manage their cattle better so that this moonscaping of the environment wouldn't happen.

Why did it look like this again?

When she was a girl visiting in the summer, she never saw tracts of hardened desert, devoid of most vegetation—except for those parts of the ranch her aunt rented out. When her aunt discovered her renters were running too many cattle, she kicked them off. But when Connie and Chuck took over the ranch after her aunt died, they had noticed whole areas of denuded desert.

Connie had once thought about trying to restore the vegetation of the ranch to what it had been like before her family started running cattle on it. But everyone told her not to worry about it. Once the cattle moved off a particular part of the ranch and went somewhere else, the desert would return to health, they said. Connie didn't know what to believe. She figured people had been running cattle in this area for so long that no one knew what the vegetation had been like before. Maybe it had been a grassy plain. Maybe it hadn't been. Maybe mesquite had grown only here and there, at the borders of these grassy plains, or maybe it hadn't.

Connie had felt inadequate to the task. Besides, the other ranchers had been living on the land for generations: They must know what to do. And the forest service was overseeing the public land that so many ranchers rented. They were the professionals.

Now, as Connie rode through the moonscaped desert, she felt sick to her stomach.

She clicked Loosey forward. She rode around the herd and headed toward Box Canyon. After a while, the cows and the moonscaping disappeared. The air felt cooler. They walked around boulders and up a slope where a patch of yellow wild-flowers grew. Connie didn't know what they were called. Some kind of buttercups? Then they headed down a bit. She watched the ground. This was one of the areas the walkers passed through. She often found garbage and discarded clothes here. She spotted something red.

She reined Loosey in, then dismounted. She kept the reins in her hands as she headed for the red.

As she got closer, she saw it was a pop can. She leaned over and picked it up. She turned it upside down and shook it, to rid it of any liquid or insects. Nothing came out.

She reached up to the saddle and opened the garbage bag she always carried with her and dropped the can into it.

She kept walking. She saw a flash of something near a boulder. As she got nearer, she saw it was a piece of green material sticking up out of ground. She reached for it and gently pulled on it until she realized she was pulling on a thumb of a glove—an empty glove, thank goodness. She kept pulling until she had the entire glove in her hand. It was small: a child's cotton glove. Looked like it might be handmade. She slapped it against her jeans to get the dust off. Then she put it in her back pocket and mounted Loosey again.

They rode north a bit, into Box Canyon. After a while, Connie stopped Loosey and got off her. She tied her to a bush. Then she walked up some scree, with Jimmy close behind, until she reached a small cave. It was more of an alcove than a cave, like a miniature of those amphitheaters where the Anasazi built their cliff villages. The sun cast the alcove into shadow and Connie stood at the edge of the shadow for a moment until her eyes adjusted and she could see that no creature had decided to make the small cave its home.

Then she stepped inside.

The cave only went back a few feet, but Connie had arranged

a taller flat rock so that it had the look of an altar in a church—like those places in Catholic churches where you go to light a candle.

Only she hadn't brought candles.

She pulled the green glove from her pocket and glanced around. She decided to put it on top of a shiny blue jacket.

Then she stepped back and looked around. Next to the jacket was an open glasses case with a pair of broken metal glasses inside. Near that was a packet of matches. A tiny deck of playing cards. One black sneaker. Several socks of different colors. A variety of backpacks. Piles of empty water jugs. Piles of empty soda and beer cans. So many water jugs and cans that she had started taking them home and throwing them out instead of bringing them here.

She stepped closer and rearranged the turquoise-colored tights. They overlapped a small blue dress. On top of the blue dress and turquoise-colored tights was one small blue shoe: The blue shoe that had fallen off Rosalia as they took her away.

At the time, Connie had picked up the shoe and shown it to the Border Patrol, asked them if they wanted it.

Shouldn't they have wanted it? Shouldn't they have taken it so that they could identify the girl?

No one said anything.

So she had kept the shoe.

Kept it with her until she went out riding again to look for the other one.

She didn't find it. But she found all these other castoffs.

So she started bringing them here.

She had heard about a woman in Tucson who picked up trash in the desert and then sold it on 4th Avenue along with her stories. She had heard about another woman near Green Valley who picked up those things the walkers had left behind and made art pieces out of them.

Connie was not a storyteller or an artist.

She just picked up discards and stored them in this cave.

She wasn't certain why.

At first she thought it was because she wanted all signs of them gone from her ranch.

Except for signs of Rosalia. Then she realized any of them could be a Rosalia. She wanted to honor Rosalia somehow. Or keep her things in case her parents ever came looking.

Sometimes she believed the dress and tights she had found belonged to Rosalia.

Sometimes she was certain they had not belonged to her.

Not that she was giving all of these people—these walkers— a pass. She resented them on her land. She resented them leaving their garbage and screwing up the environment.

Not that they were harming the land any more than the cattle were, she supposed.

Sometimes she thought of this place, this cave, as a shrine to everyone who had tried to cross the desert and hadn't made it. She thought of all the dreams these people had before they set out on their journey. Probably none of them thought about how hot it would be, or how cold. They didn't know how far it was, she was certain of that. Sometimes when migrants would make it to her house and beg for water, some of them half dead from the journey, they would ask her to take them to Phoenix or Los Angeles. When she would try to explain that Phoenix was five hours away by car, give or take, and Los Angeles was a ten hour drive, they didn't believe her.

"No, no, right up there. Not far," they'd say.

Connie knew that none of them expected to die, particularly the children. They were just dreaming of a better life. Or a better day.

So sometimes she thought of the cave as the dreaming place.

Maybe if she filled it up with all their leftovers, all their dreams would come true.

Maybe all her dreams would come true, too.

Even though she didn't recall what her dreams were.

"Remember, Jimmy," she said as she stepped back into the sun. "This is our secret. Tell no one." They walked back toward Loosey.

Connie needed to get home. She had to find out what the bank had said. She had to find out what was going to happen to the ranch. She should have gone with them to the bank. But right then she had felt too battered.

She suddenly felt like Rip Van Winkle. Had she been asleep for so long that everything in her world had changed? She wished someone had tried to wake her up long ago.

"I'm awake now," she said.

She got on Loosey. "Take me home, Jagaloosa."

Chapter Seven

When Connie got back to the house, she saw Matt's and Phil's trucks alongside hers. She took off Loosey's saddle and bridle, brushed her down, and put her in the pasture. Then she went to the house, opened the front door, and motioned Jimmy to go in first. He looked at her but stayed on the porch.

"So you desert me now," Connie said, "in my hour of need."

Phil and Matt sat at her kitchen table, drinking coffee.

"Make yourselves at home, boys," Connie said.

"I used my key, Mom," Matt said. "Hope you don't mind."

"Not a bit." She went to the sink and washed her hands. She looked over her shoulder. "So what did you find out?"

"We paid them what's past due," Phil said. "Matt chipped in. We're okay for now, until next month, or the next. They're not going to call in the note yet. They want a business plan soon, though, if we're changing anything."

Connie dried her hands and then poured herself a cup of coffee. She leaned against the counter.

"So what are we going to do?" Connie asked. "Obviously

what you've been doing hasn't worked very well."

"We've got a big herd," Phil said. "We'll do all right."

Connie shook her head. "You were right, Phil. I have been out of it and that's not fair. But now I'm back. I went for a ride today. Near Box Canyon. The land there is trashed. Looks like a fucking moonscape. How long have you been running too many cows on that land?"

"We thought we could pay off the loan quicker," Phil said, "if we had more cattle."

"And have the feds after us?" she said. "Have you been grazing them on federal land?"

"We've been breaking the herd up," Matt said, "just like we always do. Some on our land, some on the allotments."

"You've been a part of this?" Connie asked Matt. "I thought you took environmental science in school. I thought you came back here to help us turn the ranch into an ecological dream. That ground was so hard Loosey didn't leave any prints, and it's spring. What's the difference between what you've been doing here and an industrial feed lot?"

"Dad said it was temporary," Matt said. "No one would find out and we'd put it right again before they did."

"We're part of the Borderlands Ranchers Association," Connie said. "We're all supposed to be working toward conservation. We save the land so the government stops buying land and throwing out all the livestock."

"Yes, Mom, we know. I'm the one who encouraged you all to be a part of the Borderlands Ranchers."

"Chuck pretty much stopped going when you stopped going," Phil said.

"So you're saying I am to blame?" Connie asked.

"I thought you were on board with all of this, Mom," Matt said, "so I never said anything. I just figured you thought my major was as useless as Dad did."

"He didn't think any such thing," Connie said. "And I was looking forward to seeing the results of what you learned. You said you'd be able to help me get a good garden going out here, using permaculture methods. But nothing ever happened with that."

"You didn't seem interested."

Connie's stomach hurt. How many years had they all walked around not really speaking to one another about anything important? She looked at her son. She had always thought they were close.

She rubbed her face.

"What a mess," she said. "We've got to sell those cattle. They're ruining the land. We are responsible for every flower, animal, and grain of sand here, and we've made a wasteland out it."

"Connie," Phil said, "you can't just tell me what to do. I'm the injured party here. Your husband stole from me."

"And from me," she said, "and from my son and daughter. But you and my husband have been pillaging this land. What if someone from the Borderlands Ranchers Association saw what I saw today?"

"They wouldn't do anything," Phil said. "They don't all follow the rules either."

"These 'rules' are guidelines we came up with," Connie said. "I want that herd thinned down to something that the land can manage until we figure out what we're going to do next."

"What do you mean 'figure out what we're going to do next'?" Phil asked. "We're a cattle ranch. What else are we going to do?"

"It's not sustainable," Connie said. "We're not making it. It's always been tough, even before Chuck began pilfering. I almost don't blame him for stealing. He must have felt like he's been working for nothing for thirty years."

"For nothing?" Matt asked. "But this was the life he wanted."

"I know," Connie said. "Come on, Phil. You can't be happy with the way things have been going."

"Lots of ranchers are diversifying," Matt said.

The three of them sat quietly at the kitchen table.

"Are you ready to turn this place into a dude ranch?" Phil asked.

Matt shrugged. "Maybe. Teach people wilderness skills. Teach them how to survive."

"Could you teach me that, please?" Connie asked.

"Some of the ranchers take people out hunting," Phil said.

The three of them looked at each other.

"None of us is much of a hunter," Connie said.

"Niche marketing," Matt said. "We could have a small herd of grass fed cattle. There's a big market for organic beef."

"Marilyn said she saw an ad from a ranch in Montana that was selling skin care products," Phil said.

"Really?" Connie said. "Huh. I don't know nuthin' about makin' any pretty faces."

Matt smiled.

"Hey, I'm trying to get my sense of humor back," she said.

"I could kill him," Phil said.

"The problem existed whether he was here or not," Connie said. "Now we've got to figure out what to do without him."

"You could take in boarders," Phil said. "I'm sure you could find a mess o' people who'd love to live way out here."

Connie laughed. "Yes, I'm sure."

"You want to come to our place for dinner?" Phil asked.

Connie shook her head. "Naw, I'm good. You guys go ahead."

"I'm picking up Samantha and Amy at the airport tomorrow morning," Matt said. "You want to come?"

"Please don't make me," Connie said. "I'll take all the blame for everything if only I can be exempt from that chore. I'd be trapped for hours listening to Amy tell me all the ways I went wrong."

Phil and Matt pushed away from the table.

"Oops, I said that out loud, didn't I? Well, you know I love your sister, but she can be a little opinionated."

"At least she speaks up," Matt said. "If she had been here probably none of this would have happened."

"I'm sure she believes that," Connie said.

"Mom."

"Sorry. Thanks for going to the bank, both of you, and thanks for making a payment for us, Matt. We'll figure this all out. We'll figure out something."

"I'll see about selling some of the herd," Phil said. "I'll talk to Marilyn and Manuel. They might have some ideas."

Connie nodded. Now she wanted them gone. She had forgotten Samantha and Amy were coming tomorrow. She should clean out a room for them. Or something. Make the house presentable. Samantha was never any problem, but Amy seemed to turn up her nose at everything and everyone.

Phil and Matt headed for the door.

"By the way, Mom," Matt said, "I told Amy you weren't going to wait on her hand and foot. Or even clean up her room. And I'm going to stay here during her visit to make sure she's no trouble."

"What about you? You're a lot of trouble. Such a pain in the ass."

"Momma's boy," Phil said.

"Don't you forget it," Matt said. He kissed the top of Connie's head. "See you tomorrow, Mom."

Connie let Jimmy in, and then she closed the door and locked it.

She shivered. She was so glad they were gone. She wanted to be alone. Away from them.

She had felt the same way every time she had seen someone since Chuck left. Maybe she had felt that way before he left? Maybe that was why she stayed in the house most of the time when she wasn't out riding and collecting or horse doctoring.

Did this mean she didn't like being around people any more?

And tomorrow she was going to have a house full of people. Relative people.

She groaned.

How was she going to survive that?

Sometime later she heard a knock at the door. Jimmy didn't bark. He just wagged his tail. Connie went to the door and opened it. Manuel stood on the porch holding Gabriela's hand with both of his. Gabriela looked up at Connie and smiled.

"Hello, you two," Connie said. "Come on in. Isn't it supper time? You want me to make you something?"

"No, no," Manuel said. "We ate. I just wanted to stop by and see how you're doing."

Gabriela ran to Jimmy, who happily tolerated her embraces.

"Not too hard," Manuel said to her.

"Coffee?" Connie asked as she and Manuel walked into the kitchen.

"You don't have to wait on me," he said.

"I know I don't have to," she said, "but I'll get you some coffee if you like."

He nodded and sat at the table. Connie got him a cup from the cupboard and poured coffee from the pot into it. He took the cup from her, then glanced back into the living room.

"Where's Isabella?" Connie asked.

"She's away," Manuel said. He looked at Connie. "So you

okay? Phil called and told me what's happening."

Connie nodded. "Yep, it's a mess."

"He couldn't tell me whether I have a job or not."

"You have one right now," Connie said. "You'll have one unless we lose the ranch."

"Is that possible?" he asked.

"Manuel, did you know they had increased the herd?" Connie asked. "Have you seen the land southwest of Box Canyon?"

"I have," he said.

"Damn it," she said. "I thought you of all people would have told me."

"I tried talking to Chuck," he said. "He seemed so concerned about money. I understood. I've been trying to find some land myself. I've been trying to get Chuck to let me buy in for years, but he wouldn't even consider it. I've got a little chunk of money. It's not a lot, but it might help out."

"You want to buy into the ranch now?" she asked. "But it's a family ranch."

"I understand," he said. "And if you're against it, too, I'll drop it. It's been ten years and I've been waiting for Chuck and Phil to make me foreman like they promised. I've got a daughter. I've got to do something so that she doesn't end up living in a bunkhouse or out in the streets."

"I just don't know if there will be a ranch left in a month," Connie said. "If you bought into the ranch now, you might lose everything. I would gladly rent you part of the land."

He shook his head. "I don't have the capital to do what I'd like to do myself, but with this land, if it was done right, it could be an amazing place."

"Done right?"

They looked at one another. Connie turned away first.

"I told Phil to sell down the herd," she said. "And he said 'you're not the boss of me.'"

Manuel laughed.

"Can we at least all get together and discuss the possibility of me buying in?" Manuel asked.

"Of course," Connie said. "How much you got?"

Manuel smiled. "I can get together about fifty thousand."

"Wow," Connie said. "You could probably buy yourself a nice little farm for that kind of money."

"I'm not a farmer," he said.

Connie sighed. "Chuck took out a loan for a lot more money than that. What do you think we could do with this place? I've been thinking about it, and Phil and Matt and I talked about it. Maybe we could market organic beef. Or make skin products."

Manuel arched an eyebrow.

"Yeah, well, not my bailiwick, I know."

"We should do what you always wanted to do," he said. "We should raise horses, and we should look for your aunt's herd of Irish horses. She said they could save the ranch."

Connie leaned back in her chair. "There is no herd of Irish horses. You know this land better than anyone."

"I know jaguars live in those canyons," he said, pointing east and then north, "but I've never seen one. I know the bumblebee hummingbird lives in those hills—" He pointed west. "—but I've never seen them. I even think masked bobwhites live in the southern plains near the border, but I haven't seen them either. I've never really searched for them. I think the wild is all over this land, but we don't find it because we either don't look or we don't believe it's possible."

"What would we do with a herd of mythical sea horses if we found them?" Connie asked.

He shrugged. "I don't know. Maybe people would want to buy them."

Connie shook her head. "I wouldn't sell a jaguar, so why would I sell an Irish sea horse?"

"I don't have all the answers," he said. "I just have this feeling about the horses. I've always had this feeling. I always thought Delilah was telling the truth about them."

"And I always thought she was lying."

"You did not!" Manuel said. "You would never call Aunt Delilah a liar."

"All right, not lying, just . . . telling a story," Connie said. "Let me sleep on this."

"You're looking at me like I'm crazy," Manuel said.

"No," Connie said. "I've got butterflies in my stomach. Probably something I ate."

Or something she heard.

It was absolutely impossible to find sea horses in this desert. It was ignorant, stupid, silly. It was like looking for a Bigfoot.

"I better get Gabriela home," Manuel said.

Connie nodded, but neither of them moved. They listened to Gabriela giggling in the living room with Jimmy.

"Where is Isabella?" Connie asked again.

Manuel looked at her.

"Don't bullshit me," Connie said.

He sighed. "She left me."

Connie could hear her heart in her ears again.

"When?"

"Yesterday."

"Oh fuck me."

Manuel looked at her.

"Sorry," she said. "Something about Chuck leaving. My language has gotten foul."

Gabriela looked over at her but didn't say anything. She rarely said anything. Connie had actually never heard her speak. Manuel said she sometimes spoke to him. She went to school. She read and wrote. She just didn't talk.

Much.

"I know," Connie said. "I said a bad word, Gabriela. I'm sorry! Jimmy, growl louder so she can't hear us."

Connie reached for the phone on the countertop behind her. She called Marilyn.

"Yep." Marilyn.

"What do you know about Chuck and Isabella?" Connie.

"What do you mean?"

Connie got up and moved closer to the sink. She turned on the fan over the stove. Manuel went into the living room. She heard him turn on the television.

"You know what I mean," Connie said. "How many fucking secrets do you all have? It's not like I've been dead. Couldn't someone have given me a heads-up? That motherfucker left me for Manuel's wife, didn't he?"

"I don't know," Marilyn said. "I know that he was over here a lot when she was here, and he took her home a couple times. But she's so young. I didn't think. I thought he just had a little crush."

"Didn't it occur to you that Manuel is Chuck's age and he fucking well married her!"

Connie threw the phone across the kitchen, toward the back door. Then she opened the door and went outside. Slammed the door behind her. She jumped off the porch and ran. Kept running. When she was a distance from the house, she opened her mouth and screamed.

Her scream turned into a roar.

Then a wail.

She breathed the cool air. In and out. In and out. Watched the fading sunlight turn the mountains pink.

She went back into the house.

Gabriela stood in the living room holding her father's hand.

"I'm sorry if I frightened you," Connie said. "I got some bad news."

The girl nodded.

"She had some bad news, too," Manuel said. "Her mother left yesterday and told her she wasn't sure when she would come back."

Connie looked at Manuel.

"I didn't know," he said. "I didn't put it together until Gabriela mentioned a yellow truck, just a few minutes ago."

"And you couldn't tell me that before you tried to talk me into letting you invest in the ranch?" she said.

Manuel frowned. "It's not like that. You cannot believe—" He pressed his lips together. "We have taken enough of your time."

He turned Gabriela around, and the two of them walked out of the house. Gabriela looked back at Connie and waved.

Connie shut the door and locked the door behind them.

She phoned Matt. He didn't answer, so she said to his voice mail, "I don't want Amy to come. I don't want you to come. I don't want anyone here. I just want to be left alone."

She walked down the hall toward the stairs to her bedroom. She heard Jimmy following her. She turned around and pointed a finger at him.

"Not even you."

She went up the stairs and into her bedroom and slammed the door shut.

Chapter Eight

Connie fell to sleep immediately. She dreamed Manuel was on the other side of a wash that was filling up with water. She called out to him. He didn't hear her. The water kept getting higher and higher. She knew she'd never reach him.

She woke up in a cold sweat. She turned on the light and sat up in bed. She started shivering.

Why was that dream so frightening?

Shouldn't she be having dreams about Chuck leaving her?

She rubbed her face. She wished she hadn't fought with Manuel.

Or whatever it was that had happened. When she realized Chuck had run off with Isabella and Manuel had known—even though he had only known for a short time—she had felt betrayed.

More betrayed than when Chuck left her?

No.

It was different.

Manuel was her friend. Manuel had known her since she was

a child. They were supposed to look out for one another.

They always had.

She shouldn't have accused him of trying to take advantage of her. He never would. She knew that.

After she found the dead girl, he was the only one she could stand being around. He would take off time from work and ride with her. Or sit with her. They would talk about the weather, or the drought, or the sound of a bird they heard and couldn't quite identify.

Sometimes he would talk about the sea horses, remind her how they used to search for them.

Urge her to try again.

He never talked about cattle.

While everyone else was ignoring her depression, he stayed within shouting distance, always.

She hadn't realized it until now. Just now in the middle of the night after a bad dream.

Chuck had been in close proximity to her, but he had withdrawn. Her parents never mentioned the dead girl or Connie's change in behavior.

And Matt and Amy may have tried to break through to her, but she had not noticed.

Manuel had been the only one she was comfortable being around for a long time. And then eventually she let Jimmy back in—as long as he didn't bark.

And Loosey.

She would have to apologize to Manuel. Or at least call him and pretend it never happened.

She slipped down under the covers and went back to sleep.

She woke up cold. It was still dark. She never wore pajamas. She was always warm in bed, and Chuck was like a big old heater. Tonight she was chilly. She moved to the middle of the bed, hoping that would be warmer.

It wasn't. She got out of bed, switched on the light, and dug around for pajamas in her dresser. She couldn't find any.

She opened the dresser drawer that held Chuck's underwear and socks.

It was nearly full.

She opened the drawer with his white T-shirts and jeans.
Half full.

"You left your clothes?"

She went to the closet and opened the door. Most of his shirts were still hanging there. Blue, blue, blue, red, red, blue and red flannel.

He had taken his yellow shirt and probably some blue and red shirts. This closet didn't look as full as it usually was.

And his suit. He had taken his dark blue suit. The one he wore to weddings and funerals.

At least he used to wear it. She didn't think it fit him any more.

Too much paunch.

Connie sat on the edge of the bed.

Although lately, his paunch had grown smaller. He was eating less. Walking more. Asking her to cut down on the meats and fats.

When they first got married, they had both cooked, but as the years went by, Connie began spending more time in the kitchen and house, and Chuck began spending more time outside on the ranch.

She took care of the children. She cooked the meals. She paid the bills. He ran with the cattle.

After the kids left, she hadn't cooked much. Chuck had become a meat and potatoes guy, and she didn't like cooking cows. She didn't like raising them, and she didn't like eating them.

She knew she should have affection for the cattle. But she didn't. When she was a teenager on the ranch, she had viewed them rather benignly. But as an adult, she watched them and thought, "They shit where they eat and they eat where they shit."

And she lost her appetite.

She knew they had been bred to be what they were: a kind of walking meat market. Wasn't their fault. They could only be what they could be.

Sometimes she wondered if that was true of her and Chuck. They had started their lives together wanting to go on an adventure, to live a different kind of life. They had wanted to create a new way of being husband and wife and mother and father. They wanted to live on the land as a family, with their children, and build a happy little life together.

Yet once they began ranching, they had gotten overwhelmed with what they did not know, so they looked to their neighbors for help. And soon enough they were modeling their lives on the neighbors—because they were at least surviving—and they started living the way most of the ranchers lived. They weren't different from other people. They were the same.

Because the same was easier.

They knew if they were seen as strangers forever, they'd never make it. It was a small community. They had to know their neighbors and get along with them.

Connie couldn't point to any particular event or conversation or anything where she and Chuck decided they were ranchers and they needed to live like other ranchers. It just happened.

She forgot there was any other way to live.

She didn't know if she liked her life or loathed it.

She did know she was an idiot.

She should have suspected something when Chuck started losing weight. She had caught him combing his hair and looking in the mirror more than once in the last few months.

She had teased him about becoming vain in his old age.

Not so old he couldn't find some young chickie to take him in.

What on earth could that girl see in Chuck? What had she seen in Manuel? It didn't seem like she was interested in conversation—and she certainly wasn't getting that from Chuck. Neither man had any money. Neither was ever going to have any money.

Manuel was good-looking, at least.

Connie got up and began pulling Chuck's clothes out of the dresser and piling them on the floor. She took his shirts off the hangers and flung them on top of the pile.

Then she opened the door—Jimmy was sleeping in front of it—and hurried down the stairs and into the kitchen. She got several garbage bags and took them upstairs. She filled them with Chuck's clothes, then dragged them down the stairs, through the hallway, across the living room floor, and out the front door. She stood on the porch looking around at the darkness. She wanted to burn the clothes. She wanted to watch every fiber of Chuck's clothes wither in the flames and disappear into the night sky.

But she knew Goodwill could use the clothes. They never had enough men's wear.

So she dropped the bags on the porch and left them there for later.

She went back into the house and up to her room. She stood in the doorway.

It smelled of Chuck.

"Chuck, Chuck, fucking chucking. Fuck Chuck, fuck Chuck."

Jimmy watched her.

She went to the window and flung it open. Then she grabbed her pillow and went down the stairs to the room at the end of hallway, on the north side of the house—Delilah's old room. They had used it as a guest room for most of their thirty years in this house, even though they rarely had guests.

She opened the door, switched on the overhead light, and went inside. Jimmy was right behind her.

It was a large room. She had painted the walls a burnished gold some time ago and installed a big old Mexican-style bed that took up most of the room. On the south side of the room was an old wooden dresser with metal handles. On top of the dresser, an old red and yellow wooden rooster strutted. A metal lamp stood on an old wooden nightstand next to the bed. Across the room from the end of the bed, a recessed bookcase nearly filled the wall—except for where a small door opened into a tiny closet. Aunt Delilah had not been what anyone would call a clothes horse.

A large window looked out over the desert, although Connie couldn't see anything tonight.

Connie cracked the window open and pulled down the blinds. She switched on the light near the bed and turned off the overhead. Everything in the room softened as soon as she switched the overhead light off.

"There," Connie said. "Much better."

She couldn't smell Chuck in here. She didn't know if he had ever come into this room.

She pulled the burgundy-colored bedspread down to the end of the bed, and then she got into the bed and slipped under the covers.

The sheets felt cool and clean.

Spotless.

Fresh.

Like a whole new beginning.

Jimmy watched her.

Connie flung her old pillow across the room. Then she slapped the covers.

"Come on," she said to Jimmy. "As long as you don't bug

me, you can stay. But be forewarned, I am on the warpath."

Jimmy hopped onto the bed. He stood looking at her for a moment. Then he walked in a circle. And then in another circle.

And another.

Connie sighed. "Jiminy Cricket! Lay down."

Jimmy curled up on the bed, close to Connie, but not too close.

"There you go."

Chapter Nine

Connie heard a giggle. She opened her eyes. All was silent. Maybe someone was giggling in her dreams—laughing at her life. Light streamed through the blinds, but Jimmy was still curled next to her. She was surprised he hadn't asked to go out.

She heard feet on the stairs down the hall.

Little feet.

Was Gabriela in the house?

More likely Amy, Matt, and Samantha, ignoring her admonition to stay away.

Connie got out of bed. She hadn't brought any clothes down with her, so she was wearing only her camisole and underwear. She pulled a pair of old burgundy-colored pajama bottoms from the dresser and slipped them on. She opened the bedroom door slowly, quietly, and then tiptoed down the hall and up the stairs.

Samantha was standing outside Connie's old bedroom with her hand on the door knob looking at the chaos within.

Connie scooped her up from behind and then dropped her on the bed and lay down next to her.

"Good morning, you!" Connie said, kissing her five-year-old granddaughter on the cheek noisily.

"Grandma!" Samantha said. "We've been looking for you all night."

They faced each other on the bed.

"All night?" Connie said. "I've been here all night."

"On the plane," Samantha said. "We looked for you from the plane. We didn't see you. Mom said to look for you, but I knew we wouldn't see you. I think Mom just wanted me to be quiet. So I fell to sleep."

"And now you're a long way from home," Connie said. "What's your dad think of that?"

"Dad doesn't live with us any more," Samantha said.

Connie shook her head and sighed. Her daughter had failed to share that little piece of information with her.

Samantha got up off the bed. "What room can I have this time?"

Connie sat up. "Any one you want."

Samantha looked around Connie's old bedroom.

"Except this one," Connie said.

Samantha said, "I want this one."

"Ask your mother," Connie said. She got off the bed. She had decided long ago—even before Samantha was born—that it was not her job as a grandmother to argue with her grandchild. That was a parent's job. At least, that had always been her job as a parent. With Amy. Amy had been born cantankerous. She had never liked Connie, at least as far as she could tell. She wouldn't take her breast and liked it best when Chuck fed her the bottle. Then she spent the better part of twenty years ignoring Connie until she went off to college and met what's-his-name, Julian Smith. He got a job teaching at a university in Boston, so Amy went with him.

Connie wasn't certain what her daughter did for a living. She seemed to change interests and jobs like some people changed hats.

Connie glanced at her grandchild and then left the room and went down the stairs.

Her inner dialogue was beginning to sound bitter.

She didn't want to turn into one of those angry husband-less middle-aged women.

She loved her daughter. Amy had a mind of her own. That was a good thing. Amy always let everyone know her opinion. About everything.

That was probably a good thing, too.

Samantha caught up to Connie and grabbed her hand. Connie looked down at her. Samantha smiled, and Connie squeezed her hand. They hopped down the stairs together.

Matt sat at the kitchen table reading the paper. Amy stood at the stove, cooking something.

"Hi, Mom." Amy put down the turner she held in one hand and walked over to Connie. They embraced. Amy held her tightly for a moment. Connie closed her eyes, briefly. She knew the hug wouldn't last.

Amy broke the embrace, then went back to the stove.

Connie sat at the table. She heard Samantha opening and closing bedroom doors, trying to decide where she would roost. Matt pushed his cup of coffee toward her. They liked it the same: black, no sugar. She picked it up and took a sip.

Then she said, "Didn't you get my phone message?"

"Yes," Matt said as he closed the paper and looked at her.

"He told me you didn't want us here," Amy said. "What a surprise." She glanced over at the table and smiled grimly. "But we'd already bought the tickets, and we couldn't get a refund."

"You should have waited a couple weeks and gotten cheaper flights," Connie said. "Besides, what are you going to do here? Or don't you have any place else to go?"

Amy didn't answer. She brought the skillet of scrambled eggs to the table. Connie pulled four plates from the cupboard and put them around the table. Amy scooped eggs onto each plate.

"Samantha!" Amy called.

"Get up and help, you lazy ass," Amy said to her brother. She kicked his boots as she went back to the stove. She opened the oven, pulled a dish of potatoes from it, and brought it to the table.

Matt leaned back in his chair. He was able to just reach the silverware drawer on this side of the counter. He pulled out flatware while balancing on the chair's two legs. Samantha came running into the room and jumped up onto one of the empty chairs. Amy watched her brother.

"Don't you dare," Connie said. "He could get hurt."

Amy rolled her eyes as she spooned potatoes onto Samantha's plate. Then she put the pan on a pad in the middle of the table.

Matt set the chair back down on all four legs and handed out forks to everyone.

"No bread in the house, so no toast," Amy said. "No orange juice either." She pulled out a chair and sat in it.

Matt tossed the paper onto the countertop. Then the four of them began to eat.

"Dad always said grace," Amy said.

Samantha stopped eating and looked at her mother and then over at Connie.

"Your father isn't here," Connie said. She took a bite of eggs. They were good. She vaguely remembered that Amy's latest interest included cooking. "Besides, he only did that when you kids were around. For show."

"Mom, don't bad-mouth Dad," Amy said, "at least not around Samantha."

Samantha shoveled eggs into her mouth, barely chewing; then

she swallowed. A few bites later, she pushed away her plate. "I want to go out and play with Jimmy."

"Jimmy is not a pet," Amy said. "He's a work dog. Don't you want any potatoes?"

Samantha shook her head.

"Go ahead. Stay close to the house and away from the barn."

Samantha got up from the table and ran through the living room. A moment later the screen door creaked open, then slammed shut.

"Amy, this is my house," Connie said. "Don't tell me what to do or say in my own goddamn house. Your dear daddy left me for another woman, a married younger woman, and he embezzled from me, my brother, and you and your brother. I'll say whatever I want to say about him. If you don't like it, leave. I didn't ask you to come, and frankly, I don't want you here."

Amy kept eating. Connie noticed her blink quickly a few times.

Matt spooned potatoes onto his plate. "This is all very good, Amy."

Amy finished the food on her plate. Then she got up, took her plate to the sink, where she dropped it noisily; then she left the kitchen. A moment later, Connie heard a door slam.

"Well, I guess she picked her bedroom," Connie said.

"Mom," Matt said.

"Don't start," Connie said. "I'm not in the mood for her bullshit. Or yours, for that matter. Why is she even here? Did your dad ever call her?"

"No, he hasn't called her or me," he said. "And what did you mean about him leaving you for another woman?"

Connie sighed. She dropped her fork. She wasn't hungry anyway.

"Manuel stopped by last night," Connie said. "Apparently his wife has left him, for my husband. It's all pretty sordid, don't you think?"

"It is disgusting," he said. "But none of this is Amy's fault."

"I know."

"She came to help," he said.

"I'm not some old woman who needs her children to save her," she said. "Maybe one day, but not today. She didn't come to help. She and Julian have split up. She probably didn't have anywhere else to go."

"Wow, Mom," he said. "It's like you and Amy have traded places. You're the old nasty Amy, and she's like you."

"I never hid in the bedroom like she's doing now," Connie said. "I know this is very difficult on you kids. I appreciate that. But I won't be treated like shit in my own house, not any more. Not ever again."

"Are you saying Dad treated you badly?" Matt asked.

Connie looked at him.

"Besides the obvious that he stole money and left you," Matt said. "But before that."

"Before that doesn't matter any more," Connie said. "Did you feed the horses and chickens?"

Matt nodded. "I've been in contact with some buddies from school. I suggested they come out in a few days, and I can take them for a ride. I don't want to go on hunting trips, but I wouldn't mind taking people on wilderness trips. That was part of my training in college, and I've wanted to do it for some time. I can clean out the bunkhouse apartment in the barn and live there."

"You can stay in the house if you want," Connie said. "I never mind your company. You'd have more privacy out there. It's a mess. No one's lived there for quite a while."

"I'll take care of it," he said. "And Phil's arranged to have a cattle buyer come out."

Connie nodded. "How's he gonna explain it?"

Matt shrugged. "The buyer doesn't care, Mom. He's not counting head per portion."

"I don't want any more secrets," she said. "I don't want you to keep anything else from me."

"Like the fact I'm a serial killer?" he said.

"Don't even joke." She stood and began collecting the dirty plates. "And wait on bringing out your friends. I think it's a good idea, but I don't know that I can be hospitable right now."

"Mom, we've got to start something," he said. "These guys are ready to go. They might bring people out from their spring and summer classes. We can charge them. You wanted a garden. Now's the time. They could help with that."

Connie took the dishes to the sink. She sighed and growled. She wanted to go hide in her new bedroom. Or stick her head in the sand.

She had been doing that for too long. Apparently.

Now she had to face the music.

As long as it wasn't country music. She hated country music.

She started to laugh.

"What?" Matt asked. "What's so funny?"

"I just realized I will never have to listen to country music again," she said, "now that Chuck is gone."

"Are you kidding?" Matt said. "There are only two types of music out here: country and western." He grinned. "You're not getting batty on me now, Mom, are you?"

"*Getting* batty? Hah! I'm already there. Now get your ass up and do these dishes. Don't become like all these other men out here who can wrestle a cow or track a mountain lion but can't boil water to save their lives. I taught you better."

"Oh man," Matt said. "I'm going get all the 'I hate men' shit piled on me now. I didn't leave you, Mom. Remember that. Dad did. And he left me, too. And Amy."

Connie looked at her son. He was smiling, but he wasn't joking. She went to the table and kissed the top of his head.

"I know, darlin'," she said. "I'm sorry. I guess I should go apologize to Amy." She sighed. She was doing a lot of that: Sighing. Moaning.

No crying, though.

She could wrestle a cow and track a mountain lion, too. Crying wouldn't get her anywhere.

She wished she had a mountain lion or cow in front of her now. She'd prefer that to talking with her daughter.

Chapter Ten

Connie knocked on the door to Amy's bedroom. Amy had chosen to sleep in her old room, the one she usually stayed in when she visited, unless Julian was with her. Then they took the guest room. Julian rarely came out to the ranch. He said his allergies acted up in the desert. Connie figured he just didn't like it out here in the borderlands. This life was not for everyone.

Including, apparently, her own husband.

"Come in," Amy said.

Connie opened the door. Amy was taking clothes out of her suitcase and putting them into empty dresser drawers.

"Sammy wants to stay up in our old room," Connie said.

"She'll get over it."

"Is this bed big enough for both of you?"

"Mom," Amy said.

Connie went to the window and looked out. Jimmy and Samantha were running in circles together. Connie couldn't tell who was chasing whom.

"So what's going on with you and Julian?" Connie looked

back at her daughter. She leaned against the window sill.

"Nothing's going on," Amy said. "He's just working."

"Samantha said he's not living at home."

"That's temporary," Amy said. "He's got a lot of work to do, so he's taken an apartment closer to campus."

Connie pursed her lips. She had never been Amy's confidante. They didn't have the kind of relationship most mothers and daughters had. Or at least the kind of relationship she had seen between her friends and their daughters. Those daughters seemed to actually like their mothers.

"You could pretend I was your father," Connie said, "and tell me what's going on."

Amy didn't say anything. She closed the empty suitcase and put it in the closet. Then she looked at her mother.

"Do you want to tell me what happened between you and Dad?"

"I have no idea," Connie said. "He left early in the morning. I came downstairs and found a note. It's around here somewhere if you want to read it."

"Matt showed me. He didn't tell me about any woman."

"Who didn't tell you? Matt or Dad?"

"Dad hasn't called me," she said. "Or written to me. I've had no contact with him."

"Do you remember Manuel's wife? Your father apparently ran off with her. Left behind little Gabriela."

"The little mute girl?"

Connie had never thought of her that way.

"I don't know that she's technically mute," Connie said.

"She doesn't talk, right?" Amy said. "So she's mute. Or a mute. Mom, why do you always, always have to argue with me?"

"I'm not arguing with you," Connie said.

She wanted to say, *"You* are always arguing with *me."* But she knew that was childish. She was the mother and Amy was the daughter.

"Yes, she left behind Gabriela. I guess she said she's coming back for her. Probably after she's done with your father. She'll bleed him dry and then go back to Manuel. He'll probably take her back."

"Are you blaming this woman for Dad leaving you?"

"What? No. I don't know. I'd like to blame someone."

"You know you haven't been around much the last few years," Amy said. "Emotionally."

"So you're going to blame *me?*" Connie nodded and pushed away from the window sill. "I figured you'd eventually paint your father as the hero and me as the villain. 'Poor Daddy to be tied to such a hideously awful wife.' Maybe I was depressed, but I didn't leave. I was here every day. If things were so bad, he should have spoken up. Maybe he should have gotten me some help. Instead, he fucks some little *chica,* embezzles from the ranch, and runs away. And I'm the bad guy in this scenario?" She walked to the open door. "I don't need your judgments, Amy. If that's why you're here, please just pack up and leave. I'm not in the mood."

Connie left the room and walked down the hallway. She stood in her living room and tried to breathe deeply. She couldn't. Her stomach was too tight. She had no idea what to do next.

Absolutely everything in her life was upside down.

Or twisted.

Or just plain wrong.

Why *had* Chuck left? Maybe things weren't great, maybe they weren't even good. But they had each other. There had been a rhythm to their lives together.

Now what did she have?

A bitchy daughter and a gentle son who didn't speak his mind.

Jimmy was barking. Barking as he ran in circles with Samantha.

Connie could not stand the sound of that dog barking.

She went to the door and opened it.

"Jimmy," she called, "stop that damn barking."

Samantha and Jimmy both stopped running and looked at her.

"Samantha, aren't you tired after your long trip?" Connie asked. "You can go sleep on my bed if you want."

"Mom and Dad have to put a quarter in the jar every time they swear," Samantha said as she walked up to Connie. "I can't swear at all, even if I have a quarter. Does this mean in this house I can swear?"

"We have freedom of speech in this house," Connie said. "As far as I'm concerned you can say whatever you want."

Samantha smiled and ran into the house. "Momma! Grandma says—"

Connie didn't listen to the rest of it. She knew she'd get crap for it later from Amy. Right now she didn't care. Right now she just wanted to get away.

She went to the pasture and whistled. Loosey lifted her head and looked her way. Then she trotted toward her. Connie took Loosey to the barn and saddled her. Then she led her outside and got on her. Jimmy stood near them, watching. He looked up at Connie.

"Yes, you can come," she said. "No barking. Every time you bark I think someone is dead."

Oh. So that was it.

She didn't like to hear him barking because that was what he had done the day they found the dead girl. Little Rosalia.

Connie didn't want to think about that. She urged Loosey forward, in the general direction of the mountains. She didn't want to see any moonscaped desert. Phil and Matt had better get rid of the extra cattle as soon as possible. Or else she'd turn them in.

Maybe.

As soon as the cattle were gone, they would have to figure out how to restore the land. What they had done—run too many cattle—was why so many people wanted all cattle and horses off public lands. Connie hoped Phil was telling the truth when he said they had not run too many cattle on any of their federal allotment. She didn't want to think about what would happen if they had turned public land into cemented desert.

She supposed the feds would cancel their contract and they'd be thrown off all their allotments.

She wondered if she cared.

She did not want to run cattle.

So maybe it would be a good thing.

No, not a good thing if they had ruined the land.

Not a good thing for the land or the other cattle ranchers.

Connie galloped Loosey across a grassy plain. Jimmy ran to keep up. After a while, they slowed as Loosey picked her way through the desert scrub.

Connie started watching the ground, looking for anything the migrants or drug runners had discarded.

A couple years earlier, the Borderlands Ranchers Association had gotten a grant to hire someone to pick up trash on their lands and the federal allotments. For a year he worked full-time, picking up truck load after truck load of what the walkers had left behind.

It helped. He had gotten quite a bit.

Except for what was up in the mountains.

Connie could be up on some of the old trails, way up in the mountains where hardly any people ever went, and she would find trash. Sometimes at ponds and other water holes, she—and other ranchers—found diapers, pop bottles, and pieces of plastic in the water. She never understood that. She always wondered why the *coyotes* would allow it. If they used these trails over and over and had to count on these water holes, why would they ruin them?

Sometimes she felt so disheartened to be on her own land. It hadn't always been this way. But the human traffic had moved east as the border controls tightened in California and in the border towns in Arizona. Now thousands of migrants crossed the border and walked through the ranches, leaving their garbage behind.

She didn't mind the people crossing. She understood that kind of economic imperative. She did mind the drug smuggling. And she didn't understand why some of them had to destroy the land they walked through. Why pollute a water hole? Why damage solar fixtures on water troughs? Why slice water lines? Why cut fences when they could just open the gates and walk through?

It didn't make any logical sense to her.

It wasn't neighborly. It wasn't friendly.

She and the other ranchers hadn't done anything to harm the migrants. In fact, she had helped many people who had crossed and ended up on her doorstep begging for water.

All the ranchers had.

Or they used to.

She didn't want to think about this again. Or any more.

She watched the ground for a while, then looked up at the mountains in the distance, then watched the ground.

Some day she might find the blue shoe.

Every day the man who picked up the trash had stopped by her house when he was finished. She had been treasurer of the Borderlands Ranchers Association then, so she paid him. Every time he stopped, she asked him if he had found a blue shoe. After a while, he started looking for the shoe, too. He found several blue shoes: running shoes, men's shoes.

No match to Rosalia's blue shoe.

Now Connie saw an empty bread bag. She got off Loosey, picked up the bag and put it in her saddlebag. She got back on Loosey and gave her her head. Jimmy followed.

He didn't bark.

After a while, Connie noticed horse tracks in the dirt. The desert floor was so hard that the prints were barely visible. She got off Loosey and leaned over so her face was closer to the ground.

Yep. Horse tracks. Small horses. Two or three of them? Unshod.

Wild horses? As far as she knew, no wild horses wandered in this part of the country.

Except maybe her aunt's sea horses.

She got back on Loosey. She could follow sign as well as any rancher, she supposed, but it looked like these tracks went up a rocky escarpment. She'd lose them for sure.

She nudged Loosey forward.

"Jimmy, find those horses for me."

Jimmy ran up the escarpment ahead of them.

They had only gone a few yards when Connie lost sight of the tracks. She got off Loosey again. Loosey stood next to her quietly. She was a good horse. She never complained about Connie getting up and down. Sometimes Connie rode Chuck's mule, Leo, and he was always wandering away. If she didn't tie him to something, he'd be gone.

Just like Chuck, she thought as she crouched to get a closer look at the ground. Although to be fair, Chuck had only wandered off once.

Connie couldn't see any more prints or any sign that the ground had been disturbed in any way. She walked around looking for horse manure, broken twigs, or tufts of hair.

Jimmy came running back to her. He hadn't found anything either.

Connie stood up straight. "Well, if these are sea horse tracks, I guess I don't have the gift," she said, "because it seems like these horses disappeared into the desert air."

Connie got back on Loosey, and the three of them traveled through the borderlands for a while longer.

By the time Connie got back to the ranch, it was nearly dark. Jimmy ran straight for the house. She hoped someone would let him in. She heard him bark once, and that was it. She took her time brushing down Loosey. Then she fed her, the other horses, and the chickens.

She was not looking forward to facing her children. They must be wondering what had happened to their normally calm mother.

Connie sighed out loud and went into the house.

Something smelled good.

The living room was dark, but the lights were on in the kitchen, making the whole house seem golden and cozy.

She went into the kitchen where Matt and Samantha sat at the table. In the center of the table was a basket of bread and a bowl of salad. Amy stood by the stove.

"Something smells good," Connie said. She would try to make nice.

Amy carried a large glass dish to the table and set it on the hot pad.

"That looks like lasagna," Connie said. She pulled out a chair and sat in it.

"It is," Amy said. She sat next to Connie. "And before you start complaining about it not having meat, you didn't have any meat in the house. Alice had cheese and spinach so I borrowed some—she said to say hi—and you had the noodles and tomato sauce. So it's vegetarian. I'm not trying to convert you or anything. It's all you had."

"I'm not complaining," Connie said. "It was your father who

liked eating cows all the time. Until he started—well, until lately. Hi, Sammy. How has your day been?"

Matt began serving the lasagna. Amy passed around the salad.

"Good," Samantha said. "I slept in your bed, like you said I could."

"Upstairs or downstairs?" Connie asked.

"Both," Samantha said. "Upstairs was too lonely. So I tried downstairs. That was better."

They all began eating.

"Where did you go, Mom?" Matt asked.

"Just out," Connie said. "Seeing what's happening on the land."

"Looking for the blue shoe?" he asked.

Connie glanced at her children.

"This is very good," Connie said. "I guess those cooking lessons paid off."

"I went to cooking *school,*" Amy said. "I didn't need lessons."

Connie took another bite of her lasagna. Amy sounded offended. What on earth had Connie said that was offensive?

"In any case," Connie said. "It's good."

"What blue shoe?" Samantha asked.

Amy gave Matt a look. He shrugged.

"It's nothing, darlin'," Connie said. "A little girl lost her blue shoe somewhere on the ranch. I sometimes go out and look for it."

Samantha nodded. "If I ever see it," she said, "I'll be sure to bring it to you right away."

"Thank you, honey," Connie said. "So what room are you going to stay in this time?"

"I'm going to sleep with Mommy," she said, "so she doesn't get lonely without Daddy."

"That's sweet of you," Connie said. "I could never get your mother to sleep anywhere near me. When she was a baby, she wanted a room of her own. When she cried, she'd only let Grandpa rock her back to sleep."

"It wasn't personal, Mom," Amy said. "I was just a baby."

"You never grew out of it," Connie said.

Amy didn't say anything.

"Did you check out the bunkhouse?" Connie asked Matt.

"I've already started cleaning it out," he said. "It's not so bad. Sammy helped me."

"Be careful with her in there," Connie said. "It's pretty dusty."

"It's not really," Matt said. "And I found a couple of old boxes with Aunt Delilah's journals in them. And some of stuff. I left the boxes in the living room near the couch. Thought you might like to go through them."

"Grandma," Samantha said. "I had another dream when I was sleeping in your room."

Connie looked at her granddaughter. "Another dream?"

"She's been dreaming about the ranch," Amy said.

"Do you want to tell me about it?" Connie asked.

"The horses were here," Samantha said. "The sea horses. I couldn't see them very well, except for one. And it was blue. It was a blue sea horse, but it was here."

Connie looked at Amy and then back at Samantha.

"That sounds like a lovely dream," Connie said.

Samantha nodded. "I think the blue horse was for you," Samantha said. "I could smell them, Grandma. They smelled like the ocean, like where we live." Samantha took another bite of lasagna. Then she put down her fork. "Can I go play with Jimmy?"

"Jimmy isn't a pet," Amy said. "But if you've had enough to eat, go ahead."

Samantha pushed away from the table, then ran into the living room.

"Why do you always tell her that?" Connie asked. "About Jimmy not being a pet?"

"You used to always tell us that," Amy said. "Didn't she, Matt? The dogs weren't pets. They were here to work."

"She could have said that," Matt said. "I didn't pay too much attention." He grinned. Connie laughed.

"Samantha said she had 'another dream,'" Connie said. "Has she been dreaming about the sea horses since you told her about them?"

"She has been dreaming about sea horses," Amy said. "At least that's what she calls them. But I've never told her anything about Aunt Delilah's sea horses. Not a word."

Chapter Eleven

Connie spent the next few days talking to lawyers and accountants. Matt continued to fix up the bunkhouse. Amy went grocery shopping in town. She took Samantha and asked Connie to come with them. Connie declined the offer but gave Amy money and told her to get whatever she needed.

Connie asked her lawyer to hire an investigator to track Chuck down. She didn't want him back—at least she didn't think she did—but she needed him to relinquish any legal rights to the ranch.

And she wanted their money back.

She didn't see Manuel, although Matt mentioned him in passing. Apparently he was still working on the ranch despite their argument the other night. She knew she should apologize to him, but she didn't feel particularly kindly toward him—or anyone else.

The accountant advised her to either find an investor or think about selling. He thought she had only a year or two to turn it around; otherwise, they were going to lose the ranch.

After everyone had gone to sleep one night, Connie sat on the couch working on a crossword puzzle. The house felt empty, even though Amy, Samantha, and Matt were all there. Jimmy slept at her feet. In the quiet of the night, things seemed calm and normal. But she didn't feel right. Maybe she missed Chuck. Maybe she wished he would come home.

Maybe she could forgive him.

If he came home now, she would say, "I'll go have sex with some young stud, and then we'll be even."

Of course, she didn't know any young studs.

Okay. Skip the young stud.

Instead she'd tell him, "I'll have sex with Manuel. Since you had sex with his wife, it seems only fair. And then we'll be even."

After that, they could go back to their old lives.

If she had sex with Manuel, things would definitely not go back to normal.

She did not want to think about that.

She wanted to go back to a time when she wasn't constantly worried about how to save her house and the land.

Phil still believed cattle would save them.

Matt was planning wilderness trips.

None of it felt like enough.

She had to do something.

But right now, she wanted to sleep. She didn't like being awake in the middle of the night again. And again.

She looked around the room and saw the boxes from the bunkhouse Matt had brought in several days earlier. She kept meaning to go through them or put them in the office. She leaned over and dragged one toward her.

Jimmy grumbled and moved away from her.

She lifted the top off one box. It appeared to be filled with old papers. Connie took out a pile of papers and thumbed through them. Old feed bills. Electric bills. Dental bills.

All kinds of bills. Paid in full.

Letters from various relatives. A few from Connie's mother, Dorothy. Connie read a couple of them. Aunt Delilah and her mother exchanged recipes and weather news.

In one letter, her mother wrote, "Connie says you didn't mention the Irish sea horses this summer. I guess this means you've finally given up on that foolishness. They were just dreams she had when she was practically a baby. Connie does not have the gift, or whatever it was you believed she had; she is not your sea horse wrangler or whatever it is you called her. Life is a lot easier without all these impossible hopes and wishes, isn't it?"

Over the word "wrangler" someone had put an X and written in "siren."

Looked like Aunt Delilah's writing.

"Sea horse siren," Connie whispered.

What dreams was her mother talking about? Connie didn't remember any dreams that would have any meaning to Aunt Delilah.

It was too late to call her mother now.

Besides, she hadn't told her parents yet that Chuck had left her.

Maybe she'd call tomorrow.

She looked for more letters from her mother—or to her mother—but she didn't find any that were interesting to her. At least not interesting tonight.

She pushed that box away and pulled the other toward her. Inside she found several journals and record books, plus folded blueprints and diagrams.

Connie flipped through the record books. Some were money accounts, others detailed the flora and fauna on the ranch. In some journals, Delilah—and others—had made sketches of the local animals, birds, insects, and plants.

"Wow," Connie whispered.

The drawings were so clear and detailed. Connie would recognize any of these creatures or plants if she saw them in the wild, she was certain. Delilah had noted when and where each had been found. Delilah's was not the only handwriting, but Connie found no other names to indicate who else had written in the wildlife journals.

One of the journals was filled with recipes. On the inside cover Aunt Delilah had written, "Recipes from the Sky Blue Horse Ranch." She had a little legend on the second page: "v" for vegetarian, "m" for meat, "ow" for Old World, "nw" for New World. She explained that Old World recipes were ones she had gotten from her parents or other relatives.

Amy might like to see the recipe book. Connie set it on the coffee table for her. Then she opened one journal that was clearly a diary: "Jan. 15. One of the calves Buddy brought down died. Something's going around. Hope it isn't hoof and mouth.

"January 28. Too cold this winter. Hope all the cattle make it."

Connie flipped through the journals until she found entries from when she was a child. She scanned her aunt's clear slanted cursive writing for her name. She found it in an entry from when she was about five years old.

"Sept. 24: Consuelo is here with her mother. That boy Philip I can barely stand. But Consuelo, she is one of us, I believe. She told me she dreamed of the horses from the water last night. She said she could smell the sea and that she saw them up in our mountains. I had not told her about the sea horses. Her mother warned me not to fill her children's heads with these stories. I don't understand: These stories are our heritage. Consuelo came to me on her own and told me. I think it is a sign."

Connie leaned back against the couch. She rubbed the goosebumps on her arms.

She heard a sound in the kitchen and looked up. Matt stood over the sink, drinking a glass of water. She had been so engrossed in the journal that she hadn't heard or seen him.

"Matt," she said. "Did Samantha see these journals? Or did you read them to her?"

Matt looked at her and shook his head. He set down the glass and shuffled over to her. He looked sleepy.

"Why? What's going on?" He sat on the couch next to her. She handed him the journal and pointed to the paragraph about dreams. Matt took the journal and read.

Then he looked at her.

"Wow. That's kind of spooky. Do you remember this?"

"No."

"Maybe it means you should look for the sea horses," Matt said.

"What would I do if I found them?" Connie said. "If they existed, I wouldn't sell them. What use would they be?"

"Oh man, Mom, that's cold. Do they have to be of some kind of economical use? Can't they just exist?"

"*I* can't just exist," Connie said. "I've got to figure out some kind of economical use for myself. Why should they be able to just exist?"

Matt shrugged. "I don't know how to explain it to you if you don't see it. The sky exists. It's this amazing blue thing above us. We can't buy and sell it. It's of no economical use."

Connie growled. "I know. I know, I know. I just feel like I have to do something to save us."

"Save us from what?" Matt said. "We're not drowning or anything. We're okay. Dad's gone. We've got some financial trouble. But we're okay. If you want to look for some wild mythical sea horses in the Sonora Desert, I say go for it, Mom."

Connie smiled. "Manuel wants me to look, too," she said. "And he wanted to invest in the ranch."

"He's got real live moula to give us?" Matt asked.

"Yep."

"Well, hell, Mom. Dad and Phil promised him a promotion for years and didn't deliver. Let's let him invest. Right on. That'll help us."

Connie laughed. "How did you get to be so positive with a mother like me, a father like Chuck, and a sister like Amy? You're just a little pot of sunshine." Connie pinched his cheek.

"I'm like this because you always encouraged me to follow my dreams," he said. "You told me money wasn't everything. You said I should find beauty in the world and follow it to the ends of the Earth if need be. And to me, there is beauty all around in this place, at the ends of the Earth."

Connie looked into the face of her second born. "I said that? I don't remember. I'm glad I did. I hope I encouraged both of you. Sometimes it seems like—" She stopped.

"Seems like what?"

She shook her head. "Nothing. Go to bed. I'm going to read some more of these."

"Naw," he said. "I'm not sleepy. I want to read with you."

She handed him another journal, and she sat back and continued reading the one she had.

"Sept. 30. Took Consuelo out to see if we could find the place in her dreams. She couldn't be sure. We looked for tracks. A couple times I thought I saw horse tracks. Then I'd look again and they were gone. She feels bad that she can't help, I know. Her mother has warned me not to push her. I believe she wants to find the horses as much as I do. I've always thought it was my destiny. It is hers, too."

Connie read the last two lines out loud to Matt.

"That's tragic," Connie said. "She wanted to find these horses her whole life and she never did. She thought it was her 'destiny.' Clearly if such a thing as destiny exists, finding the horses was not her destiny because she never found them! No wonder Mom thought it was all foolishness. What a waste of a life!"

"You don't know that," he said. "Maybe Aunt Delilah loved and lived and had a good time always believing that these amazing horses roamed this land."

"But she wanted to find them," Connie said. "She wanted me to find them."

"Listen, Mom," Matt said. "Here's a passage from when you and Phil were here one summer. You were fifteen, I think. Aunt Delilah writes, 'It's good to have the children here. I've had the privilege of watching my niece and nephew grow into young adults. They are good people. I've done what I can to protect this land. There is so much visible and invisible that happens: We have no idea. I have smelled the sea in this desert. I know what is here, and I have done my best to preserve it.' She sure sounds happy to me. She didn't think her life was a waste."

"I wish you had known her. She was a strange and wonderful woman. She was thin and tall and she almost always wore something purple, mostly long purple skirts. She often looked as though she was ready to go out to some place fancy—some place fancy from another century. The only time she wore pants was when she was riding. She told me it was because she came from a long line of sirens and she was still shy about showing her legs."

"Sirens?"

"Mermaids," Connie said. She laughed. "My mother hated it when she started talking about that kind of thing. The Emericks were all a bunch of liars, my mom said. And one was worse than the other."

"But isn't your mom an Emerick, too?"

Connie nodded. "Yes. On her mother's side, which was the same side as Delilah. Almost all the Emerick women kept the name, even after they married."

"That reminds me," Matt said. "I saw some kind of coat of arms and a family tree. I didn't look at it closely." He dug around in the open box and pulled out a piece of paper. "Here it is." He spread it out on the coffee table. Connie and Matt leaned over it.

On the page was a green and white coat of arms for the Emerick name. At the top of it was a mermaid holding a trident. On either side of the coat of arms shield were two black rearing horses. Their manes were white with a green tinge and curly, like sea foam.

"Aunt Delilah used to talk about our Irish relatives," Connie said. "She said it was a common belief amongst the Irish in their villages—especially the villages near the sea—that some of their people were descended from mermaids. Aunt Delilah called them sirens. Sometimes she had friends visit from Ireland and other places and she called these women her siren sisters. There was something about them. They visited a couple times when we were here. They seemed like they were from another place, obviously, and yet they fit in here. They were exotic to me, these women. When they walked, it seemed like they floated above the ground." She laughed.

"Do you think they actually believed they were descended from mermaids?" Matt asked. "I mean, mermaids weren't real. Maybe it was a metaphor for being descendants of fishermen, or sea folk."

Connie nodded. "Sure. But Delilah thought it was the sirens who brought the sea horses here. Doesn't make much sense. Why would they leave the ocean all around Ireland to come to this desert—even if it did used to be an ocean?"

"I think our ancestors bring their stories with them," Matt said, "from the old world, from wherever they're from. Maybe they bring their spirits with them, too—like the fairies, in the case of the Irish, which would include the sea horses—and mermaids. Not literally, of course. But figuratively. The stories just get transferred onto this land."

"So you don't think there were any real horses?" Connie asked.

"No sea horses," Matt said. "No fairy horses. Maybe real horses."

"She believed so strongly that these horses were the answer to everything," Connie said. "I had forgotten so much of this. Just since your dad left, I've started to remember. Aunt Delilah said we came from a long line of sea horse sirens—like horse wranglers. It was our heritage to protect and preserve these amazing creatures, she told me. She said being a 'sea horse siren' was like being a horse wrangler only it required a belief in the existence of magic—and the ability to sing your own siren song. She'd tell me this stuff and I'd listen with one ear. With the other ear, I was thinking 'there goes crazy Aunt Delilah.' She said the men in the family never understood, at least not the ones who married into the family. That's why she never remarried."

"Do you think she was ever in love?"

"She loved this land," Connie said. "She loved this place. She was married once, but I don't know anything about him. I really know nothing about her love life. She definitely marched to the beat of a different drummer."

Connie pulled more papers out of the box. She unfolded one that turned out to be an old diagram of a house.

She spread it out on the table. She recognized the landmarks. The sycamores down by the creek not too far from where the house was now. There was the *acequia madre*—the mother ditch—running out to where the gardens had been and beyond. The rock outcropping just east of the house that was called Willie's Corner, for some unknown reason. But the house was not the house as Connie knew it, although it was in the same place where the house sat now.

Beneath the bird's eye view of the building was the name: Sky Blue Horse Ranch House, complete 1850. It was a large house, hacienda style, rectangular with a courtyard inside. A side panel showed an arched porch going all around the house.

"Do you think it was actually built?" Matt asked. "It looks like it's on the footprint of this house."

"I never heard anyone talk about another house," Connie said. "Although I suppose that could have happened. "Look at this courtyard. There's a fountain in the middle and gardens all around."

"Looks like they had permaculture before there was permaculture," Matt said.

Connie looked at him. "What is permaculture anyway? If we're going to try it here, I should understand it."

"It's a blend of the two words 'permanent' and 'agriculture'," he said. "But it means we build and plant with nature, so that the ecosystems are sustainable, self-sufficient, and resilient. You do a lot of work in the beginning, understand the climate, weather, microclimates, what grows naturally in an area, then you design the gardens and buildings, put them in, and eventually you have to do very little work. You know, this whole house could run on solar generated electricity."

"I'm for it," Connie said. "You design it and we'll put it in. I'm not sure where we'll get the money for it all, but we'll do it." Connie looked at the house plan. "I like the feel of this much better than this house. I wonder if this house was a part of the original or if they tore down the other and built this one."

"Or it burned down," Matt said. "Seems unlikely they'd just tear down a perfectly good house."

"I'm ready to pull this one down," Connie said. "And it's a perfectly good house."

"Why?"

Connie shrugged. "It stinks of your father."

Matt grimaced.

"Sorry. I'm a little bitter."

Matt laughed. "Yeah, me too."

"Hey."

They looked up. Amy came into the room, wrapping her robe around her. She sat in the easy chair across from them and pulled her legs up underneath her.

"It's cold," she whispered. "What are you guys doing up?"

"Did we wake you?" Connie asked.

Amy shrugged.

"We're looking through some old journals of Aunt Delilah's," Matt said. "Apparently Mom had dreams about sea horses when she was a kid, too, just like Samantha, before anyone told her about the horses. Spooky, eh?"

Amy frowned and yawned at the same time. "You're making that up," she finally said.

Matt shook his head. "It's right here in black and white."

"Could Samantha have read the journals?" Amy asked.

Matt shrugged. "I didn't see her looking at these boxes. They were only in the house for a little bit before she told us about the dreams. Can she read?"

"Sure," Amy said. She leaned over and picked up one of the journals and opened it. "You know, like a five-year-old reads. I don't think she could read this cursive handwriting. Maybe there's such a thing as communal dreams. Or relative dreams. I don't know. I'm babbling. I wanted to tell you both—I meant to tell you earlier, but I—I wanted to tell you Dad called me today."

Connie and Matt both sat back against the couch. Neither said anything. Amy cleared her throat. "He called to see how everyone was doing. He told me he was sorry for leaving without saying good-bye. He asked me to tell you he was sorry, too, Matt."

Matt glanced at Connie, who stared at her daughter.

"Apologized to *me?*" Matt said. "What about Mom?"

"I know," Amy said. "He didn't say anything about Mom, except to ask if you were okay. And I told him you were."

"Did you happen to mention the money he stole?" Matt asked.

"I told him the ranch was in trouble," she said. "I did mention the money."

"And?" Matt asked.

"And, he didn't answer," she said. "Just said he was settling into a new place and he'd let us know more later."

"Did you get his number?" Connie asked.

"Why?" Amy asked. "Did you want to talk to him?"

"I want to know where he is," Connie said. "I'm paying an investigator to track him down. We need his signature on some documents. Plus, I'd like to get back the money."

"It was one of those throwaway phones," Amy said. "At least that's what he said. But I can give you the number."

"A throwaway phone?" Matt said. "Isn't that what drug smugglers use? Isn't that what criminals use?"

"Matt," Connie said. She rarely heard her son upset, let alone angry.

"It's just so creepy what he's done," Matt said. "And then he calls Amy because he knows she won't give him any shit."

"That's not fair," Amy said.

"To him or to you?" Matt said.

"To me," Amy said. "I told him I thought it was really lousy what he had done, especially him leaving Mom in the lurch. I told him what I thought." Her voice broke. She stopped. "But he is my father. I don't want to lose all contact with him."

"I'd appreciate it if you didn't tell him we're looking for him," Connie said. "I understand your loyalty to him, but if I don't get some of that money back, I'm going to lose the ranch.

It's not your home. But it is mine. It is your brother's. It is Samantha's legacy."

Amy stood. "You can both go to hell. I didn't even have to tell you he called. I'm not the enemy. No, I won't tell him you're looking for him. I so appreciate how welcome you've made me feel in this place that is not my home. We'll leave as soon as we can so you won't have the burden of our company. I've been cooking and cleaning for you for days and you haven't even said thank you."

"Now you know how I've felt every day for the last thirty some years," Connie said.

"She says thank you every time she sits down to the table," Matt said. "I've heard her."

"Well, she doesn't mean it," Amy said. "You and her in this little clique together that I'm not a part of. I get it. But you know, I haven't been having an easy time in my life either. Did you ever consider that I might need my mother?"

Connie looked up at her daughter. "No, it wouldn't occur to me. You've never needed me before. I asked you about Julian, but you didn't want to tell me anything. Don't play the victim here, Amy. You are my daughter, and you're welcome here. I told you that before. But your attitude has been that I did something wrong to cause your father to leave. I put up with your scorn when you were a child. I won't do it now."

"Scorn?" Amy said. "I don't know what you're talking about! I just wanted us to have a relationship. But you pushed me away again and again. Just like now. I try to get close to you and you won't have anything to do with me. Never mind. I don't want to talk about it. I'm going to bed. I'll make the plane reservations tomorrow."

She strode out of the room.

Matt and Connie sat in silence for a moment.

Then Matt said, "What a drama queen."

Connie smiled but kept herself from laughing. "Don't make fun of your sister."

"Why not? She loves these little dramatic scenes where she can play the martyr. Then we all walk around on eggshells trying to make her feel comfortable and happy, until she decides we've done something wrong again. She's cried wolf with this stuff for too long. I'm not going to fall for it. Don't you either, Mom."

"I'm sorry if she's not feeling welcome," Connie said. "I have appreciated her cooking for us. I haven't felt like eating, that's for sure." Connie folded up the diagram. "Come on. It's late. I'm going to bed."

"Me, too," Matt said. "See you in the morning." He kissed her cheek, then got up and left the room.

When he was gone, Connie opened Aunt Delilah's journal and started to read again.

Chapter Twelve

Connie slept in. She lay in bed and listened to the house. All was still. Quiet. It was strange not to hear Samantha's giggles or Amy's murmuring. How quickly she had gotten used to everyone being around.

She looked out the window at the mountains in the distance. They appeared especially clear this morning. Everything was sharp. Distinct. A puffy cloud seemed to bob slightly, just above Craggy Peak. Connie smiled as she stared out at the wild beyond her window. The view was much better from here than it had been in the bedroom she shared with Chuck.

And the bed was better, too.

Every morning she opened her eyes and felt wide awake.

She couldn't remember how long it had been since she felt awake.

It was as though she had been Sleeping Beauty and Chuck's note had pricked her awake.

Something.

She was lost and afraid. Terrified, actually.

But she was also awake.

She got out of bed, left her room, and went to the kitchen. Amy had left a note on the kitchen countertop, "There's a quiche in the oven. Love, Amy."

Amy's way of making up? Connie wondered if her daughter was actually going to leave today.

She doubted it.

She got the little quiche from the oven, pulled a fork from the drawer, and took the phone from its cradle. Then she sat at the table. She took a bite of the quiche.

Not bad.

She pressed in her parents' phone number.

Her mother answered. Darn. She was hoping to talk to her father.

"Hi Mom," Connie said. "How are you?"

"Hello, Connie," she said. "I'm fine. Dad and I just got back from taking a walk. What's up?"

Her mother always wanted to get to the point. With her father, she could talk about sports or politics. Even art or philosophy. Her mom wanted to know the point of any and all conversation. At least that's what it always felt like.

"I wanted to let you know that Chuck has left," Connie said. She put down the fork and pushed the quiche away. "He didn't say why, except that he couldn't take it any more. Or couldn't do it any more. He's actually run off with another woman." She tried to sound matter-of-fact. "Manuel's wife." Her mother didn't say anything. "Anyway, he's left." She started to tell her mother that Chuck had stolen money from them, but then she realized if she and Chuck ever reconciled, her parents would not welcome him back if they knew he had taken money from the ranch.

"Mom," Connie said. "Are you there?"

"It's a lot to absorb," she said.

"Matt and Amy are here," Connie said. "We're figuring it out.

Hey, Mom, I wanted to ask you about Aunt Delilah. We found some papers of hers. There were letters from you to her. You talked about me dreaming about sea horses. I don't remember that."

"I don't remember either," she said. "That was ages ago. You were just five years old."

"Good thing you don't remember it."

"It was just part of that sea horse nonsense of Delilah's," she said. "The women in our family were crazy. I've told you that. That's why we need to be especially grounded and practical, always. Delilah was not. She believed fairy tales and myths were real. Our ancestors—the supposed sirens—were probably whores, prostitutes, and mad women who managed to finagle passage to the new world from some old men willing to listen to tall tales about sea horses and mermaids."

"Wow, Mom," Connie said. "It's like you've been sitting there waiting for me to ask this question so you could say all that. I don't remember anything about the women in our family being crazy. Where did that come from?"

"No, I told you," she said. "I warned you to be practical. You wanted to travel the world and find the poetry in life. I suggested you find one place and make it your own. I didn't think that one place would be the ranch, but Chuck seemed like a good down-to-earth man."

Connie ran her fingers through her hair. She knew her mother had wanted her to settle down when she was younger, but she didn't remember anything about the mad women of the Emerick clan.

"I suppose in a way I have been waiting to say it," her mother said. "After you found that dead girl, you seemed to go a little off your rocker."

Connie laughed. She couldn't help it. No one said "off your rocker." At least not seriously.

"You thought I had gone crazy?" Connie asked.

"Hadn't you?"

"I was a little depressed, I guess," Connie said. "I think it's interesting to find out you all thought I was crazy, but no one tapped me on the freakin' shoulder and asked me if I needed help. Nobody said anything until Chuck left me. Now you're all anxious to tell me how weird I've been acting."

"Don't play the martyr, Consuelo," she said.

"What?"

"You used to do that when you were younger," she said. "Everyone was always wrong, everyone was always mean to you, and you were the injured party."

Connie made a noise. Really? Maybe Amy had learned it from her.

"Okay, Mom," she said. "I just wanted to let you and Dad know what was up. By the way, I found a diagram, like a blueprint, of a house that used to be where my house is now. Do you know anything about it? It kind of looked like a hacienda—square with a courtyard in the middle."

"That was the original house," her mother said. "I think it was already here when the Emericks came and bought it. Or stole it. I'm not sure how they got it. But it was destroyed. Fire, earthquake, storm. I'm not sure what happened. Or when. It was before my time. Then the ranch house was built over it."

"I'd like to know more about the sea horses," Connie said.

Her mother sighed. "I know as much as you do. They were stories I heard when I was a child. Delilah believed them; I didn't."

"Did you ever see any signs of them?"

"You mean the disappearing hoof prints?" she said. "Sure, I saw signs of wild horses. Delilah said we couldn't track them because we didn't have the gift, whatever that gift was. I really think our parents told us those stories to get us out of their hair. It was like sending us off to search for treasure. It's funny, though, when I was maybe ten, or twelve, I got sick and had a pretty high fever. It was too hot in the house so they put me outside. I must have been hallucinating because I could have sworn this strangely colored horse—a small horse—came up to me and put her muzzle on my chest. I remember I could hear her breathing. And I could smell fish, or the ocean, or something. Even then I thought how real Delilah's delusions were!" She laughed. "I got better. Delilah told me there were horse prints around my bed. She was a good storyteller."

"Mom, did you ever consider the possibility that she wasn't lying?"

"I didn't say she was lying," she said.

"I'm not tape recording you," Connie said, "so I can't play it back, but you said she wasn't telling the truth. You said she was delusional." Connie stopped. Why was she arguing with her mother? Did she want a confrontation or did she want to have a conversation? "Sorry, Mom. I realize you weren't calling her a liar. I guess I'm wondering if you ever thought maybe she was right. Maybe there were horses. Not magical horses, per se, but maybe our relatives did bring over a boatload of Irish horses."

"I don't even know if the Irish had horses," her mom said. "Weren't they poor?"

Connie laughed. "Mom."

"I don't know if I ever thought she could be right," she said. "Maybe. Maybe I did. But I couldn't spend my life chasing a fairy tale. She was so alone, you know. No family. Just us. And we didn't come down much."

"I read her journals last night," Connie said. "She didn't seem lonely. And it didn't seem like she was writing about fairy tales. I think she thought the horses really existed. And I'm wondering if maybe they did—or do. There's so much of this part of the country that we don't know about."

"So you want to go out on a wild goose chase instead of figuring out why Chuck left you?" Dorothy said.

"It's a wild *horse* chase, Mom," Connie said. "And yes I think I just might go on that chase."

"Maybe you should—"

"What, Mom? What are you going to suggest? He ran off with a woman half my age. I ain't ever gonna be half my age. And I was never girly like you or like Amy. I'm not going to tart myself up just so some fat slob like Chuck will want to have his way with me. That ain't me."

"I was going to suggest you come up here for a visit," Dorothy said.

"Not that I was implying you were a tart," Connie said. "Or anything."

"Peter," her mother shouted away from the phone. "I think your daughter wants to talk with you."

"Good-bye, Mom," Connie said. "Love you."

Her mother was gone.

"Hi, honey" her father said. "How's life on the farm?"

She had to say the whole thing over again for her father. He listened sympathetically and offered to help in any way he could.

"You can always come live in Scottsdale with us," he said. "We've got a spare room. Just don't tell Phil. I'm not crazy about him or his wife." Her father laughed.

Then they talked about the upcoming baseball season.

By the time Connie got off the phone, she knew what she was going to do.

She called Manuel.

"Hello," she said when he answered the phone. "I've decided to forgive you."

"Not a great way to begin an apology, Consuelo," he said. "I just went into town to pick up Gabriela, so I'm not in a very forgiving mood. She doesn't want to be in school any more. The ride in makes her sick. The ride back makes her sick. She misses her mother."

"Bring her here," Connie said. "Samantha could use someone to play with."

"I'll be there in a few."

She put down her phone, smiled, then walked into the living room. Delilah's recipe journal was still on the coffee table. She picked it up and carried it outside. She looked around. Where was everyone?

She went to the bunkhouse. The door was open. Her family was inside.

"Wow," Connie said as she stepped over the threshold. "This looks great. Maybe I'll come live out here and you can go live in the house."

It was shaped like a "7" with a bunk bed in the short part of the number. The bathroom was near the bed, but not too close, and the kitchen was at the other end of the room, with a small table and chairs near the stove. In between, on either side of the narrow room, were tall bookshelves, a small sofa hide-a-bed, and a coffee table.

Samantha and Amy sat at the kitchen table. Matt was on the sofa with his feet on the coffee table.

Connie raised an eyebrow.

"Hey, my house, my rules," he said.

Connie shrugged. Jimmy came and put his nose in her hand. She rubbed his head.

"Hey, Manuel is bringing over Gabriela," Connie said. "As company for Samantha."

"Mom, she doesn't talk," Amy said.

"I understand that. But she's very good company. She's having trouble in school since her mother left. Speaking of such things, doesn't this little one need to be in school?"

"I'm homeschooling her," Amy said, "until we get things figured out."

Connie started to say she hadn't seen any schooling going on, but she decided it was none of her business.

"If Manuel wants, I can homeschool Gabriela, too, for a while," Amy said.

"That's generous," Connie said.

"It gives her another guinea pig for her food experiments," Matt said.

"You've got that right," Amy said. "Jimmy's starting to shy away when I come around now."

Matt, Samantha, and Amy laughed. Jimmy looked up at Connie. She smiled. She was glad they were all getting along.

"Okay, well, that would be great," Connie said, "because I want to talk with Manuel about some things, so if you could look after Gabriela, I'd appreciate it."

Samantha jumped up from the table. "There she is!" She ran out the door.

"I guess she heard his truck," Amy said. She got up from the table, too, and passed by Connie.

Connie touched her elbow, and she stopped.

"Thanks for the quiche, darlin'," Connie said. She kissed Amy's cheek. "And for looking after Gabriela. I found this in Aunt Delilah's papers. It's filled with recipes. Some of them are hers that she made up or got from people around here, but some are family recipes. She has a little story about each of them. I thought you might like it."

She handed the recipe journal to Amy.

"Thanks, Mom."

Then she left the room. Matt looked at his mother.

"She got to you, didn't she?" Matt said.

"She's my daughter," Connie said. "I want her to feel comfortable being here."

"She's not going anywhere," Matt said. "I asked her."

"Leave her be," Connie said. "No sense you two fighting."

"We don't fight," Matt said. "She does what she wants and I ignore her. So you look like a woman with a purpose today."

"I am," Connie said. "I'm going to let Manuel invest. As long as your uncle agrees. You, too. You should be on the deed if you want. You've worked here all these years. You paid part of the mortgage."

"I don't know, Mom," he said. "After reading Aunt Delilah's journals, I think this is women's land."

Connie kicked his feet on the table.

"Well, if Amy wants a part of it," she said, "I would love that. But for now, it's us. I want Manuel in, and we're going to look for those imaginary horses. I'm hoping Delilah wasn't crazy and that I'm not crazy. In the meantime, you get that wilderness stuff going and the permaculture. I want to find out about the original house, too. Maybe we could rebuild it. Make this a kind of education place for workshops and such, like you were talking about."

Matt stood. "You woke up on the right side of the bed, eh?"

"According to your grandma," Connie said, "I woke up on the crazy side of the bed. I swear sometimes she drives me crazy."

Matt put his arm across Connie's shoulders.

"You sound just like Amy when she's talking about you."

"Hey, what about those bunk beds?" Connie said. "What if you want to have someone over. That's not very romantic."

"Then I'll bring them to your house," he said. "You've got lots of beds."

"I dare you," Connie said.

"Unless you already have someone over," he said. "You can put a sock on the front door or something."

"Ew," Connie said.

"Too early, eh?" He shrugged. "You wait. You're gonna want

some alone time with someone one of these days."

Matt and Connie left the bunkhouse. Gabriela was already outside of Manuel's white truck, standing a few feet from Samantha. Samantha was saying something Connie couldn't hear. Then she took Gabriela's hand and they ran toward the house. Jimmy ran after them. Amy waved to Manuel and went into the house.

Matt said, "Well, I bet you and Manuel need to kiss and make up, so I'll leave you alone. But I'll tell you right now if you're hatching any harebrained ideas, I'm all in." He started to walk away, and then he stopped and looked back. He rubbed his chin. "Why do they call it a harebrained idea, anyway? I've seen jackrabbits, I know jackrabbits, and they seem pretty smart to me. Or at the very least, they look really cool." He grinned, turned on his heel, and went toward the house.

Manuel was leaning against the truck with his arms crossed when Connie reached him.

"You've known me practically your whole life," Manuel said. He shook his head.

"I shouldn't have accused you," Connie said. "I'm sorry. I do know you. And *you* married her. Christ, Manuel, she's nearly half your age, talk about harebrained."

"Her or me?" he said.

"Both."

"Hey, you were the love of my life and *you* married him," he said, "and then I had to work with him—for him—and I had no choice if I wanted to be near you." He smiled.

"I can never tell when you're joking or not," Connie said.

"I'm not joking," he said. "What better way to piss you off than by marrying her?"

"Quit it, Manuel," Connie said.

He kicked the dirt. "Naw. I thought I loved her. I guess. Couldn't pine for you forever."

"What would you do if one of these days I responded to your flirting?" Connie said. "You'd go running for the hills."

Manuel looked around.

"You ever see me running from anything?" He shrugged. "Not me. I don't run from nuthin'. You know I've been waiting right here for you since we were kids."

Connie looked at him for a moment. He returned her gaze.

"I called you because I want to take you up on your offer," Connie said. "To invest in the ranch. To become partners. That is, if I can get Phil to agree. Matt has already said it's okay with him. Matt's going to start a kind of wilderness school, I think, and maybe a demonstration farm—or ranch—for desert permaculture—creating sustainable self-sufficient gardens—"

"I know what permaculture is," Manuel said. "Matt talks about it all the time."

"He didn't talk to me about it," Connie said. "Not much." She shook her head. "That doesn't matter. I think we should look for the sea horses. Maybe they do exist. Maybe they're beautiful and wonderful and people will want to see them. Maybe they'll pay to see them. I don't know. Right now I don't care. I just want to look for them. Finally and for sure. You're a good tracker. I'm fair to middlin'. I figure, let's give it a shot."

Manuel unfolded his arms and looked at her. "I am ready. If you got the plan, I am the man."

Connie giggled. Then she laughed. "Okay, I guess I've got da man. Time for the plan."

Chapter Thirteen

Connie had to argue with Phil, privately, for a time before he would agree to let Manuel invest in the ranch. Then they all went to the lawyer: Connie, Phil, Manuel, and Matt. They asked Amy to come, but she said she trusted them to do whatever needed to be done.

"Don't do that," Connie said. "Don't trust anyone when it comes to money. Look at what happened to me."

"But Mom, the ranch doesn't belong to me," she said. "It belongs to you and Dad."

"Not for long," Connie said.

Connie didn't want to go either. She wanted to stay out of town, stay out of banks and lawyer's offices, but she went. She needed to understand every bit of their business. The lawyer started the paperwork to make Manuel a partner and to turn the whole ranch into a partnership.

They went to the accountant, and he showed them how to start a business plan.

They put Manuel's money in the bank.

Two of Matt's friends came out from the University of Arizona and stayed several days. Every morning, Amy packed them gourmet lunches, and they went out on horseback. Connie was glad to see the mules and horses getting out more. Matt brought his horse, Kalamazoo, over from Phil's stables to board permanently at Connie's ranch. Kal was a gelding who didn't always play well with others, but he and Loosey were old friends, and she quickly helped acclimate him to pasture culture at C&C Ranch. Since Manuel and Connie were planning on riding out several times a week, Manuel brought his horse, Major, over to her stables, too. Major got along with everyone, human or horse.

Connie knew that if they actually started a wilderness business, they would have to get more mules. They were much more sure-footed in these mountains than the horses. Chuck and Phil used mules whenever they needed to go far up into the mountains. Lately, Chuck had been using Phil's ATV rather than riding at all. Connie hated those things. Whenever he proposed getting one, she always told him she thought they were for fat, lazy ranchers. She didn't actually believe that—probably—but she knew if she said it to Chuck, he wouldn't get one.

Perhaps she had not always been as kind to him as she ought to have been.

Connie and Manuel got out a topographical map of the area and plotted their search for the Irish horses. Connie decided to just call them wild horses if anyone asked what they were doing. Or maybe Irish horses. Calling them sea horses just sounded too strange. And she didn't want anyone to think she was crazy.

No one asked.

One day, Alice came over with Jamie from the bank. They brought coffee cake and some kind of newfangled coffee from Phoenix that Amy oohed and ahhed over. After the second cup of coffee—which Amy made after she ground the beans—Jamie and Alice wanted to talk about Connie's problems. Connie was not inclined to do that.

"I love you both," Connie said unexpectedly, in the middle of their visit. "And I'm so glad you came over. But Manuel and I have work to do today." She stood. "You see, we're so upset by what our spouses did—you knew it was Isabella that Chuck ran off with, right? Anyway, we're so upset that we've decided we're going to find a spot on the land and build our own little love nest, away from town, the ranch, and my children, who keep coming back home to roost. So if you'll excuse me—"

Jamie giggled, and Alice smiled.

"I wish you were telling us the truth," Alice said. "I like the image of you and Manuel shacking up. Yep. Childhood lovers come back together after thirty plus years. It's very romantic."

The two women got up to leave.

"We were never lovers," Connie said as she escorted the women to the door.

"Please, don't spoil the fantasy," Alice said.

"I don't want you fantasizing about me and Manuel," Connie said. She opened the front door.

"You started it," Jamie said. "He is a nice looking man. Mmm-mm."

Manuel's truck drove up just then. Dust billowed for a moment and then settled back down.

"When you're ready to tell me what you're really doing," Alice said, "give me a call."

Connie smiled. "I do appreciate you visiting," she said, "and especially you, Jamie, driving down that awful road. I'll see you soon."

Samantha ran around the women and out the door to greet Gabriela. The two girls had become fast friends despite their age difference—and the fact that Gabriela didn't speak.

The women went out to Alice's car. They both waved to

Manuel. Samantha and Gabriela ran up onto the porch and sat on the rattan couch together. Jimmy sat near them.

"Stay close by," Manuel said to Gabriela. "Always let Amy know where you are."

He and Connie went into the house.

"Hey, Manuel," Amy called from the kitchen. "You and Gabby want breakfast?"

"No, thank you," he said. "We've eaten."

"You're not feeding her cereal all the time, are you?" Amy asked. "That's really not good for growing children."

"Amy, he's a grown man," Connie said. "He knows how to cook for his child." Connie rolled her eyes. Then she said quietly, "You do know how to cook, don't you?"

He nodded.

"I wasn't talking to you, Mother," Amy said. "I was having a conversation with Manuel."

"That's not a conversation," Connie said. "That's telling someone what to do."

Amy made a face at her. Lately they had been able to spar with each other without either of them getting angry. Connie wasn't exactly certain why. Maybe it was because she had given Amy Delilah's recipe book.

"Mom, are you hungry or not?"

"Dear, you've made me coffee and scrambled eggs," she said. "You are not my slave. You are not Manuel's slave. You are a guest in my house. Relax a little."

"A guest? Cool. Does that mean you'll cook for me?"

"No, not a chance."

Amy brought two cups of coffee to the table and set one in front of Manuel. Then she sat at the table with them. Connie spread out the map.

"I'm going to try one of Delilah's recipes tonight for dinner," Amy said. "Did Mom tell you about the journals she found?"

"They were Delilah's?" Manuel asked.

Amy nodded.

"Oh, she was quite a cook," Manuel said. "Do you remember her feasts, Consuelo? People came from miles on both sides of the border for her fiestas."

"I remember a few of them," Connie said. "They were fun. Didn't she sometimes call what she made 'desert sea food?'"

"Yep," Manuel said. "She stopped saying that because she got sick of Phil sticking out his tongue with food on it every time she said 'sea food.'"

"Phil was always so gross," Connie said. "I think Aunt Delilah wanted me to help out with the cooking, but I thought cooking was women's work, so I wasn't interested. What a little idiot I was."

"Can't argue with that," Amy said. "Providing nourishment for other people is a great act of healing, of love. And putting the dishes together so they taste good and so they provide nourish-ment—well, that's magic."

"I don't think any of you thought my cooking was magic," Connie said.

"No, and neither did you," Amy said. "You hated cooking. And we tasted your hate."

"No!" Connie said. "Don't say that! I never fed you hate. I disliked cooking because I wasn't very good at it. Like I said, I thought it was women's work and I didn't like that I had become the designated cook because I happened to have ovaries."

Amy nodded. "I understand that. It wasn't fair. But it would have been nice if you had made some effort."

"I did make an effort. For one thing, I did it! I made sure you were fed three squares a day. Are we going to have one of those 'bad mother' conversations? I'm really not up to it."

"No," Amy said. "No! I wanted to tell Manuel about the rec-ipe book."

"Good, recipes are better than fighting," Manuel said.

"We're not fighting," Amy said. "We're exploring our relationship."

"It feels like fighting to me," Connie said.

Amy sighed. "Okay. I can see now is not the time for this conversation."

"I want to hear all about her recipes," Connie said. "I do. But Manuel and I need to get started."

"Be back by seven," Amy said. "I don't know where we're going to put ten people."

"Ten?"

"I invited Uncle Phil and Aunt Marilyn," she said. "Plus Matt's friends. Manuel, you and Gabriela are welcome."

"Thank you," he said.

"We'll be back," Connie said. It was dark by 7:00 p.m., or close to it, and at this time of the year, the desert got so cold so quickly at night. She didn't want to be out there after dark.

"How about up here?" Connie said to Manuel.

She pointed to a spot on the map, near Box Canyon. "You've seen prints there. I was nearby the other day and saw something." Without thinking she moved her finger to the spot on the map where she had found Rosalia.

She generally avoided that area. She came close to it sometimes because the canyon shrine was near it.

She quickly moved her finger to a different place on the map.

"We're burning daylight here," she said.

Amy handed them each a small cloth lunch sack. Connie knew Amy had made them herself, stitching a little pocket on the side of the sack for the box of frozen gel. She filled the inside of the sack with food.

"Have a good day," Amy said.

"Thanks for these," Connie said.

Soon, Manuel and Connie were out riding the range. Jimmy ran alongside them.

It felt good to be away from the house and outside in the bright sun and cool morning. Soon a coyote ran out in front of them. A rabbit followed. Connie and Manuel looked at one another and laughed. It should have been the other way around: rabbit and then coyote.

"The rabbits around here have a lot of cojones," Manuel said.

"That implies they are manly rabbits," Connie said. "My guess is she is a momma rabbit telling the coyote to get the hell out of her space and away from her children."

"Just like you?"

"Just like me," Connie said. "Amy may not like to remember it but I was—and am—a fierce momma bear. I was always watching out for them, but I didn't let them know. I wanted them to be able to stand on their own feet. Especially Amy. Girls have it tough in this world. I wanted her to be able to do anything. I just don't understand why she wants to do the things she does."

"You mean because she likes to cook?" Manuel asked. "And sew. Consuelo, someone who has practical skills can go very far in life."

"I guess I was hoping she'd be able to pay someone to do those things for her," Connie said. "You know, she'd be a lawyer or a doctor."

"Just like your mother wanted you to be anything but a rancher," Manuel said.

"Yep," Connie said. "Just like."

They rode together for several hours. They found prints, separately and together, but they were shod horse prints, so they didn't follow them.

Sometimes Manuel and Connie talked. Sometimes they were silent. The sky was clear blue. Hawks and crows circled overhead. Jimmy wandered away now and again. Once he came running back like a bat out of hell.

"What's wrong, buddy?" Connie asked. "Cat got your tongue?"

For a while Jimmy walked between Loosey and Major. Connie watched him for a bit to see if he was limping or bleeding. He seemed fine, just spooked. Probably stuck his nose in the wrong hole. If a rattlesnake had gotten him he'd either be howling or dead.

They stopped for lunch at the head of Black Canyon, near Spring Creek. The creek was running strong this time of year, and the air felt fresh and cool. The sound of water over rocks was soothing to Connie's ears after hours of listening to the near silence of the desert. They tied Loosey and Major underneath a young sycamore and then sat on flat rocks near the water.

"This is a great sandwich," Manuel said. "The bread has a particular flavor. I don't know what it is. It's infused with something."

Connie started laughing. She covered her mouth with her hand. *"Infused?* You been watching the food channel or something?"

"Can't a man better himself?"

"This *is* good," Connie said. "She should open a restaurant. Her talents are certainly wasted on me. I eat food because I have to. I don't feel any particular attachment to it."

"What about flavor?" Manuel asked. "Don't some things taste better or worse to you?"

Connie shook her head. "No. Not really. It's like breathing. I don't notice the air. I don't notice food."

"But you were always such a sensual girl," Manuel said.

"I haven't been a girl for a long time," Connie said.

"I bet you notice more than you think," he said. "Close your eyes."

"No."

"Come on."

She groaned, then closed her eyes.

"What do you smell?"

"Nothing."

"Try again."

She sighed and breathed deeply. "Mud. I smell mud."

"And?"

"It's spring mud," she said. "Not winter mud. The air is getting warmer, not getting colder. It almost has a spicy smell to it, though not quite. Earthy. Deep dark muddy earthy smell." She breathed again. "I smell Jimmy. A kind of wet dog smell. And the sandwich. Or maybe I taste it. It's an onion garlic smell or taste. And sweat. I smell a bit of sweat. Not me. You. Musky. It's gone now."

She opened her eyes. Manuel was watching her.

She grinned.

"Now try listening."

She closed her eyes.

"I hear the horses breathing." She was silent. "And Jimmy chewing on something on his paw." She listened. "The sycamore leaves brushing against one another. It's so quiet, as though someone is very quietly brushing crumbs off their hands, only there's hundreds of them, all trying to be quiet. I hear my heartbeat in my ears. And of course, the water running over the rocks in the bottom of the creek." She smiled. "I know this sound. I recognize it. The creek bottom and the stones are very happy. They love this water. They love this constant shower, this drowning in luxury, and the water is happy, too. Like two lovers: one constantly on the move, the other still. And I hear a bird somewhere in these sycamores. Not a song. Just moving from limb to limb."

She opened her eyes again.

"Now, take one bite of your sandwich and chew it slowly with your eyes closed," Manuel said.

She looked at him, made a face, and then did what he asked.

She took a bite of the sandwich and closed her eyes.

She really wanted to swallow. But she made herself chew.

She could hear the creek. It was speaking a language of its own.

She could almost understand it.

Loosey snorted.

Jimmy sighed.

Connie tasted cilantro, avocado, garlic, olive oil. Cumin? An ingredient she did not recognize. Part of it stung the inside of her mouth.

"Keep chewing," Manuel said.

She chewed. The tastes went down her throat. Now she was just chewing a ball of something in her mouth.

"Okay," he said.

Connie swallowed.

She opened her eyes.

Everything seemed sharp and clear, like it often did right after a rain. Jimmy looked over at her. A vermilion flycatcher flew out of the sycamore tree. Connie squinted and watched the flash of color disappear from view.

The creek flowed.

Connie looked at Manuel.

"Make a difference?" he asked.

"No," she said.

"Liar."

She laughed. "I must admit it did taste pretty good. Or I guess I should say I actually tasted it. Makes me want to eat the rest of it."

She tried to eat her sandwich slowly. She tried to savor every bite of it.

When she was finished, she said, "I feel like I've been this way all my life. Not really enjoying things. I can't remember when I stopped enjoying life. It feels like it's always been this way. Do you remember me being different from this?"

"What do you mean 'this'?" Manuel said. "You are Consuelo, as I have always known you. Complex and beautiful."

"Hah!"

"You have never known how to take a compliment," he said.

"It's because I don't believe them," Connie said. "I was never queen bee. Never someone who turned men's heads."

"I meant every compliment I've ever given you," he said.

She shook her head.

"Why would you doubt me? Have I ever lied to you?"

"Except for all the nice things you've said about me?" She shrugged. "No."

"You never took me seriously."

Connie got out the apple slices Amy had put in the pack and began eating one. She chewed slowly. "I think she put cinnamon on it. Tastes like apple pie without the pie part."

"We don't have to talk about this," he said. "Ever. I told you that ten years ago."

"It's been longer than that," she said. "Hasn't it?"

"Yes, let us debate how long it has been," he said.

Connie sighed.

Ten years ago, more or less, she and Manuel had been out looking for strays on a day much like this one. They had decided to camp out rather than return to the ranch. That night as they sat in front of the fire, he told her he loved her and he always had. He had asked her to leave Chuck, to leave her children, to leave this place and run away with him.

She told him she didn't believe him. She told him he shouldn't keep flirting with her. It wasn't right.

Then she had thrown up.

She never understood why what he said frightened her so much.

He was her best friend. He wasn't supposed to have feelings like that for her. She was married with children.

But she had liked the idea of running off with him more than she would admit.

She had lain awake most of that night, waiting for him to come into her tent.

Wanting him to come into her tent?

Later they made a joke of it. He claimed he had had too much tequila. And then they pretended it never happened.

"Do you really want to talk about this?" she asked now as they sat next to the creek. She had a knot in her stomach. Maybe it was time she started talking about those things that made her uncomfortable.

"No," he said. "It was humiliating enough the first time. I opened my heart to you, and you threw up."

Connie chuckled. Manuel smiled.

"I suppose it is funny," he said.

"I didn't take you seriously," she said again.

"I think you did," he said.

"How could I believe you?" she asked. "You were always flirting with me. Always complimenting me. I thought that was just who you were with women."

"That is who I am with you," Manuel said.

They were silent.

"Didn't you ever wonder what kind of life we could have had together?" he asked. "If you hadn't married Chuck."

Connie shook her head. "No. No."

Her eyes started to water.

No.

She was not going to do this.

"Before you went away to college," he said, "we talked

about our life together. How we would create this amazing place where people could come and see what the desert is truly like. We'd spend several weeks a year looking for the sea horses. We didn't know if we would or wouldn't find them. We didn't care. We would bring artists, poets, writers, and others here. I know you wanted a life of poetry. Instead you settled on a life of . . . tax codes."

Connie stared at the water.

"I didn't believe you," she said. "Then or later. I didn't believe it was possible."

She could see Manuel shaking his head on the periphery of her vision.

She wiped her eyes and then shook out her hands.

"What do you want me to say, Manuel? Maybe I didn't believe you. Maybe I didn't believe *in* you. Maybe I didn't believe in myself. Maybe it was never Chuck's fault that we fell into this dauntingly boring unfathomable rut. Maybe it didn't have anything to do with that dead girl. With all her lost potential. Maybe it was just that I am not capable of living a life of poetry. I don't even know what that means now. Maybe this is just who I am. I don't stop and smell the roses or anything else. I don't notice the world around me. I don't feel anything. That girl you loved is long gone. Just like the dead girl."

"When I heard about you and Chuck getting married," he said, "I felt as though my entire world fell apart."

Connie put her head in her hands for a moment. Then she said, "I'm sorry."

"At least tell me you and Chuck have had lousy sex all these years," he said.

"Yes, terrible," she said. "Why do you think we've only got two children?"

He laughed, but she could see the pain in his eyes.

"Aren't you glad we didn't run off together ten years ago?"

Connie said. "Chuck and Isabella did what you wanted us to do. It has not brought happiness to anyone."

"Maybe it brought happiness to them," he said.

"I don't give a fuck about them."

"I tell you what has changed," he said. "You never swore before. You suddenly talk like Ernie Bidwell. Do you remember him?"

"Oh yeah," Connie said. "I remember." She put away the rest of the apple slices and picked up her lunch bag. She and Manuel walked over to their horses.

"His wife said he only swore in public," Manuel said. "He thought it would keep people from being too sociable with him."

Connie laughed. She briefly put her hand on Manuel's right arm and squeezed it. Then she stuffed the lunch bag into her saddle bags and went to Loosey's head. She untied her and led her to the stream. Manuel did the same with his horse. The two horses stood side by side, sipping water from the stream.

"I was thinking I'd go up that backbone near Box Canyon," Manuel said. "On the north side. You want to go back to where you found the tracks a few days ago?"

Connie nodded. "Sounds good. Should we meet at the crossroads in a couple of hours?"

Major lifted his head. Manuel brought the reins up to the saddle horn. Then he put his left foot in the stirrup and swung his right leg over the horse.

"By the way," he said, looking down at her. She put up her hand to shield the sun from her eyes as she looked at him. "I never said I wanted to run away with you. I wasn't asking you to leave this land or your children. I only said that I loved you and I wanted to be with you. I don't think that's anything like what Chuck and Isabella did. I'll see you in a while."

Then he rode off.

Connie stood still for a moment.

Jimmy walked over to her. She looked down at him.

"For the life of me, I can't seem to say the right thing to any-one."

Chapter Fourteen

Connie followed horse tracks for a time before she realized they were shod horses, probably Matt and his group. Apparently her talk with Manuel had thrown her a bit off balance.

"Gotta pay attention," she told herself.

One way to get killed on this land was to be lost in thought.

Or lost in something besides paying attention.

She was surprised she didn't see any other human beings and very few animals. Except for occasional bird sounds and the constant quiet clip-clop of Loosey's hooves, the desert was quiet.

Connie started looking around for color, for some tossed garment. That calmed her. If she found something, she could take it up to the shrine—to the dreaming place. It wasn't far from here.

She watched the ground and let Loosey go where she wanted.

After a while, she spotted a piece of black, or something, in the near distance. She looked up and around.

She wasn't sure where they were.

She squinted. She could see a sand bar, as if once, long ago, a pond or river had lived here.

Her heart started racing.

"We have to get out of here," she said out loud.

But Loosey was trotting toward the black.

Jimmy began barking.

"Stop it," she said.

They were near the place where she had found Rosalia.

Loosey was walking straight for the black.

Only it wasn't a piece of black cloth.

Suddenly Loosey stopped and began backing up.

"Loosey, stop," Connie said.

It wasn't black cloth. It was black clothing. On a person sprawled on the ground.

Jimmy went near, growled, and came running back.

Loosey stopped. Connie reached for her cell phone inside the saddle bag. No signal.

She got off the horse.

"Stay here," Connie said, "both of you." She walked closer to the body. It was a young man. He wore black clothes. A black backpack and what looked like an empty plastic water bottle—painted black—lay near him.

He looked dead.

"I cannot fucking believe it," she said.

She knew she should check his pulse.

She didn't want to.

She gently nudged him with her foot.

"Hello, are you all right?"

The wind shifted, and she smelled him.

She didn't need to check his pulse.

She walked around him. The backpack was empty. If he was dressed in black, with a painted black water jug, he was most likely a drug smuggler—or he was a migrant forced to be a drug mule.

In any case, he was dead.

He couldn't have been eighteen years old.

His left arm was flung out in front of him with a watch still on it. Looked like a child's watch, the kind with a buckle that you had to put on and take off like a belt.

A red second hand went around and around.

Connie stood watching the second hand. She couldn't make herself move. She was sure she could hear the watch ticking.

Tick, tick, tick, tick, tick.

She suddenly wanted to take the watch off of him and run up to the shrine, to the dreaming place, and set it there. Maybe the boy's dreams could still come true.

She was surprised that the people who had been with him hadn't taken the watch. His shoes were gone. His socks. Looked like something had starting nibbling at his toes.

Connie bolted. She ran toward the horse.

Loosey looked frightened—her eyes wide—but she stayed still. Connie got on her, and they galloped off. She let the horse run for a bit, and then she slowed her.

She needed to meet Manuel at the crossroads.

Maybe she should have checked his pulse.

That would have been respectful.

She felt sick to her stomach.

How had he died? Hypothermia? Must have been.

Must have been.

What was there about that place?

Nothing. Nothing at all.

David Emmett had found dead walkers on his place every summer. Mostly in the same spot. He had started leaving water in that spot, in the hope that water would prevent any more deaths. It had, for a while.

But now he was dead.

Killed by who knows who.

A drug runner like this kid she had just run from?

The dead kid.

A dead girl. Now a dead boy.

She wasn't going to name this boy.

She was *not* going to name this boy.

Loosey and Connie came to the crossroads. It was just two paths intersecting in the desert. Nothing to mark it. Not a stone, not a tree, a bush. Nothing except the giant X marks the spot of two animal trails lapping over one another.

She wanted to keep thinking about this useless trail. This crossroads.

She did not want to think of the dead boy.

The dead man.

Maybe if she thought of him as being a dead man it would be better.

She got off Loosey and began pacing. Jimmy walked beside her. The desert seemed to go on forever in all directions. Desolate.

What the hell was she doing here?

At the crossroads.

Someone.

Come.

Help.

Me.

She opened her mouth and screamed.

The effort made her dizzy.

Loosey trotted a few feet away from her.

Jimmy whimpered.

She went to Loosey and took out the cellphone again.

One bar.

She called Manuel.

It went directly to voice mail.

She tried home.

Amy answered.

"Amy, I need you to call Border Patrol," Connie said.

"Mom? I can barely hear you."

"Call Border Patrol," she shouted.

"Call Border Patrol," Amy repeated. "Are you okay?"

"Yes. Someone has died though." She tried to give Amy directions for the Border Patrol.

"That sounds like it's near where you found the girl," Amy said.

"Same spot," Connie said.

"What?"

"Same spot. We'll wait there for the Border Patrol."

"Okay. Be careful," Amy said.

Connie tried Manuel again.

Nothing.

She stood still and looked in first one direction and then another. And another. Looking for any sign of Manuel.

She got back up on Loosey and looked.

There. A dot on the horizon.

Was it a bird?

A plane?

No. A person on a horse.

Connie rode toward whoever it was.

She hoped it was Manuel.

Maybe it was a drug smuggler.

Maybe it was whoever had killed David Emmett.

Jimmy began barking.

This time Connie was glad for it. She knew that was a bark of recognition.

"Go get him, Jimmy. Bring him back to me."

A few minutes later, Manuel came riding up on Major.

"What's happened?" he asked. He knew right away that something was wrong.

"Someone has died," she said. "In the same spot where I found the girl. I was able to get a hold of Amy. She's calling Border Patrol. I told her we would wait for them."

He nodded. They started riding back toward the spot where she had found the dead man.

"You okay?" he asked.

"No," she said. "But it's not like with the girl. I'm pissed off. People should not be dying out here. I don't want that happening on my land. They're out here without water. Without any way to communicate with anyone. I don't like it. We should do something."

"Change immigration policy? Legalize drugs? Put a welcoming booth at the border? What?"

"Maybe all of it. I don't know. I just know I don't want to keep stumbling over young people who have died on my land."

Jimmy began whimpering when they neared the body. Connie reined in Loosey before they got too close. Manuel got off his horse and went over to the young man. Connie watched him check his pulse, then look into the pack. He reached into the boy's shirt pocket, pulled something out, and looked at it. Then he put back whatever it was and walked over to Connie.

"Looks like he was probably running drugs," Manuel said.

She nodded. "What was in his pocket?"

"St. Christopher medal."

"I guess it got pretty cold last night," Manuel said. "Noticed there was ice on the water trough this morning."

A breeze made a tiny dust tornado near them.

"That's nice," Manuel said. "Takes away the dead smell."

"What?" Connie asked.

Then she smelled it.

Smelled like the sea.

"Smells a bit like the creek," Manuel said. "Or like the ocean."

Connie breathed and looked around.

No sign of the sea horses.

Connie wondered if Delilah had stood out in this part of the desert with her siren sisters, trying to sing the sea horses home—or at least back to the ranch.

Siren sisters.

Sirens.

A siren.

All little towns had sirens. A way to signal when something was wrong.

"Manuel, what if I put a siren here? Then if someone is in trouble they could push a button. It would make a loud noise, so anyone within the sound of it could come help, or they could set it up to signal at my house. Then no one would have to die. At least not in this spot."

"Consuelo, he was a drug runner," Manuel said.

"You don't know that," she said. "But who cares? He's a human being. We don't know why he was doing what he was doing."

"So if some drug smuggler pushed this button and activated the siren, you'd come out and help him?"

"Yes."

"What if you got here and he shot you and took your truck or your horse?"

"I guess I'd have to risk that," she said. "Just think if Rosalia had had that option. She'd be alive. Or this boy. Maybe I could talk all the ranchers into putting sirens up on their land."

"It might work," he said. "But I don't like the idea of drug smugglers running around this ranch."

"They're already here," Connie said.

Manuel and Connie waited out in the sun for a long while until Border Patrol got there. Connie watched them put the young man on a stretcher.

She thought she could still hear the tick, tick, tick of his watch.

She resisted the urge to ask Border Patrol for the watch.

Then they were gone.

They left behind the black water jug.

Connie walked toward the jug. "Why'd they leave this here?" She reached for it.

"What are they going to do with it?" Manuel answered.

"Don't be reasonable," she said. She picked up the jug.

Something shiny was in the dirt near where the jug had been. Connie nudged it with her foot.

It turned on its side.

The watch.

It must have been loose and fallen from the young man's wrist when they moved him.

Connie crouched and picked up the watch. She carried it over to Loosey and dropped it in the saddle bag.

Manuel watched her, but he didn't say anything.

Connie mounted Loosey.

"You'd tell me if you ever found the blue shoe," Connie said. "Right?"

"Of course," he said. "I might take it up to the shrine and leave it there. But then I would come get you."

"The shrine?" she asked.

They turned their horses around and started toward home.

Manuel looked at her.

"It's beautiful," he said. "Sometimes I go up there and just sit."

Connie felt a lump in her throat. She should have known Manuel would find it. She should have known he would understand.

"You're welcome to add to it," Connie said.

Manuel nodded. "I appreciate that."

Chapter Fifteen

Amy and Matt were standing in the door when Connie and Manuel came into the house after putting away the horses.

"Are you all right?" Amy asked.

"What can we do?" Matt asked.

Gabriela and Samantha sat on the couch together, their eyes wide, their mouths turned down. Connie glanced at them and then back at Matt and Amy.

"Good grief," Connie said, moving past them. "Nothing happened to me." She walked into the kitchen. "Where is everyone? I thought we were having a fiesta tonight."

"I figured we'd call it off," Amy said. "Because of what happened."

Connie shook her head. "No. Let's do it. Come on!"

She looked at her children. Manuel stood with his hands on his hips watching them all. Jimmy walked in a circle around him.

"Last time this happened, you were mad because we didn't notice something was wrong," Amy said. "This time—"

"This time is not the same," Connie said. "I am older and wiser."

"Or tougher and—" Amy started.

"Hey," Connie said. "Besides, I wasn't mad because you didn't notice. I was mad because you all noticed and didn't point it out to me; you didn't try to help me."

"So we're trying to help," Amy said.

"Then help me eat," Connie said. "I'm starving. Did you decide where to put everyone?"

Amy shook her head. She looked at her brother, who shrugged.

"Probably too late to get Uncle Phil and Marilyn over," Matt said.

"Darn." Connie snapped her fingers.

Matt laughed.

"Unless you didn't make anything," Connie said. "Matt's friends have to eat."

"We were just going to eat in the bunkhouse," Matt said, "but hey, I'm game. You need any help, Amy?"

"Ah, sure. Mom, did you want to take a shower or anything before dinner? Manuel, you and Gabriela are staying?"

"Sure, sure," he said. He seemed to be trying not to look at her, while Amy and Matt kept staring at her.

Connie put her hands up. Then she said quietly, "I am fine. Nothing happened to me. I'm not going to crack up or get depressed again. Let me go wash up. When's dinner?"

"Thirty minutes?" Amy said.

Connie nodded and walked toward the hall and her room.

"Hi Grandma!" Samantha said as she walked through the living room. Connie smiled and waved. Gabriela and Samantha both waved at her.

She went into the bathroom first and splashed her face. She looked at herself in the mirror and sighed. She looked gaunt.

Haunted? Hollow? She rubbed her face and looked again. No difference.

She dried her face and then went into her room, shut the blinds, and lay on her bed. She wanted to close her eyes for a moment.

She dreamed an ocean was rolling over the Sonora Desert. The desert floor soaked up the water, like a sponge that's been dry for an eternity and now it was "hallelujah we've got water!" If a sponge could sing hallelujah. Connie thought all this as she watched the sea coming. Every dead twig it touched sprang to life. Every bone it picked up grew flesh and either swam, flew, or ran with the tide. Then it reached the shrine. Water lapped into the cave, touching first a little jacket and the girl who had once worn it. Then the water rose until it was at the green glove and the woman who wore it grabbed the girl's hand and then a boy's and then a man's and they were all running for their lives. And then they were swimming, swimming, flying, running. They all made it to safety. When the water touched the blue shoe, Rosalia was there, only she wasn't like the others: She didn't run or swim or fly. She was not clothed.

She was just dead, floating next to the dead boy dressed in black.

Connie gasped. She opened her eyes. It was dark in the room.

"Mom?" Amy's voice. There she was, coming out of the darkness.

"Is dinner ready?" Connie asked. She sat up. Amy sat next to her.

"We started without you," Amy said. "Couldn't get you up. You kept telling us to go away."

"But I wanted to hear your stories of the recipes," Connie said. "Weren't you going to tell us about each dish?"

"I'll do it another time," Amy said. "But now, come and eat. I will tell you that Aunt Delilah believed that this particular meal was good for new beginnings. It was to be prepared on the New Moon and I couldn't start until I heard a coyote howl and then I would know it was the right time. And if I saw a hawk flying overhead I should make apple pie. If I heard an owl, it should be an apple crisp."

Connie rubbed her face. She wanted to cry.

"So?" Connie asked.

"I stood outside last night until I heard the coyotes begin their chorus," Amy said, "and then I went in and started peeling the apples. In the morning I saw a hawk so it became pie. I also made dew stew. I had to find a drop of dew somewhere on the ranch before I could make it. It would have been okay without it, but with the dew, magic happens. At least that's what Delilah said."

"And?"

"I went out very early for a couple of mornings," Amy said, "before everyone got up, and I looked for dew. It's been so dry. But then I thought I saw a cloud settle over West Midnight Ridge just before nightfall yesterday."

"Fog," Connie said.

Amy nodded. "Yep. I figured there'd be some fog. How often do we see that?"

"But if we do it's almost always over West Midnight Ridge."

Something about the rhythm of their conversation was chasing away the nightmare. It was as though the tide of it was going out, way out, and leaving behind this land Connie knew so well.

"So in the morning," Amy said, "very early, I drove out to the ridge, to that meadow west of the creek, and I found me some dew near the ground on the tall grass. They were big drops. I could practically see my reflection. I could hear quail not far from me, annoyed at my intrusion. After I got the dew, I followed the sound of the creek; I mean, who can ever ignore an invitation from a body like that?"

Connie smiled and leaned, just slightly, against her daughter.

"And guess what I found, Mom?"

Connie shook her head.

"I looked down and I saw deer tracks," Amy said. "And mountain lion tracks. And then I saw a set of horse prints, small ones. The horse wasn't shod. I could see the frog of the hoof pressed into the mud. The stream was wide, and I didn't want to cross it, but I looked around. I didn't see any horse or horses. But I did see a clump of hair that had gotten caught on one of the cottonwood branches. I walked toward it. As I got closer, I realized it was blue. I could hardly believe it. I thought it must be a feather. But it wasn't. I was a foot away. I could see it was hair. Blue hair. Not like dyed blue hair. Not gaudy. Not fluorescent."

"Sky blue," Connie said.

"Yes," Amy said. "I was ready to go out and get it, to pick it off that branch, like picking blue cotton. But just then, a breeze came through. It lifted up the blue clump of hair and took it away. Just like that. I looked all around for it. But it was gone. I found a clump of rabbit hair nearby, but it wasn't blue. Maybe some trick of light fooled me. But I don't think so. Because at the same time the breeze blew through, I smelled the ocean, Mom. I smelled it. And I shivered. It was spooky and beautiful all at the same time. I felt like something was watching me. Maybe the mountain lion. Who knows? But I got into the jeep and came on back. And I made the dew stew."

Connie looked at her daughter. She could barely see her in the darkness.

"Mom, I think you should look for those horses," Amy said.

Connie put her arm across Amy's shoulders.

"Thank you, darlin'," she said. "I appreciate it. Now let's go eat."

Around the crowded table sat Samantha, Manuel and his daughter, and Matt and his friends: Greg, the engineer and permaculture specialist; Carlos, the gardener; and Sergio, the biologist and wilderness trekker.

Connie sat next to Matt and Samantha and tried to listen to the conversation. Amy brought her a bowl of dew stew. She took a spoonful of it and put it in her mouth. Instead of chewing once and then swallowing, she let the liquid go down her throat, and she slowly chewed the potatoes, carrots, and celery slowly. She closed her eyes. She could almost hear the water gurgling over the rocks again. Could almost hear the dry leaves rustling near the creek bed. She chewed.

She tasted the dew.

She was certain of it.

She could taste the meadow. She could taste the cloud that had turned into fog.

She could taste her daughter's love as she prepared the dish.

Connie smiled and opened her eyes.

"This is fabulous," she said. "I can taste the magic. Yessir. Excellent. You should open a restaurant. Let everyone experience what you do."

Amy smiled. She looked almost shy.

"Thank you, Mom."

"I'm serious," Connie said. She suddenly felt buoyant. She grinned and kept eating. Manuel and Amy talked quietly about something. Samantha laughed, then smiled at her grandmother. Greg, Carlos, and Sergio talked about their trip into the mountains. Connie didn't actually listen. She watched her son. Who was watching Greg. He smiled at whatever Greg was saying, then ate more stew, then smiled some more. He seemed almost proud.

Or something.

Manuel looked at her for a moment and then back at Amy. It was just a glance. Connie watched Matt. He was looking at Greg the same way Manuel looked at her.

Oh good grief.

Matt smiled at her. "You okay?"

She nodded. Her eyes started to water.

Why couldn't her children tell her about the important things in their lives? Or had they tried and she wouldn't listen? Matt hadn't brought girls home—or boys. He never dated as far as she knew. She didn't ask, figured it was his business. But now he was in love.

And he hadn't told her.

And Amy. She had this talent. She had a gift.

She probably didn't talk about it because Connie would belittle it as women's work.

Oh crap. Crap. Crap.

She sighed.

"I want you all to take down that C&C sign," Connie announced. "Seven adults. We can do it."

"Don't need seven," Matt said. "Two of us could do it."

"I want it down," she said. "And I'd like someone to make a sign that says 'Sky Blue Horse Ranch.' That sound good to everyone?"

She looked around the table. Gabriela nodded. Connie laughed.

"Sounds good," Matt said.

"I like it," Amy said.

"Always have," Manuel said.

"Now, you," Connie said, looking at Greg. Greg looked at her. He was a little older than Matt and the other two young men. His black hair was thick, his eyes blue. His hands looked a little soft, but that could be remedied.

"Do you love him?" Connie asked.

Greg glanced at Matt. Then he said, "Yes."

"Okay, then you have to do something for his mother," Connie said. "That's a tradition in our family."

"I've never heard of this tradition being part of our family," Matt said.

"It's a new one," Connie said.

"I'll do whatever you like," Greg said.

Connie grinned. She rubbed her hands together. "Oh good. He wants to make an impression." Everyone laughed. "I want a siren out in the desert. Not a mermaid siren but an alarm. Way out on the land. I want it set up so that people can press a button if they're in trouble. I want the siren up high so the sound will go far, but also so it won't be easy to get to and destroy. And, this is the important part—if someone pushes the button on the siren, I want it to come into here, into the house, so that we know someone is there and needs help. Can you do that?"

Greg pursed his lips. "You want it state of the art?"

"I want it to work," she said. "And my husband just left me and stole most of the money I had, so it would be nice if it didn't cost an arm and a leg."

"We can do it," he said.

"Where do you want this, Mom?" Matt asked.

"Out where we found the . . . girl," Connie said. "Near this sand bar." She glanced at the children. Perhaps it was best not to say "where we found the dead girl and the dead boy."

"I want signs on it in Spanish and English which explain simply that if they're in trouble, they can push the button and someone will come and help. And maybe a trunk with blankets and water in it." Everyone at the table was staring at her, except for Samantha and Gabriela who had their heads together, giggling.

"I know the blankets will probably get taken whether they're needed or not," Connie said, "and the trunk and the siren might all get destroyed. But I want to do it. I don't want to find any more dead children on this land."

The two girls looked at her.

"Oh crap," Connie said.

"What's Grandma talking about?" Samantha asked.

"Some people from another country have been walking through the desert without water or warm enough clothes," Amy said. "And because of that, they got sick and died."

"So Grandma wants to leave them water and warm clothes?" Samantha asked.

"Yep."

Samantha nodded. "Good. If the sea horses came, the people could ride them to safety," she said. "Couldn't they, Grandma?"

"If the horses let them," Connie said.

"They would," Samantha said. "They're magic horses. They would save people."

"Are they magic like this stew?" Matt asked. "Maybe Amy fed us sea horse stew."

"Matt!" Amy said. She picked up a piece of bread and threw it at him. He threw it right back at her. Samantha and Gabriela each picked up a piece of bread and raised their hands to throw it.

Connie quickly said, "No more of that! Look at our guests. They look stunned. They're going to want to run away before they get a chance to do all the work I want them to do."

"No, no," Sergio said. "I was just wondering where this sand bar was. I wouldn't mind a beer."

"I think you should let Sergio paint the sign," Connie said. "I sense an artistic flair under there."

"Either that or a beer gut," Matt said.

After pie, Connie went outside and watched from the porch as the five men tried to take the sign down. Amy stood next to her, her arms folded. "I'd offer to help, but they look so disorganized that I'm afraid they'd drop something on my head."

They had pulled Matt's truck underneath the sign, and Matt and Sergio stood on top of the cab. Each held one side of the sign and tried to lift it off of the hooks. It wouldn't move.

"Seems like a ladder would have been easier," Connie said, "but I guess the beers loosened them up for an adventure."

They moved the sign back and forth. Finally it became unstuck, and they lifted it up and off. And then suddenly, it dropped out of their hands, fell on the cab, and then slipped into the dirt.

In the near dark, Connie saw a puff of dust rise up as it hit the ground.

Matt jumped into the bed of the truck from the roof of the cab and then climbed out of it. He bent over. A moment later, he straightened.

"It's broken to pieces, Mom," he said.

"Good," she said. "Burn it, crush it. I don't care. C&C Ranch no longer exists! Woo-hoo! Long live Sky Blue Horse Ranch."

Chapter Sixteen

A kind of rhythm returned to the ranch. Connie liked that: She liked rhythm. She liked a particular kind of sameness. A routine. She wanted to get used to life again, so that everything didn't feel so new. So that everything didn't hurt.

She showed Matt and Greg where she had found Rosalia and the dead boy, near the sand bar. Then Greg and Matt went off to figure out how to put up a siren in the desert.

Sergio and Carlos created a new sign to hang over the gates. They painted a piece of wood the color of the sky and then burned "Sky Blue Horse Ranch" into it. They hung it up. It swung back and forth for a bit and then settled into place.

Connie liked it, but the sign didn't make everything feel okay again and that was what she wanted.

She still had the ache in her stomach. Or her heart. And the nightmares had started again. In them, she kept finding bodies in the desert.

Just like in real life.

Greg, Sergio, and Carlos came and went and came again.

Sometimes different friends of Matt's showed up. None of them were paying anything yet, and Connie wondered how they were ever going to make any money.

Sergio and Carlos installed wildlife cameras and began taking an inventory of the wildlife on the ranch. Another group of students and a professor—botanists—from the university were due at the ranch any to study and identify the area flora.

One morning when Connie was having breakfast with Matt and Amy, Connie gave Delilah's flora and fauna journals to Matt to show to his friends.

"I don't want them taken from the ranch by anyone but you," she told him.

"We should think about turning these into books," Matt said. "Start our own little ranch industry out here. 'Flora and Fauna from the Sky Blue Horse Ranch.' Amy could put together 'Recipes from the Sky Blue Horse Ranch,' using her recipes and Aunt Delilah's. Once we get the garden and permaculture plans going, we could write about that, too."

"If it's something you kids are interested in, go for in," Connie said. "I'll help in any way I can. What do you think, Amy?"

Amy nodded. "I do like the idea of putting together a cookbook. I think it would be fun to have a restaurant, too. The 'Sky Blue Horse Ranch Restaurant.'"

"That's a mouthful," Connie said.

"The Sky Blue Cafe?"

"Better," Connie said. "They'd have to fix that damn road."

Matt grinned. "Doesn't it feel like suddenly everything is opening up? Falling into place?"

"Or falling apart," Connie said. "I still can't shake these butterflies in the pit of my stomach. They arrived when your father left. Speaking of such things. Why didn't you ever tell me about Greg?"

"You never asked."

"What do you mean I never asked? What was I supposed to say: Who are you sleeping with this week? Are you sexually attracted to men or women? I wanted you both to have a sense of privacy. I felt like my mother was too involved in my life when I was young. She was always telling me what I should and shouldn't do. She was afraid of so many things. And I got afraid. I got afraid I'd end up alone with no money and no prospects."

The three of them looked at each other and then started laughing.

"Wow," Amy said. "I better be careful about what I'm afraid of. It might come true."

"Naw," Matt said. "You're not alone and you're not without prospects."

Connie smiled at her son. Her children were the ones with the ideas: a restaurant, books, wilderness training, permaculture. What was her purpose in all of this?

"I always thought you weren't interested in my life," Matt said. "Because you never asked."

"Me, too," Amy said. "Of course in my case, I also figured you didn't like me."

Connie felt a lump in her throat.

"I was interested," Connie said. "But I never wanted to pry. And as far as your sexuality, that was your business. I tried to let you both know that I was here if you needed me. I tried to make the way as clear as I could. I was interested in your life, Amy, of course! I'm your mother. I love you both."

She did not like this conversation. The butterflies in her stomach were worse.

"It felt like you didn't want to be here," Amy said. "Like you were going to disappear at any moment."

"What?" Connie said. "You mean the last few years?"

"I mean forever," Amy said. She looked at her mother. "I'm not trying to hurt you, Mom. That's just the way it felt."

Connie looked at Matt. He shrugged and nodded.

She expected this from Amy but not from Matt.

She wanted to push away from the table—and from them. She wanted to run away. But she held her ground, breathing in and breathing out so they wouldn't know how hurt she was. So they wouldn't know how much she wanted them all to leave.

"Well, I better get going," she finally said. "I've got work to do."

She left the table and walked through the living room. She patted the side of her thigh and Jimmy jumped up from the floor near Gabriela and Samantha.

"It's a beautiful day," Connie said to the girls. "Why don't you go out and play. If you keep watching this television, I'm going to get rid of the service, and then all you'll see is snow."

The girls looked at her. She felt foolish and stupid. What a mean thing to say.

She kept walking out onto the porch. She heard Matt yell, "Mom, don't forget we're christening the siren today."

She went out to the barn, whistled for Loosey, and then saddled her. She didn't wait for Manuel. Not today. She headed toward Box Canyon and the shrine.

She didn't look back.

She watched Jimmy run ahead and then come back every once in a while to check on them. She watched the ground for more items for the shrine. She didn't find much. Maybe it was because her eyes burned with tears.

"Let's tally this up, Loosey," Connie said. "My husband couldn't stand me, so he left. Manuel let me know I ruined his life thirty years ago, and I'm still ruining it. My children both say I was a terrible mother and ruined their lives."

Loosey did not respond.

"This shit is hard, Loosey," Connie said. "I think I'd like it better if I just lived alone."

They rode out to the shrine. Connie got off Loosey, pulled the dead boy's wristwatch out of the saddle bag—it was still ticking—and she and Jimmy climbed up the ridge to the alcove.

She touched first one and then another item to make certain no part of her dream had been true. No great sea had washed through this part of the Sonora. Or any other part, she guessed.

She laid the watch next to the blue shoe.

"May your journey be good," she said. "May you find wisdom and peace and love and whatever else you needed and didn't get while you were here."

Like a blanket. Or warmer clothes. Or a stronger heart.

Or whatever.

She didn't know why the boy had died.

"Good-bye, Roberto."

Oh shit. She had named him.

Roberto and Rosalia.

Had they known each other?

No. Rosalia wouldn't have known any drug smugglers. Besides, she died years ago.

Connie shook her head. Rosalia could have known many drug smugglers.

"Just legalize the damn stuff," she said. "Then we wouldn't have young men or women dying in this desert. Maybe my friend David would still be alive."

Jimmy looked up at her.

She stopped talking.

She rode Loosey to the creek. She got off the horse and followed the stream bed for a while, looking in the mud along the shoreline.

She saw lots of prints. None of them belonged to horses. She wondered if Amy had made up the story of the blue horse hair and the smell of the sea just to make her feel better. She couldn't decide if that was a kind or a cruel thing to do.

Eventually she turned Loosey in the direction of the sand bar where she was supposed to meet Greg and Matt. That's what she decided she was going to call it now: the Sand Bar. That was better than thinking of it as the place where she had found the dead girl—and now the dead boy. Maybe once the siren was up, she would call it the Siren at the Sand Bar.

Or maybe just the Desert Siren.

She hoped she could talk the rest of the ranchers into putting up their own sirens.

She spotted the long white pole rising up from the desert floor long before she was near it. It looked like a strange kind of light, and it wavered, almost like a mirage.

Then she saw two pickups and people milling around. Jimmy looked up at her. "Go ahead," she said.

The dog ran toward the people. Loosey began trotting.

As they got closer, Connie could see a siren at the top of what looked like a flag pole. Near the siren was a small solar panel.

Matt waved to her. Greg was kneeling down and adjusting something near the trunk. The trunk was next to the siren pole. A little shelter, like a mini-car port, shaded the trunk. Amy, Phil, and Manuel stood nearby.

Connie stopped Loosey and hopped down. Loosey wandered away a bit and began grazing.

"Hello," Connie said. "Where are the girls and Marilyn?"

"Marilyn's watching the girls and hanging out at the house," Matt said, "so that when we push the siren, she'll see if it works at the house."

Connie nodded. It was a good idea. She probably would have thought of it earlier if she hadn't stomped out of the house because her feelings had been hurt.

Not that she had stomped.

"Hello, brother," Connie said. "I'm glad to see you. I thought you'd think this was a crazy idea."

"I do," he said. "I like to be around when crazy ideas come to fruition. I'm so sorry you found another body."

Greg straightened up and said, "So here's how it goes. First there's this trunk. On the lid is this sign. It reads in English and in Spanish, 'if you are cold, please use these blankets with our blessings. If you are thirsty, please drink this water with our blessings.'"

"With our blessings?" Connie asked. "Really?"

"We could change it to 'please use these blankets with our scorn,'" Greg said.

"It just sounds a little religious to me, that's all. But I see you're trying to be kind. Don't let me interfere with that."

"Mom, this was your idea," Matt said.

"I know," Connie said. "I'm sorry. Go ahead."

Greg opened the trunk. Inside were several blankets, two down jackets, and several water jugs.

He closed the lid again. Connie heard it latch.

"We're hoping the latch will keep it wildlife proof," Greg said. "We'll see how clever the bears and jaguars are out here. And this overhang here is to provide some shelter from the sun and cold. Now here's the 'save me' button."

He pointed to a rectangular piece of thick plastic on the pole a few feet off the ground. A black button was the most prominent thing on the plastic. Alongside the button were three small lights and one small black button with the word "reset" written below it. The top light was red, the next one yellow, then green. The yellow light was on.

Above the black button were instructions in English and Spanish: "If you are in trouble, push the black button and an alarm will sound. When you the green light come on, that means someone on the other end has heard you and is on the way."

"It's just what I wanted," Connie said. "Was it difficult?"

Greg and Matt glanced at one another.

Greg said, "We'll tell you that story over tequila one night. The pole goes into the ground several feet. It was difficult to get it in. We had the well digger out here."

"He thought we were crazy," Matt said.

"We finally had to put it in the sandbar," Greg said. "Would you like to do the honors?"

Connie said, "Sure."

She held out her baby finger—to see if the smallest child or someone without much strength could push it. She pressed the black button. Immediately the red light came on and the siren blared. Connie imagined the sound waves rippling out further and further, across the grasslands, scrublands, over the mountains and through the canyons. They put their hands over their ears as it sounded again, then again.

Connie grinned.

"Perfect."

An instant later, the green light came on, and the siren stopped.

Marilyn had gotten the signal.

They all clapped.

"When someone gets the signal in your house," Greg said, "they press a button which then turns this green. When the rescuers come, they should push the reset button, which will then turn it yellow again. If they forget, it will return to yellow in twenty-four hours."

Connie suddenly felt a bit giddy. "This is great," she said. "The idea that this might save someone's life gives me such a lift. Let's see if there are any other places on the ranch where people are particularly vulnerable. Maybe we can put up another one, or at least leave water and blankets. Thank you both so much."

"It was your idea," Greg said. "You're the genius behind it."

Amy went to one of the trucks and retrieved a bag from it.

She returned to the group and pulled a thermos and paper cups from the bag, then passed around the cups.

As she poured the cinnamon colored liquid from the thermos into their cups, she said, "This is peppermint sun and moon tea. The sun baked it and then the moon cooled it and whispered stories to it. I added a drop or two of tequila and a drop of two of agave syrup. The story goes that the agave plant holds the wisdom of the ages in it. Aunt Delilah called this Sun and Moon Know It All Brew. It was only to be made and drunk during special occasions because it is powerful and heady stuff. So here's to this siren. May it help save lives. And here's to my mom, for her brilliant idea." Amy held the glass up and looked at her mother. "To the desert siren."

The others said, "To the desert siren."

Connie blinked away tears and took a sip. She closed her eyes and kept the tea in her mouth for a moment.

She could taste the claws on the agave—or the tequila.

She swallowed and opened her eyes.

"That is good," she said.

Everyone laughed. Connie smiled.

Maybe everything would work out after all.

Chapter Seventeen

Connie felt better knowing the siren was there. The nights were still killer cold, and hotter weather was coming.

The siren "receiver" sat on the kitchen counter. It looked like a short wave radio. A small light on it was lit green. When the alarm on the siren sounded, the box made a ringing sound, like a telephone, and the light blinked red. The ringing stopped and the light went back to green once someone hit its reset button.

Almost daily Connie rode out looking for the sea horses. She and Manuel often rode together, but something had changed between them. Connie wasn't certain what. She had probably withdrawn from him. That was her *modus operandi*—according to her children.

She wanted her and Manuel to be friends again, but she did not want to talk about what a disappointment she was to him.

And she did not want to talk about when they were kids, when they had promised each other to live an exciting beautiful life together. Didn't everyone make promises like that to someone? To themselves?

Anyway, that was so long ago.

She had made the right decision then.

And even if she hadn't, what could she do about it now?

Her stomach hurt to think about it.

She had been a wild child out on this ranch. Fearless. Then she went away to college. The world was different there. More stable.

More normal.

Out in this wild place, anything could happen at any time.

Only what had happened was that she had married a dull man who left her because she was too dull herself.

Or something like that.

He was dull, and yet she still ached for him.

Ached for the normalcy of their life together.

Not feeling anything had become normal.

She did not want to think about any of this.

When Connie and Manuel went out looking for the sea horses together, they talked about the weather and the drought. But Manuel didn't flirt with her. He didn't compliment her. He was nice to her the way a good man was polite to a woman he didn't know.

She began to feel lonely on their rides together.

Often they would split up early on, and sometimes not even come back together at the end of the day.

Manuel was still around the ranch as much as he had ever been. But something had changed.

Now Connie missed Chuck *and* Manuel.

Besides all that, they found no sign of the sea horses.

At night, Connie's nightmares continued.

Sometimes she woke up in a cold sweat and listened to the darkness until she heard Samantha talking in her sleep or Jimmy whimpering beside her. Then she would get up and go down to the kitchen and look at the siren box.

The light was green, always green.

She kept wondering if someone was dying out in the desert.

Kept wondering if someone needed her help.

Connie went with Phil, Matt, and Manuel to the next Borderlands Ranchers Association meeting which was at the Ellis ranch house. Alice and a few other women put out a buffet dinner: beans, rice, beef, tortillas, salad, soup. About twenty of them sat around two long tables. First Howard said grace. Then the women lined up and filled their plates. Once they were done, the men went and filled theirs.

After they all finished eating, Alice cleared the plates, and then they conducted their regular business. Each rancher talked about what was happening on their ranches. How the frogs were doing on the Dunnett place. How the water troughs were drawing a variety of animals to them. When it was Connie's turn, she told them about finding the dead boy and how she decided to put in a siren.

"I'd love to show any or all of you how it works," she said. "And Matt and Greg, the engineer who created it, would work with you to put any on your property."

"I heard you've been overgrazing south of Box Canyon," Bill Conner said. "Someone catches you and films it, you'll give us all a bad name."

"I just found out about it myself," Connie said. "We've sold those cattle and we're now down to about ten head per portion. I know we're behind in the conservation work that you've all been doing. As you now know, Chuck left. He took some of our money, so we're kind of in a tough spot. We're trying to figure out a way to make it."

"And you think giving water to the drug lords will help?" That was Joseph Williams. "I don't mind the Mexicans any more than anyone else. I know they're coming here to work and I've hired quite a few over the years, but this new breed. They just seem destructive to be destructive."

"I don't particularly want to give shelter and water to drug smugglers either," Connie said, "but that girl I found was so young. And this boy the other day. He probably didn't even understand what he was doing. I don't want any more children dying on my land."

"We need to get the government to fix the border," Dunnett said. "Get the worker pass program going again. Legalize marijuana. Fix that damn road!"

"Here, here," someone called out.

Someone else said, "What's happening with that road is a crime."

"Well, I just wanted to tell you about the siren," Connie said. "And Matt's starting a wilderness company. We're having scientists and students and tourists come out to the ranch. He's figuring out the details. Phil's taking care of the cattle part of it. Manuel's a partner now. We're working out who's doing what."

"I heard you're looking for Delilah's horses."

That was Howard, Alice's husband. Connie looked at Alice. She shrugged, as if to say, "What can I do about him?"

Connie hadn't told Alice she was looking for the sea horses. She hadn't told anyone, except her family.

But she wasn't surprised word had gotten out.

Connie nodded. "We are looking for the wild horses."

The other ranchers looked at her. She could tell some of them knew about the sea horses and some did not. Should she tell them herself or let them guess?

"My aunt Delilah, who owned the ranch before us, believed that our relatives may have brought some horses over from Ireland. I recently found some of her diaries and she seemed fairly convinced. So I thought I'd look for them."

"I've not seen wild horses around here for a long time," Dunnett said. "What are you gonna do with them if you find them?"

"Sell Irish horse meat," Williams said.

The others laughed.

"Maybe I'll train them and sell them to you for a whole lotta money," Connie said.

"She does have a way with horses," Alice said. "Everyone knows that."

"She's no horse whisperer," Dunnett said. "I don't believe there is any such thing. But she is good with horses. When are you going to come out and see my colt? He still won't hardly let anyone around him."

"She's a horse cajoler," Alice said. "If those horses are out there, she'll find them."

"Is anyone interested in putting a siren on your land?" Connie asked.

"We'll watch how it goes with you," Howard said, "and then we'll see."

The ranchers talked a while more about business. Then they ate pie and drank beer. Some of the ranchers asked if Connie had heard from Chuck since he left. Some of them noted what a good man Chuck was.

Connie said, "I thought so too, until that day."

Dunnett said, "If I ran off with another woman, Bernice would shoot me dead. Especially if I ran off with a younger woman."

"No, I wouldn't," Bernice called from across the room. "I figure a younger woman wouldn't put up with your crap for too long and she'd shoot you herself."

Connie heard scattered laughter. She excused herself and left the meeting. She went outside into the dark cold night. She could hear the horses in the barn, snorting, stomping, eating. Normally she would go talk with them, spend some time in their presence.

But she no longer felt that urge.

Did that mean every urge she had had, every delight, every joy, was now lost to her?

Manuel stepped out onto the porch and went and stood next to her in the near dark.

"You did really well in there," he said. "I was ready to punch a few of them. I can take you home now if you want."

"I didn't know you were speaking to me," she said. She stepped off the porch and walked toward his truck.

"I see you every day. I talk to you every day."

"You know what I mean," she said. She jerked open the passenger door and got inside. Manuel got in next to her and started the engine.

"I don't know," he said. "You're the one who has been quiet and sullen."

"And why shouldn't I be?" Connie asked, her voice raised. "You practically told me I had ruined your life. What can I say to that? You're the one who brought *her* into our lives. Everything was fine until she came along. It's all your fault." She was yelling. She wanted to hit Manuel. Or hit something. She kicked his glove compartment.

"And you shouldn't have brought *him* into our lives," Manuel said. "Everything was fine until *he* came along."

"We were children," Connie said. "Did you really think we were going to get together and live happily ever after? You couldn't have! That would have been naïve and—"

"And what? Stupid? Idiotic? Insane? Well, guess what?"

"No," Connie said. "I don't want to hear this again. I can't be responsible for how your life turned out."

"I never said my life was ruined," Manuel said. "Where did you get that?"

"Maybe because my fucking life is ruined."

Connie got out of the truck, slammed the door shut, and ran into the darkness.

She soon slowed to a walk. She knew she shouldn't be out here alone. Any number of predators could decide to jump her. She could fall. She could—

She stopped listening to all the various things that could happen to her. She didn't care. She had never figured Chuck would leave her. She had never worried about that particular thing, and off he had gone.

Leaving her.

Leaving her in the lurch.

Leaving her alone to deal with her own crap.

The darkness got darker.

And silent. She heard her shoes crunching over dirt.

She knew Manuel would not follow her. He knew she wouldn't appreciate it. She wanted to be alone. She wanted to be gone. She never liked to face anyone once she had revealed some truth about herself.

Suddenly she felt a hand on her arm. She stopped and turned. Manuel folded her into his arms, pressing her gently against his chest. He was only a couple of inches taller than she was, and they fit together perfectly. She put her face in his shoulder.

"I'm sorry," she said. "I'm sorry."

"It's not too late," he said softly. "We're still young."

"It is too late," she said. "You've got a child with her. She's always going to be part of your life."

"You've got two children with him," he said. "I don't care."

Connie stepped back, and Manuel's arms dropped away from her. She could barely see him in the dark.

"It's too late," Connie said. "I'm not that teenager any more, thank god. I don't feel the same way. I don't feel much of anything. I don't think you can have me close my eyes and chew slowly to regain emotions and passion."

"We could try," he said. "It worked with food. You seem to be enjoying food more."

"But you're not my healer," she said. "Or my therapist. You are the boy I once loved now all grown up. And I failed you. I betrayed you. That's pretty unforgivable."

"I've never felt that way," Manuel said. "Maybe you need to forgive yourself."

They stood together in the dark desert, breathing.

"I'm tired, Manuel," she said. "I've been tired for so long. I latched onto the sea horses so I'd have something to do, to save me. But they won't save me. I'm just so tired."

He put his arm across her shoulders. "Come on. I'll take you home. You can sleep for as long as you like. And when you're ready—or if you're ready—we'll go out and look for the sea horses again."

She leaned against him, and they walked back to the truck.

Chapter Eighteen

Connie slept in the next morning. Amy brought her breakfast in bed. Then she slept some more. Amy brought the phone into the bedroom, and Connie woke up long enough to talk to her lawyer.

"The detective found him," Shaw told Connie. "He's bought a bar in Scottsdale."

"He's in *Scottsdale?*" Connie said. "His great adventure is going to *Scottsdale?* And buying a bar?" She started to laugh. "Oh my god. No fucking imagination at all."

"He was just here," Shaw said.

"What?"

"The investigator served him with papers. So he came down here today, out of the blue, and I spoke to him. I got him to sign the papers. He's out of the ranch. He didn't ask for any money. And he's agreed to pay you two thousand dollars a month until he pays off what he stole. He won't be able to sell the bar without me knowing it. He gave me the first installment."

"Just like that?" Connie said. "He just did all that?"

"He was afraid of going to jail," Shaw said. "He knew what he had done was wrong."

She wasn't sure if she was relieved or angry.

No, she was sure: She was angry. He didn't even have the courtesy to fight with her after all these years.

"I can't believe he was here and he didn't try to see the kids." *Or me.* "Did he say anything else?"

"He asked how Matt and Amy were," Shaw said.

She wanted to scream.

"Thanks, Bennett."

She turned off the phone, threw it across the room, then went back to sleep.

She dreamed someone was pushing the alarm on the siren, but it wasn't working. While she slept, a young girl collapsed on the sand bar. Someone else pushed the alarm, and still Connie didn't hear it. An old man turned to dust. One person after another pushed the button. One person after another died. And then Samantha came to the button and she pushed and pushed it. No sound came out. She began to turn to dust.

Connie bolted up in bed.

It was morning. She jumped out of bed and hurried out of the room, down the hall, and to the kitchen.

"Samantha!" she called. "Amy!"

She found a note on the kitchen table.

"Samantha and I have gone into town for groceries," Amy wrote. "Call me if you need anything."

Connie leaned her head back and sighed deeply.

She returned to her room, got dressed, then went out into the cool morning. She had been riding Loosey too much lately. Leo looked like he could use a ride. Connie liked mules and usually had one of her own. They were sure-footed and stable. But Loosey had been her favorite for so long that she hadn't bothered to buy her own mule after her last one died.

Connie went out and got Leo, brought him back to the barn, and saddled him.

"How you been, Leo?" Connie asked as she put her foot in the stirrup and swung her leg over the saddle. "Let's check out Box Canyon."

She called for Jimmy, but he didn't come. Matt or Amy must have taken him. That was all right. He had probably gone stir-crazy waiting for her to wake up for two days.

She wanted to gallop Leo to the siren. She wanted to be there as soon as possible. She knew it had only been a dream; still she wanted to make certain no one else had died on her land.

She saw the siren on the pole for some distance before she got close to it. Soon she spotted the sand bar and the trunk. All looked well. She stopped Leo and got off him. She walked toward the siren slowly, looking at the tracks on the ground. Lots of animals. A cow. Horse—a shod horse. People tracks. Maybe from when they'd all been there a few days earlier.

The yellow light was on.

She went to the trunk and opened it. Everything was still inside, safe and sound. No one had been by, or else they had been by and hadn't needed anything.

She could relax.

All was well, all was well.

Connie turned around to get back on Leo.

Only he wasn't there.

She turned all the way around.

The mule was gone. He must have walked off. She knew he sometimes did that, but she had forgotten to tie him or keep a hold of the reins.

"Leo!" she called. "Leo!"

She looked for his hoof prints, found them, and followed them, walking as quickly as she could.

"Leo," she said. "Goddamn it, you better come back here."

The prints began breaking the ground.

He was running.

"If you weren't already sterile!" she yelled.

What was she going to do now?

She turned around and followed the tracks back to the siren pole.

She hoped Leo would return to the ranch. She didn't like the idea of him out in the desert by himself all night. Of course, he'd probably kick to death anything that came near him.

She went to the trunk and sat on it.

She tried to figure out what to do next. She could walk back to the ranch. She couldn't get there by dark, though, and she did not relish walking in the dark.

She could not stay here. It would get too cold. Of course, she could bundle up in all these blankets. She couldn't make a fire. That's what she should have put in the trunk: matches and kindling.

"Hah!"

She chuckled. Guess she couldn't think of everything.

She didn't want to sound the alarm. She wasn't dying. She wasn't freezing to death. Her mule had just stranded her.

But it was her damn siren. She could use it any way she wanted. She wished she had brought Jimmy with her. He would have been good company.

She got off the trunk and looked around. A little north was a dry riverbed. If they did some restoration on it, they could probably stop some of the erosion that happened when the water poured down the canyon during the monsoons. She vaguely remembered they had put in a series of large stones at certain places on one of the creeks on Alice's ranch. This slowed the water so it stayed longer in the creek and that helped raise the water table.

She wondered why she had hardly paid any attention to the

conservation work the Borderlands Ranchers Association was doing. It wasn't that she didn't care.

She had loved the ranch when she was a girl.

Why had she come back here after college and turned into some kind of ranch wife zombie?

Because she hadn't wanted to remember. She didn't want to remember walking along the creek with Manuel when they were kids. She didn't want to remember all the plans for the future they had made. She didn't want to remember all the mistakes she had made.

She sighed.

Right now if she stayed out here under the sun by herself on this land her aunt had given to her, stranded near this siren she had planted in the desert, she would have to face her life.

And she didn't think she could do that.

She leaned over and pressed the black button on the pole. She put her hands over her ears as the siren blared once, twice, three times.

She watched the lights. She waited for the third one to glow green.

It didn't. It stayed red.

They probably weren't home yet. Once Matt or Amy got back to the ranch, they'd figure it out.

Or once Leo got home.

She waited.

And waited.

She danced in the sand.

She remembered the dead girl and boy and danced a mourning dance for them. Then she began to sing. It was a wordless song, happy at first, and then more like a dirge or a wail. No tears came. She just let the sound pour out of her body.

At the end of her song, she noticed the sun was beginning to set. It was chilly out.

She was getting cold. She glanced at the light on the pole. It was still red.

She sighed. Well, she had been in tougher situations than this. She reached down to open the trunk.

She stopped: She smelled the ocean.

She looked around: young mesquite to the east and south of her. Grassland to the west. North east was Box Canyon and the shrine.

And something else.

Something was walking toward her. Or away from her.

She could hear footfalls on the dry grass.

Then she saw—or thought she saw—the bobbing of the head of a horse.

And then suddenly it was there, as clear as day—as though one moment it had been invisible against the desert and then it was visible.

A small blue horse stood three feet from her. If she leaned forward and stretched her hand out, she could touch it.

She knew the horse could not be blue. She squinted. Its hair was whitish blue. She glanced up. Just like the sky right now. Its mane and tail where long and black. It had bright blue eyes and hooves the color of a dark green sea.

Connie put her hands over her face.

Then she dropped them.

The horse was still there. It stared at her.

Connie bent over to look under the horse.

"I know," Connie said. "That was rude. I just didn't want to call you an 'it.' That seemed even more rude."

She started to laugh.

"You have to be an illusion," Connie said.

The horse pawed the ground a bit. Connie slowly walked toward her. The horse had a burr in her tail and a cottonwood leaf in her mane.

Seemed pretty real.

Maybe something about the near dusk light made her look bluish.

Who cared? Who cared?

Why was she trying to disprove the existence of this extraordinary creature?

She did that. She experienced something wonderful and then found ways to pick it apart.

It wasn't a great day: *I'm just easily amused.*

She couldn't have a happy life: *That's not possible for people like me.*

He couldn't really love her: *Crazy love doesn't last for people like me.*

People like who? *People who see blue horses.*

"May I touch you?" Connie whispered.

She stepped closer and put out her hand. Her fingers got closer and closer. She was certain the horse would disappear.

And yet . . .

Her fingers touched hair. Horse hair. She felt the familiar oil she often found on her own horses. It was soft. *She* was soft. The horse turned her head to watch her.

"What can I call you?" Connie asked. "How about Blue? Or Sky? Yes, Sky Blue. How do you do?"

The horse looked at her. It seemed wild and tame all at the same time. How was that possible?

Connie could see the setting sun in the horse's eyes as the horse looked west. Her ears were forward and she watched everything Connie did. Then her nostrils flared. She pranced a bit. Snorted.

Connie put her hand on Sky's neck.

"It's okay," she said. "It's okay."

She followed the horse's gaze. She didn't see anything, but she heard something.

A moment later, Manuel came out of the shadows riding Major, with Leo following behind, a rope securing him to Major and Manuel.

Manuel pulled Major to a stop as soon as he saw Connie.

"You okay?" he called.

She nodded. She could feel Sky trembling slightly under her hand.

She whispered, "It's just Manuel and Major and Leo. He's called Leo because he's a leopard Appaloosa. See all those spots. I was riding him today and he ran off when I checked the trunk." She kept talking, her voice low, until the horse stopped trembling. She didn't think her words mattered. It was her tone, her calmness.

"Can I come closer?" Manuel asked. That must mean he saw Sky. She was flesh and blood, not a figment of Connie's imagination.

Connie nodded.

"Leo ran off, didn't he?" Manuel said quietly as he got off his horse. "I figured. I'll tie Major up just to keep Leo from giving him any ideas." He led the horse and mule to the siren pole and tied Major to it. He pushed the reset button and the yellow light began to glow.

Then he walked slowly toward Connie. The last rays of the sun were pulling away from the desert. Gray dusk replaced the fiery sunset.

Manuel stopped a few feet from Sky and Connie.

"Isn't she beautiful?" Connie said.

"She's impossible," Manuel said. "And exactly how I imagined. Where are the others?"

"I don't know," Connie said. "Maybe there are no others."

Sky watched them both. She whinnied softly. Connie felt the hair on the back of her neck stand up.

"Did you see the alarm at the house?"

"No," he said. "I found Leo wandering around the desert. I followed his tracks and then I heard this amazing song. It was so beautiful I almost wept."

"My siren song," Connie said. She smiled. "I don't know why I did it. I was feeling alone and lost, I suppose. I wonder if she heard it too?"

"Maybe that's why she came," he said. "I know you want to stay here with her, but it's going to get cold tonight. We need to get back to the ranch. Or we can gather some wood and try to spend the night here. It's going to be pitch dark soon and any wood is pretty far away."

"I was thinking we should put wood and matches here," Connie said. "So the walkers can either get warm or burn the ranch down." Connie kept her hand on the horse as she spoke. Sky bobbed her head. "I bet she'd let you touch her," Connie said.

Manuel stepped closer. He stood on the right side of the horse and reached out and touched her back. Her skin twitched slightly, as though trying to rid it of a fly, but she didn't move. Manuel smoothed his hand across her back.

"I'm calling her Sky Blue," Connie said. "Sky for short. I think she's okay with that."

"Maybe she'll follow us," Manuel said. He walked to the siren pole and untied Major and led him and Leo over to Connie. Sky moved back a bit, pranced a little more, but she didn't bolt. The horses whinnied, snorted, and then obliquely ignored one another.

Connie reluctantly moved away from Sky. She untied Leo from Major.

"You are a bad mule," Connie said. "I should not have trusted you. You give mules a bad name." She stroked his neck. "But I'm glad you are all right." She looked at Sky. "Would you like to come home with us?"

"You're not going to put a rope around her neck?"

Connie shook her head. "No. That doesn't feel right."

Manuel nodded.

Connie got on Leo. Manuel turned Major around and headed in the direction of the ranch. Connie and Leo followed. She glanced behind them.

Sky followed.

"Manuel," she whispered.

He looked back at her and then beyond. He nodded.

Could it be that Sky would follow them all the way home?

When they got to a spot where the cell phone would work, Connie called home. Amy answered.

"Hi, Mom. We just got home."

"So you didn't hear the siren?"

"No, and it's not blinking or making a sound or anything," she said. "It's green."

"We reset it," Connie said. "I'll tell you about it later. Manuel and I are on our way home." She said good-bye and turned off the phone. "I figured out a flaw in our system today, that's for sure. I'm going to ask Greg to put a siren box in the bunkhouse and in the barn. And I'll see if we can get it forwarded to my cell phone if no one responds at the house."

"Mine, too," Manuel said.

She nodded. She glanced behind her. She couldn't see Sky. Her stomach lurched. She stopped Leo.

Manuel stopped, too, and looked behind them.

Connie's eyes had adjusted to the darkness, but she couldn't see Sky. Had she run off?

"Sing," Manuel said.

"What?"

"You know, your siren song," Manuel said.

"I don't know if I can," Connie said. She had done that spontaneously, when she thought no one else was around.

She opened her mouth and tried to sing.

Her voice cracked.

She breathed deeply and tried again.

This time, she was able to begin the wordless song, a kind of lullaby to the night.

A few moments later, Sky trotted up to them. She got so close, Connie was able to stroke her neck.

"Stay close, little sister," Connie said.

And so they continued their journey home. Every once in a while, Sky disappeared from view and Connie would sing again until the horse reappeared out of the darkness.

Finally they reached the ranch.

Connie and Manuel got off their mounts and walked them into the barn. They pulled off the saddles, brushed the animals, and put them in the stalls with feed and water.

When they went outside again, Sky was standing nose to nose with Loosey, with the fence between them.

Connie laughed. "Of course Loosey would be the first to make friends with her."

Connie unlatched the gate and walked into the pasture. Sky followed her. Manuel closed the gate behind them.

"That was easy," Connie said.

Loosey and Sky walked toward one another. Loosey looked so much bigger than Sky. They walked away together and soon began grazing.

Connie went back to the barn. As usual, she left the stalls open in case the horses wanted to come in out of the cold. She went through an empty stall and out into the barn. Manuel waited for her.

"Thanks for finding me," Connie said. "I appreciate it."

"Any time," he said. "My goal in life is to be there when you need me."

"That doesn't seem like much of a goal," Connie said.

Manuel laughed. "I didn't say it was my only goal."

Connie put her hands on either side of Manuel's face, and then she kissed his lips.

Her stomach fluttered.

Manuel returned her kiss.

Then she let him go.

"What was that for?" he asked.

"Are you complaining?"

"No."

"Then stop asking so many questions."

Chapter Nineteen

Jimmy ran up to Connie and licked her hand when she and Manuel came into the house. Connie rubbed the top of his head.

"Boy, did I miss you today," Connie said.

Amy was putting two plates of rice, beans, vegetables, and chicken on the kitchen table.

"This is for you two," Amy said. "Gabby and Sammy have decided on a sleepover here, if that's all right with you, Manuel. I hope it is because they're already asleep. And Matt's gone to the bunkhouse. I'm ready for bed myself. All set? Okay. I'm off."

"Thanks, Amy," Connie said.

Amy left the kitchen.

Manuel and Connie ate in silence.

After a while, Connie asked, "Are you going to go back to her?"

Manuel shook his head.

"What if she begs you?" Connie said. "What if she says it would be the best thing for Gabriela? What if the only way you can see your daughter is if you go back with her?"

Manuel put his right hand over Connie's left hand.

"There are no guarantees about anything," he said. "But I don't love her. I've contacted a lawyer and filed for divorce. She left the marriage and the child. I won't lose Gabriela."

"What if the doctors say that's the only way she'll talk again," Connie said.

Manuel laughed. "Well, that would be odd since she didn't talk to her mother at all. At least sometimes she speaks to me. And to Samantha, you know."

Manuel held Connie's fingers in the palm of his hand.

Her stomach did somersaults.

"What about you?" he said. "What if Chuck wants you back?"

"I don't think that's going to happen," she said.

"But what if it did?"

She shrugged. "I don't know. Everything feels so up in the air since he left. Now that we have found one of Delilah's horses, I feel better. Nothing feels normal, but at least we have the horse. They do exist."

"Let me spend the night," he said. "With you."

"I'm not sixteen any more," Connie said. She twined her fingers with his.

"I never saw you naked when you were sixteen," he said. "So I won't know any difference."

Connie smiled. She shook her head. "Okay, show me what you got."

"That's a lot of pressure," he said.

She smiled. They both stood and faced one another.

"I don't know about this," she said. "I make no promises."

"I didn't ask for any."

They went into her room, into the darkness, and closed the door behind them. Connie opened the blinds. The moon had risen, and silvery light poured into the room. Manuel put his arms around her and kissed her. Then he slowly undressed her, and she undressed him.

Soon they were on the bed together, making love, and Connie tried not to think about anything else, or anyone else, as she followed the rhythm of Manuel's body against hers. But then she began to cry. Manuel stopped moving and looked into her eyes.

"What's wrong?" he whispered.

"I thought this would make everything all right," she said. "I thought once we were together, thirty years would disappear. But they haven't. I'm still the woman who left you and chose Chuck. I made a life with him."

They moved away from each other, just a few inches, so that Manuel was no longer inside her.

She wept. No tears fell, but she wept.

"Were you doing this to make me feel better?" he asked. "As some reward for coming to your rescue tonight?"

"No," Connie said. "No! I wanted this because I wanted you. I've wanted you for as long as I can remember—until I stopped wanting anything. It just seems hopeless. I ruined everything. I ruined any possibility for us. I ruined our lives."

Manuel put his arm beneath her and pulled her to him. She laid her head on his chest. He smelled of sweat. She breathed deeply.

"You found one of Delilah's sea horses today," he said. "Doesn't that make you feel like anything is possible?"

Connie sighed. "Sometimes I feel as though I'm nothing. I'm just taking up space. Like I'm Rosalia. She died in this desert; I died when I left this desert, when I decided—"

"Decided what?"

"Decided I could not live a life of passion," she said. "I blamed my mother for urging me to be safe. I blamed Chuck for being so passionless. But it was me. It was my choice. This is the life I created for myself. I have to take responsibility for it."

"You're too hard on yourself," Manuel said. "You've had a long day. Let's just go to sleep."

"Sleep? Could you sleep now?"

Manuel laughed. "Yes. I am not sixteen any more either. And what could be more delightful? I am finally going to rest next to my beloved."

"Yikes. That sounds like we're about to die and be buried."

They laughed and turned to face one another.

"Shhh," she said, giggling. "We can't let anyone hear. They might burst into the room to see if I'm all right."

"You can just tell them we were celebrating."

"Celebrating what?"

"Finding Sky Blue," he said.

Connie got out of bed and walked to the door. She turned the lock. Then she jumped back into bed.

"How about we really celebrate?" Connie said. "Why don't we try this thing called sex again?"

"'Making love' is much less clinical," he said.

She leaned over and kissed him.

"Whatever," she said. "Let's just do it."

Connie dreamed she was making love with Chuck. She looked away and when she looked back, she was making love with Manuel. She began to cry, and he melted away.

When she opened her eyes, it was morning. Manuel slept next to her.

He was not Chuck. He couldn't be. They were not interchangeable. Her dream was wrong, wrong. *Wrong.*

Connie slipped out of bed quietly and got dressed. Manuel shifted in his sleep, but he didn't come awake. She opened the door and tiptoed into the hallway. Amy was walking by just then.

"Good morning, Mom."

"Shhh!" Connie said as she shut the door behind her.

"Everyone's up," Amy said. "We can shout to the rooftops."

"Oh," Connie said. "Good."

She followed Amy into the kitchen. Samantha and Gabriela sat at the table eating oatmeal. Both were swinging their legs.

"Hi, Grandma," Samantha said. Connie kissed the top of Samantha's head, then Gabriela's.

"Good morning, girls," she said.

"Mom, you want oatmeal or eggs?" Amy asked.

"You don't have to wait on me," Connie said.

"I know," Amy said. "I'm feeding everyone else so why not you? This is oatmeal made with fairy dust, straight from Aunt Delilah's recipe books. She cooked her oatmeal with a bit of cinnamon and honey. The secret is to talk to all of the ingredients, of course, and to do a little jig as you're stirring it."

Samantha and Gabriela giggled. "That was funny," Samantha said.

Amy grinned.

Connie hoped Manuel would sleep until everyone was out of the house.

"Grandma, I dreamed of the blue horse again last night," Samantha said.

"Did you?" Connie said. She went to the stove and scooped some oatmeal into her bowl. "Well, I've got a surprise for you this morning."

Just then, Manuel walked into the room, stuffing his shirt into his jeans. He looked surprised to see everyone.

Gabriela waved. Samantha said, "Hi, Manuel. Did you have a sleepover too?" Amy's mouth dropped open.

Manuel glanced at Connie and then looked away, sheepishly.

"Oh good grief," Amy said. She threw the towel she was

holding onto the counter. "How long has this been going on? And in front of the children. Have some restraint. So this is why Daddy left. I knew there had to be some explanation."

"Samantha, Gabriela, take your oatmeal and go eat on the porch," Connie said.

"It's cold out there, Grandma."

"Then take it to your room."

"I can't eat in my room," Samantha said.

"This is an exception," Connie said.

Gabriela glanced at her father, and he nodded.

The girls got up from the table and carefully carried their bowls out of the room and down the hall. Connie listened to the door to Samantha's bedroom open and then close.

"Amy, this is my house," Connie said as she stepped closer to her daughter, keeping her voice low. "Don't you dare talk to me that way. It's none of your business, but nothing has been going on between Manuel and me, not until last night."

"That's a lie!" Amy said. "I've been talking to Dad every day. Yeah, I didn't tell you. I can talk to him. I can tell him that Julian and I have split up. I can tell *him* and not you. And he's told me lots of things. Like how when he was in the room with you, he felt so alone. He said you were always someplace else. You were thinking of Manuel all those times, weren't you? You were always out riding with him. Now we know what you were doing all those hours and days. Because he was lonely, because of you, Dad took up with that slut of Manuel's."

Connie slapped her daughter across the face.

She couldn't believe she had done it, and she immediately stepped back.

"I'm sorry, Amy."

Amy put her hand on her cheek.

"I'm sorry," Connie said again. "I shouldn't have done that. But don't talk about Manuel's wife that way. If your father slept with her because he was lonely, what does that say about him? He broke up two families and took a mother from her daughter."

"I hate you," Amy said. "I always have. You were a bad mother and you are a bad person." She ran out of the room.

"Amy!" Connie called.

A moment later she heard Amy's door open and then slam shut.

She glanced at Manuel.

"I'm sorry you had to see that," Connie said.

"I should have slipped out the window or something," he said. "It just didn't occur to me."

Connie nodded. He reached for her hand.

"Are you okay, about last night?" he asked.

"I am," she said. "But clearly we need to wait, or step back, or something. Maybe wait until we're divorced."

"We've done nothing wrong," he said.

"Would your mother agree with that?" Connie asked.

Manuel smiled. "I'm not going to change what I do or feel based on what my mother believes is right or wrong. Besides, she's Catholic. She'll light a lot of candles for me."

Connie smiled. Manuel put his arms around her, and she let him. It felt good to be embraced. She closed her eyes for a moment and breathed deeply.

Then she gently pushed away from him. "Sky! I almost forgot about Sky. Let's see how she's doing this morning."

Manuel and Connie went outside. Jimmy came running up to them. His nose was cold as he pressed it against Connie's hand. They walked toward the pasture. Loosey was eating grass next to Leo. Where was Sky? Connie looked quickly around the pasture.

The other horses were there but no Sky.

She hurried to the barn.

The stalls were all empty.

She ran back outside.

"She's gone," she said.

Manuel touched her arm and pointed. There was Sky, on the other side of the ranch house, pulling at the sparse grass. The horse looked up, stared at Connie and Manuel for a moment, and then continued grazing.

"I hope she doesn't teach the others how to get out of the pasture," Connie said.

Just then she heard the sound of a truck and trailer coming down the drive. She looked over at the open gate.

Charlie Dunnett.

He stopped the truck in front of the barn. Connie hoped he couldn't see Sky from there. She hurried over to him. Dunnett got out of his pickup and came toward her.

"I've got that colt I was telling you about," Dunnett said. "You wouldn't come to me so I thought I'd bring him to you. Mornin', Manuel."

Manuel nodded.

"What colt?" Connie asked. "Oh, the one who got swiped by the mountain lion."

"A skittish horse doesn't do me any good," Dunnett said. "If you can't fix him, he's headed for the glue factory."

"There's a lot going on," Connie said. "I don't know if I've got time for this."

"If it's about the other night," he said, "I am sorry about that. Bernice said I had the brains of half a jackass. And she called me some other things."

"No, it's not that." Connie glanced at the house. Sky was still out of sight. "Awright, let me look at him."

The three of them went to the back of the trailer. Dunnett put down the ramp and went inside. A few moments later, he backed a chestnut-colored horse out of the trailer. The horse quietly stood in front of Connie, his head hanging low.

"What's wrong with him?" Connie asked.

"I couldn't get him into the trailer without doping him up," Dunnett said. "He'll come out of it. He's a sure-footed thing, almost as good as a mule, but if I can't hunt with him, he ain't much good to me. His name is Bear. You'd think with a name like that he could stand anything, even a mountain lion attack."

Connie bent over and put her hand down by his nostrils.

"How you doing, fellah," she said. "Are you having a tough time?"

"I'll put him in the barn," Manuel said. He took the tether from Dunnett and led the horse away.

"I'll pay ya," Dunnett said. "Whatever you say. I've got a lot of money into this colt. I don't want to put him down."

"I'm not going to charge you," Connie said. "I'll just do what I can."

"Consuelo, Chuck has left you high and dry," Dunnett said. "You've never been partial to cattle, and Phil doesn't exactly have a penchant for this line of work." He emphasized the word "penchant." Connie smiled.

"I've been practicing that word," he said. "It was in a crossword puzzle and I try to use the words I find in crossword puzzles. Just to broaden my horizons, you know. Anyway, you're going to have to figure out a way to make a living. This could be part of it."

"But I don't have any training in it," Connie said. "I just talk to them. I hang out with them."

"I don't care what kind of training you've had," he said. "I don't care if you put the damn horse on a couch and make it talk about its mother. I just know you can fix them. So do it. Then charge me. Charge me a little extra because I'm an asshole. If you can't fix him, put a hole in his skull and wish him good night."

He held out his hand. "Is it a deal?"

Connie shook his hand. "It's a deal."

The screen door opened and then slammed shut. Connie looked over and saw Amy hurrying out of the house, a bag slung over her shoulder. Samantha followed her mother. Connie leaned to the left a bit to see if Sky had come into view, but she couldn't see the horse.

"Mr. Dunnett," Amy called. "Mr. Dunnett, are you going into town by any chance?"

"I am actually," he said, "after I drop off the trailer. Whatcha need?"

"I need a ride into town," she said. "No taxi will come out here. No car service will go down that road. I need to catch a bus or rent a car or something to get up to Phoenix."

Samantha scratched her leg and looked up at Connie.

"Amy, just wait until I finish here," Connie said. "We can talk. If you still want to leave, I'll take you into town. I'll take you all the way to Scottsdale."

"Scottsdale?" Dunnett said. "What's in Scottsdale?"

"Her father," Connie said. "He's bought a bar with the money he stole."

Amy opened the back door of Dunnett's truck. "Go on and get in, honey," she said to Samantha.

"Good-bye, Grandma," Samantha said. Amy helped her up into the truck.

"Yes, and Dad left because Manuel and my mother are having an affair," Amy said.

Dunnett looked at Connie, an eyebrow raised.

"Amy, that is absolutely untrue," Connie said. "You can't say stuff like that, especially when there's the custody of a child involved."

Amy opened the passenger door and got into the truck. Connie went to the door and held it open as Amy tried to shut it.

"Amy," Connie said. "Don't act like a spoiled child. What you're saying isn't true. Please don't repeat that to anyone."

Amy glared at her and jerked the door one more time. Connie let go of it. She walked over to Dunnett. "What she's saying isn't true, Dunnett."

Dunnett reached out and patted her arm. "This is a family matter," he said. "I won't be repeating none of what I heard. I remember when you and Manuel were kids. You were sweet on each other then. It 'bout broke his heart when you married Chuck." He shook his head. "We were glad when he finally got married, so we knew he wasn't still pining over you. And now this. I hope you do get together, but I'm sure nothing was going on before Chuck did what he did. It's not in Manuel's character, or yours."

"You mean everyone knows about—"

"Everything," Dunnett said. "There are no secrets out here, Consuelo. Don't you know that yet? Now I better get going. You let me know how that colt does. I won't tell anyone about anything that's going on out here. Not even about that blue horse over yonder. But it'll get around, eventually."

Dunnett got into his truck, started the engine, and then drove out of the ranch. Samantha waved as she went by.

Matt and Manuel came out of the barn and walked toward Connie.

"Amy just left with Samantha," Connie said. "She told Dunnett that the reason Chuck left me was because Manuel and I were having an affair."

"What?" Matt said.

"I told her she couldn't say things like that," Connie said, "especially since you were trying to get custody, Manuel. But she's mad. I don't know what she'll do."

"It will be all right," Manuel said. "It is a false accusation."

"That doesn't always make a difference," Connie said.

"Why did she say it in the first place?" Matt said. "What happened?"

"It's a long story," Connie said.

"She figured out your mother and I slept together last night," Manuel said.

"Or not so long," Connie said.

"It was the first time," Manuel said. "Nothing happened when we were married."

"Um, you are both still married," Matt said.

They looked at him.

"Not that I'm keeping track," he said. "I'll go after Amy. Maybe I can calm her down."

"She's going to see your dad," Connie said. "She'll tell him all of this."

"Something else must have happened to get her so mad."

"I hit her," Connie said.

"You hit her?"

"She called Manuel's wife a slut."

Matt looked at Manuel and then at his mother.

"I'd think you'd agree with her," Matt said.

"She's just so disrespectful," Connie said. "I lost my temper."

"I don't think you ever hit us before," Matt said. "You must have scared the shit out of her. I'll try to catch up with her."

Connie nodded. "Thanks."

Matt hurried to his truck. A few moments later, he was driving down the road toward town.

Then the day was silent.

Sky Blue walked up to Connie and Manuel. Connie held out her hand and Sky put her muzzle in her palm.

"Awww," Connie said. "I needed that."

"Dunnett's horse is coming out of his stupor," Manuel said. "And he isn't happy."

Connie nodded. "Okay, I better see to him."

She heard footsteps and she turned around. Gabriela was walking toward them. She reached for her father's hand, and he took hers. Her eyes were wide as she stared at the blue horse.

"This is Sky Blue," Manuel said. "We think she is one of the sea horses I've been telling you about."

Sky nickered. Gabriela let go of her father's hand and stepped closer to the horse. Sky ducked her head. Gabriela reached out and put her hand on her neck. She gasped and then put her other hand on the other side of her neck.

She hugged the horse. Sky nibbled on Gabriela's hair.

After a moment Gabriela stepped back and looked into Sky's eyes.

"She smells like the sea," Gabriela said.

Connie glanced at Manuel, who smiled.

"She does," Manuel said.

"Could I stay with her today?" Gabriela asked. She looked at Connie.

Connie was so startled to hear Gabriela speak that she didn't know what to say.

"Of course," Connie said. "If it's all right with your father." She started to say, "Sky is not a pet," but she stopped herself. She didn't know what the horse was.

Sky turned around then and started walking toward the old sycamore growing in the back of the house. Gabriela walked beside her with one hand on the horse's back. She turned around and waved to Connie and Manuel. "I'll be over here!"

"Okay, honey," Manuel said. He grinned at Connie and hugged her waist. "I can't believe it. It's too good to be true."

"No, no," Connie said. "Believe it, believe it. Do you want to help me with Dunnett's horse? His name is Bear. And I think he's going to be trouble."

Chapter Twenty

Connie and Manuel got Bear into the small pasture. Connie kept the gate open so he could run into the barn and into his own private stall if he got too afraid. He looked terrified. His eyes were opened wide, his ears were flat half the time, he jumped at every sound. The mountain lion attack had left four claw-shaped scars on his right hip. White hair was starting to grow around the scars.

Manuel threw some hay down in the pasture. Bear ran around the relatively small enclosure, whinnying and snorting. His eyes were so wide Connie thought they would pop out.

She straddled the fence and talked to him quietly the whole time. Manuel sat on the fence across the pasture from her.

"It's a beautiful day," Connie intoned. "Look at the clouds over the mountains. That's where you used to go. I bet you liked being out there . . . ."

Eventually Bear stopped prancing. He drank some water, his eyes relaxed, and then he began chewing on hay. His ears flicked back and forth, listening first to Connie and then to something else she didn't hear, or didn't notice. Maybe Manuel breathing.

Maybe the other horses.

Maybe the sound of a cougar up in the mountains.

She needed to calm his nervous system. Or actually, to get him to calm his own nervous system. His hooves barely stayed on the ground. He was ready, ready, ready for another attack.

She understood that. After she found Rosalia in the desert, she had felt like she was shivering for weeks. Trembled for months. She couldn't quite explain it: It was as though electricity was coursing through her body, and it didn't feel good. It felt as though she was going to burn out.

And the nightmares hadn't helped.

"I understand, Bear," she said softly. "More than you can know. Do you have dreams? Nightmares? Think of fields of grass and clover. Or imagine being able to run free. No burden of a rider or saddle. You can just run for your life. Be free, be free." She closed her eyes for a moment as she talked. A saddle on the horse's back would no doubt remind him of the cougar attack. Cougars often jumped onto the back of their prey.

After a while, Connie slowly climbed down and stood in the pasture. She leaned against the fence. The horse ate and watched her with his ears. He looked like he was going to bolt any second.

"What would make you feel better, Bear? A big pasture where you can run? A smaller place so you know the boundaries? What do you need?" She stayed against the fence for a long while. At some point, she nodded to Manuel. He got off the fence but stayed on the other side of it, away from the horse. Bear twitched and danced a bit, but then he continued eating. Manuel went to the other pasture and called to Loosey. Loosey trotted over to him. He took a hold of her halter and led her to the pasture where Bear and Connie were.

Loosey nickered. Bear ran around the pasture. Connie kept

talking. He kicked up dirt as he went by her. He galloped by once more, and then he slowed to a trot. He stopped near where Loosey stood. The two nickered to one another.

"You can let Loosey in," Connie said to Manuel. "We'll let them spend some time together."

Manuel opened the gate and Loosey walked into the pasture. The two horses nuzzled each other.

"Don't get any romantic notions," Connie said. "She's too old for you."

Connie climbed over the fence. Then she and Manuel walked toward the house.

"I haven't been around horses much since Chuck left," Connie said, "except for riding. Felt kind of nice doing this again. Bear will be okay."

"I don't know what you do," Manuel said, "but it's something! That horse was having nothing to do with Matt and me. You come along and he starts to calm down."

"Just my natural born charm, I guess," she said, grinning.

They went toward the sycamore where Sky grazed and Gabriela sat on the picnic table, watching the horse.

"She's been telling me all kinds of things," Gabriela said when her father and Connie came near.

Connie went to Sky and put her cheek against her neck. She breathed deeply. Sky smelled like the sea.

"What did she tell you?" Manuel asked.

"That her eyes change color depending upon the phase of the moon," Gabriela said. "Or the clouds in the sky. She said not everyone can tell she's blue. And she is magic. Absolutely."

"Gabriela," Connie said. "It's so nice to hear your voice."

"It's like Sky," Gabriela said. "Not everyone can tell she is blue. I was talking, but not everyone could hear me. Now, they can hear me. Dad, do you think Mom will come back now that everyone can hear me?"

"Mom didn't leave because you didn't talk," Manuel said.

Gabriela pursed her lips. "I'd like to see her. I'd like her to know. Maybe if she saw Sky, she would be all better, like me."

"You think Sky made you better?" Connie asked.

Gabriela nodded. "That's the way she is. Just like how you are with horses, she is with people."

Connie nodded. "I never knew you were so wise."

"Yep," Gabriela said.

Connie and Manuel laughed.

"Where did Samantha go?" Gabriela asked. "I didn't get to say good-bye."

"You'll see her again," Manuel said. "It's about lunch time. Let's go inside and see what we can rustle up. Maybe we'll try one of Aunt Delilah's recipes."

Gabriela jumped off the table and took her father's hand. They walked toward the house.

"Aunt Delilah has one recipe called fairy soup," Gabriela said. "We were trying to figure out if there really was a fairy in it. I don't think I'd like to eat a fairy. Seems kind of rude."

Manuel glanced over his shoulder at Connie. He looked deliriously happy.

Connie smiled and leaned against the horse.

"If you had anything to do with that," Connie said, "thank you."

Matt drove into the ranch. He stopped the truck, got out, and walked toward Connie. When he was halfway to her, he stopped, squinted, stared at Sky, then kept walking.

Sky whinnied.

"Sky, this is my son, Matt," Connie said. "Matt, this is Sky."

"This is a freakin' blue horse," he said. "May I?"

He held his hand out. Connie shrugged. "How would I know? Ask her."

Sky didn't move, so Matt touched her.

"She's beautiful," he said. "Amazing. Is she one of Aunt Delilah's sea horses?"

"I assume so. I haven't heard reports of any other kind of blue horse."

"Maybe someone dyed her blue," Matt said, "and they're trying to fool you."

"For what purpose?"

"I have no idea," he said. "Mom! You found the horses."

"One horse. And she found me. Gabriela saw her and now she's talking a blue streak."

Matt laughed. "A *blue* streak. I get it."

"No, really. She's talking almost nonstop. She's been healed or fixed or something."

"What are you going to do with the horse?" Matt asked.

"I don't know. What happened with your sister?"

"She wouldn't listen to me," he said. "Samantha was crying. Amy was very angry."

"I wish she had seen Sky," Connie said. "She encouraged me to look for the horses, you know."

"You should call her and tell her about the horse," Matt said.

Connie shook her head. "Nope. She knows where I am."

"You are both so damn stubborn," he said.

"Do you think she'll say anything about me and Manuel?"

He shrugged. "I don't know. She's in her teenage fury mode."

"She really needs to grow the fuck up," Connie said.

"You go, Mom," he said.

"Sky seems to like it here," Connie said. "It is a nice day. Let's eat out here. We can have some lunch and forget all about Amy and her tantrums. I need to talk to you about the siren. I want Greg to make some alterations."

"He's coming down this weekend," he said. "We can talk to him then."

A few minutes later, Manuel and Gabriela brought grilled cheese sandwiches, carrot sticks, and water out to the picnic table where the four of them sat down for lunch.

Sky trotted away, and they all watched her. When she moved, it seemed as though she was there and not there at the same time.

"She's not leaving," Gabriela said. "She just wants to say hello to Loosey and Bear."

"Did you find grilled cheese sandwiches in Delilah's recipe book?" Connie asked. "Or did Amy take the book with her?"

"She did not," Manuel said, "and yes, we found a recipe for these sandwiches. In fact, Gabriela told me about them."

"Aunt Delilah called it the Grilled Cheese Healing Surprise," Gabriela said. She sounded so much older than she was. Or maybe that was how a ten-year-old sounded. Connie didn't know any more.

"What's the surprise?" Matt asked.

"You slice the cheese very thin and put some on each slice of bread so that you really have two pieces of cheese," Gabriela said. "Then you sing to the cow to thank it for the cheese."

"Oh, I wish I had heard that," Connie said. "You and Manuel singing to a cow."

"Yep, we sang," Manuel said. "It was very nice. Shall we show them?" He looked at Gabriela. She smiled. He said, "One, two, three."

They sang together, "How now brown cow thank you for the cheese, if you please."

Connie and Matt laughed and clapped.

"I bet you made that up," Connie said.

"How'd you guess?" Manuel asked.

"Then we put some greens and slices of garlic on the bread before we put them in the oven," Gabriela said. "That was the surprise."

"We brushed a little olive oil on the non-cheese sides, too," he said. "Then we baked them."

"Wow," Matt said. "He can cook, Mom. You better snatch him up."

"I wouldn't call grilled cheese sandwiches cooking," Connie said.

"Why? We grew up on grilled cheese sandwiches," Matt said.

"Yeah, because I wasn't much of a cook. But I bet these are great." She winked at Gabriela, picked up a half sandwich, and then bit into it.

She closed her eyes and chewed slowly. She could taste the cheese, the lettuce, garlic, wheat flour. Olive oil. And she could smell the sea.

She swallowed and opened her eyes. Manuel smiled at her.

"Best grilled cheese sandwich I have ever had," Connie said.

They ate in silence for a while. Connie watched Loosey, Bear, and Sky. Leo had wandered over to the horses, too.

"I have an idea," Connie said. "Actually, Gabriela gave me the idea. She said I fix the horses and the horses fix people. I remember hearing about something called equine rehabilitation centers. People take care of horses to help themselves heal from addictions. Other places rehabilitate the horses. What if we did something like that? I loved working with Bear today. I had forgotten how much I liked just being with the horses. And Dunnett said he'd pay me. Other people might, too."

Matt nodded. "Sure. Uncle Phil might be interested. Didn't he start out in psychology? And Aunt Marilyn is a social worker. Maybe it would be something they'd be interested in."

"Would Sky be a part of this?" Manuel asked.

Connie looked over at the horse. "I don't know. What do you guys think?"

"She's a wild horse," Manuel said, "despite how she appears right now. It seems wrong to cage her."

"We could take the cattle off the ranch completely," Connie said. "We could restore the land to what it was before, if we can figure out what it was like before."

"I know this rancher in Mexico who converted his whole ranch into what he calls a 'conservation ranch,'" Matt said. "He does amazing work. Ten thousand acres devoted just to wildlife conservation. He wants to make it a paradise for wildlife. I would love to do that here. And it's what we talked about before. We'll have people come in and do restoration projects, learn permaculture, go on nature expeditions. It's like in archaeology. They go on all these digs, and they charge volunteers to come and help them out. We can do that here, too."

"I want to rebuild the old house," Connie said. "Once it's built, we can live in part of it and visitors can stay in the other part. You can use your permaculture and energy efficiency training, Matt."

"Where would we get the money?" Matt asked.

"Let's do as much as we can with volunteers at first," Connie said. "What a great opportunity for those students in Tucson. They can help design and build an eco-friendly hacienda ranch house. They can get credit for it, I imagine. They can write articles about it. Whatever they need."

"'Sky Blue Ranch Eco-tours,'" Matt said. "And 'Sky Blue Ranch Wilderness Retreats.' I like it. We'll need a bigger barn, too, for the horses. We're going to need a lot of money."

"I know," Connie said. "We can start small. I'll research how other people do this kind of thing." She looked at Manuel. "What do you think, Manuel? We're all talking about our heart's desires. As far as work goes. What's your heart's desire?"

"Don't you remember?" he asked.

Connie frowned. "What do you mean?"

"The last summer you were here," he said, "we talked about what we'd do. We talked about our hearts' desires."

They looked at each other. Matt picked up another cheese sandwich and bit into it.

"I don't remember," Connie said. "Can't you just tell me?"

Manuel looked down at his plate and then up at her again. He shrugged. "Whatever you need me to do," he said. "I wanted us to find the horses. You found one of them. There. That's done."

"Manuel can do what he's always done," Matt said. "He takes care of things. Makes sure they run well."

Manuel looked at his daughter as he ate his sandwich. Matt made a face at his mother. She shrugged and finished her sandwich. She did not remember what he had said when they were children. Was there something specific? They wanted to be together. Was there something else?

When they finished lunch, Manuel told Gabriela to say good-bye to Sky. It was time for them to go home.

"I'm gonna call Greg," Matt said. "I'll be back in a few."

Gabriela got up and ran toward the blue horse. Bear ran away to the other side of the pasture. Loosey followed him slowly. Sky turned to the young girl and nuzzled her when she got close enough.

"Did I hurt your feelings?" Connie asked Manuel. "Because I don't remember exactly what you said thirty-five years ago?"

Manuel shook his head. "No. I think you do remember. You don't want to say it out loud." He nodded. "I understand. I'm just not sure I can go through it all over again."

"What? What can't you go through? You sound like Chuck. He wrote in his note 'I can't do this any more.'"

"I am not Chuck," he said. "Please don't compare me with him. I don't think you can commit to me, just like you couldn't commit to me all those years ago. If Chuck returned, I bet you'd take him back. I cannot tell you in words how that makes me feel." He got up from the table. "Excuse me. Gabriela and I need to go home. I want her to talk with her mother, now that she is talking. Isabella called and asked if she could visit."

"What did you say?" Connie asked.

"I won't keep my child from her mother," Manuel said. "I will let her visit. I hope we can work out everything without going through too many lawyers or judges."

"You want to go back to her, don't you?" Connie asked.

"Would it matter?" Manuel asked.

Connie rubbed her mouth. She shook her head. Then she said, "You've got to do what you've got to do."

"I'll be back in a day or two," he said. "I'll call."

Connie nodded.

Manuel went over to Sky and Gabriela. Gabriela waved good-bye to the horse and then to Connie. Connie nodded.

Sky galloped around the yard. What on Earth was Connie going to do with this one little blue horse?

She heard the truck doors slam shut. Heard the truck start up and drive away.

She knew she should look. Should wave good-bye. But she didn't. She had too much to worry about. She couldn't be thinking about some broken promise from thirty-five years ago.

Chapter Twenty-One

"Connie, I don't know anything about horses helping people or people helping horses," Phil said.

He sat at Connie's kitchen table with Matt and Marilyn, a few hours after Manuel had left with Gabriela.

"It's what you trained to do," Connie said. "You've been seeing clients all these years. Marilyn still works as a social worker. Wouldn't it be great if you could do that here, on our ranch? It's a way we could get rid of the cattle."

"I don't want to get rid of the cattle," Phil said.

"He likes being a cowboy," Marilyn said. "You know that."

"You can still be a damn cowboy," Connie said. "It just won't involve cattle. Hey, if cows could make people feel better, we could work with cows, but I've never heard of that particular therapeutic method."

Phil shook his head. "There's so much happening. Things keep changing."

"I like the idea," Marilyn said. "I'd love to get some training in that area. At least see how I feel about it."

"We were thinking we'd go talk to the accountant," Matt said. "We could come up with a business plan, combining all these different ideas: the therapeutic use of horses, wilderness outings, rebuilding the house, permaculture gardens. And Greg's going to fix the siren, Mom, so it'll go to your cell phone, the barn, and the bunkhouse."

"This will be a huge commitment," Connie said. "It'll take years. We might lose the ranch. But wouldn't it be something if we could actually pull it off?"

"I think you've gone a little crazy," Phil said. "All of you."

"I want to show you something," Connie said. "Maybe it'll change your mind. You, too, Marilyn."

Matt grinned. He and Connie got up from the table.

"What's going on?" Phil asked.

"Just follow me," Connie said. "Why are you limping? You look like an old man."

The four of them—with Jimmy tagging along—headed for the back door.

"Cow stepped on my foot," Phil said. "Then my horse stepped on it. Thinking of getting me one of those quads so I don't have to deal with this crap. I might have broken a bone or something."

"He doesn't want to go to town to the doctor," Marilyn said. "I wish we could figure out some way to fix that damn road."

Connie opened the back door and motioned Marilyn and Phil to go out first. Jimmy stayed back with Connie and Matt. He didn't seem to know what to make of Sky. He didn't bark at her. She tried to be friends, but Jimmy was still shy around her.

"Oh my," Marilyn said.

Sky was grazing just beyond the sycamore, with Loosey beside her. The horses had become instant buddies, so Connie had let Loosey out, too. Bear seemed content to eat hay in the pasture and look up and gaze at the other horses every now and again.

"You found one of Delilah's horses," Phil said.

"She found me," Connie said. "Leo had wandered off and I was out by the siren by myself."

"You really should put one of those boxes in our house, too," Marilyn said.

"That would be great," Connie said. "Obviously I didn't think it through enough when we first installed it. We need to set up some kind of backup in case I'm not around."

"Or in case you're the one in trouble," Matt said.

"Yes, son," Connie said. "Go on, you two. You can touch her."

Marilyn and Phil stepped off the porch and slowly walked toward the horses.

Connie talked softly to them from afar, murmuring sweet nothings. Sky raised her head. Marilyn reached out and touched Sky's neck.

"Hello, you," Marilyn said. "We've heard a lot about the possibility of you." She glanced at Connie. "It's like there's electricity under my hand."

Phil touched the horse's forehead. He leaned closer. "It's really blue."

The horse tolerated all of this, her ears forward. She seemed as curious about them as they were about her.

"Her name is Sky," Connie said. "Sky, this is my brother Phil and my sis-in-law, Marilyn."

"Phil, what's wrong?" Marilyn asked. "Are you crying? Oh for Chrissakes, he's having a breakdown." Marilyn went to him and put her arms across his shoulders.

"I'm not having a breakdown," he said. "The horse is beautiful. I've heard about these horses since I was a child. Aunt Delilah thought if she found them they could save the ranch. And look, now we've found them." He wiped his eyes, then patted Sky's neck. "Beautiful. Were you thinking of using her to help people? As one of the therapy horses?"

"I don't think so," Connie said. "I can't imagine training her. Or putting her in a corral. Well, I tried that. She got out." She shrugged. "I'm not sure what to do with her. She seems like a visitor. So I'm trying to make her feel as comfortable and welcome as possible."

They spent a few more minutes with the horses. Then Connie brought Loosey back to Bear. Bear hardly flinched when Connie opened the gate and Loosey trotted back inside. Connie talked to him the entire time. She glanced back at the house. Phil, Marilyn, and Matt were walking toward the house.

Phil was not limping.

Connie looked at Bear. "Good boy," she said. "Look how far you've come in less than a day. You are a good boy. You are so much easier than my own children, yes, you are."

Bear calmly ate the hay.

Connie looked back at her brother.

He was not limping.

Bear was not as afraid.

Gabriela could talk.

"Excuse me, Bear," Connie said. She hurried toward the house. Marilyn, Phil, and Matt stood on the back porch, talking animatedly.

"Connie, honey," Marilyn said. "I'm so excited! I can't wait to research this and get training. I want to quit my job today!"

"Phil," Connie said. "You aren't limping."

Phil looked down at his foot. "I know. It's all better."

"You got better after you touched Sky," Connie said. "Didn't you?"

Phil glanced at the blue horse, who had walked over to the trough and was now sipping water.

"Yes," he said. "I did."

"When Gabby saw her or touched her," Connie said, "she began to speak. And Bear—the horse Dunnett brought to me to cure—is so much better. I'm good but not that fast and or that good."

"My shoulder doesn't hurt either," Marilyn said. "It's been bothering me for months and now the pain is gone. Oh my word. She's a miracle. That's why Delilah said the horses would save the ranch. They're healers or miracle workers or whatever you want to call them. People will come from all over, bring their pets, their livestock, their families—and this horse could cure them all!"

"Wait," Matt said. "Let's not get too excited. It's a horse. A blue horse, but she's just a horse. She's not Jesus. Or whatever. How could a horse cure people or animals or anything?"

"I don't know," Connie said. "I don't even know if that's what happened, but what if it is? We don't know the reasons for everything under the sun and moon. But Marilyn's right: This could save us."

"How?" Matt asked. "If this horse can cure people, would we charge them? That doesn't seem right."

"Why not?" Phil said. "Doctors charge."

"We're not doctors," Matt said.

"Okay, we were talking about getting training so that we could pair people with horses so that they would get better," Connie said. "This is the same kind of thing, only we're pairing everyone with Sky, until we find the other horses."

"Mom, you said you wouldn't cage her," Matt said.

Connie glanced at the horse. "But that was before," she said. "Think of all the good she can do."

Matt shook his head. "That's what always happens. Once someone figures out how to make money off of some precious part of nature, all promises, all high ideals, go right out the window."

Connie put up her hands. "Calm down. We're just speculating here. We don't even know if Sky was responsible for any of this. Let's go slow. Marilyn will find out where she and Phil can get training on using horses to facilitate healing. And we'll all put together a business plan. Step by step."

Just then, Bernice Dunnett pulled her jeep into the driveway. The jeep had barely stopped before Bernice and Charlie Dunnett got out.

"I heard, I heard," Bernice said. She strode over to them and stared at Sky. "Oh my, oh my. So Delilah wasn't crazy after all." She shook her head. "She's little, isn't she. Fifteen hands? What's her name?"

"Sky," Connie said.

Bernice strode right up to Sky. Sky lifted her head and nuzzled Bernice's palm when she held it out.

"Oh my," Bernice said.

"Sorry," Dunnett said when he reached Connie. "But you know whatever a man knows, the wife must know. It's the law of the jungle."

"Dunny," Bernice said. "You have to touch her. It's amazing. She smells like the ocean. I remember Delilah said that. She said they smelled just like the sea."

"But she never actually saw them," Connie said.

"Sure she did," Bernice said. She motioned to Dunnett. He walked over to his wife and began stroking the horse.

Phil and Connie looked at each other.

"She sent us out looking for them nearly every summer," Connie said. "We thought she'd never seen them."

"Yep, she saw them," Bernice said. "Something about them eased her mind. After that she was much happier. That's when she started having the fiestas. And she had her affair with Mr. O'Brien. I can't remember his first name. Oh look, she's nibbling your fingers, Dunny. Too bad you didn't have a carrot." Bernice breathed deeply. "Something about this animal. You know, I'm breathin' easy. Been having trouble with asthma today. Or was. I guess seeing a blue horse just knocked the breath back into me."

"Dunnett, you have anything bothering you?" Connie asked.

He continued stroking the horse. He shook his head. "Naw, nothing I can think of straight off. Little worried about Jolly. She's been taking prescription drugs, but they're not her prescription, if you know what I mean. I'm so afraid she's gonna turn up dead one of these day. But seeing this horse, I don't feel so worried any more."

Bernice nodded. "Maybe we could bring her to see Sky. Might brighten her day. I wonder if she would come all the way down from Phoenix for this?" Bernice kissed Sky's forehead. "Thank ya."

Then she and Dunnett turned away from the horse and started walking back to the jeep.

"Bear's looking better already," Dunnett said. "Keep up the good work."

A minute or two later, they were gone, and Sky trotted to the pasture. With little effort, she leapt over the tall fence and walked over to Leo and Loosey. The three of them trotted over to Bear.

"Wow," Matt said. "That seems too high for a horse her size. And yet, she jumped it like a deer. A very big deer. Or an agile mountain lion."

"She jumped it as though it wasn't there," Phil said. "And as I watched her, I could almost swear the fence disappeared for an instant."

"Dunnett stopped worrying," Marilyn said, "and Bernice's asthma got better." She rubbed her hands together. "This is a miracle. I can't believe it. I don't know what to do or say. I keep thinking of all the people I know who are sick. I want them to see Sky."

Phil nodded. "Hell, I could bring my clients out here."

"You have clients?" Connie said. "Plural? I thought you just saw one. The same one for the last thirty years."

"Hey, if you want me to be a part of this," he said, "you can't be so mean to me."

"I'm not mean to you," Connie said, laughing. "But you're right. I need to cultivate a different attitude. I think you'll be great at this, Phil. Especially since Marilyn will be here with you. She'll keep you from making an ass out of yourself." Connie grinned.

Marilyn said, "You got that right." She leaned over and gave Connie a kiss on her cheek. "You take care. Don't let that horse out of your sight. This is a great gift for us and for the whole community. Come on, Phil."

Marilyn took Phil's arm, and they went around the house and got into their truck. Connie and Matt waved good-bye.

"You're not really going to try to cage Sky are you?" Matt asked after Marilyn and Phil left. "You want me to get Greg to engineer a fence that a sea horse can't jump over? Or should I figure out how to hobble her? Probably just like any other kind of horse."

"I don't want to hurt her or cause any harm to her!" Connie said. "We have to be practical. I don't have any skills, Matt. If this ranch disappears, I don't know what I'll do. Samantha said she dreamed of a blue horse and the horse was for me. Maybe Sky came to me to help me save the ranch."

"That seems an odd kind of miracle," Matt said. "Shouldn't miracles be larger than life?"

"I think a blue horse that makes people feel better is pretty freakin' larger than life."

Matt stared at her. She looked over at the horses and rubbed her face.

"I'm just trying to find a way through all this."

"Mom," Matt said, "it's going to be all right. Slow down.

Breathe. Nothing terrible is going to happen."

"Something terrible already happened," Connie said. "And something else terrible is down the road. Isn't that pretty much the definition of life?"

"Wow," he said. "When did you get so cynical?"

"It's realism," Connie said.

"Where's Manuel, anyway?" Matt asked. "You're always in a better mood when he's around."

"He's gone," Connie said.

"You say that like he's gone for good."

She shrugged.

"What did you do, Mom?"

"I didn't do anything," she said. "Come on. Enough talk. Let's get busy on that business plan."

Connie couldn't sleep. The house felt strangely empty, even with her and Jimmy wandering around it. She sat on the couch, with Jimmy next to her, and listened to the silence throbbing all around her.

Amy hadn't called. Neither had Manuel.

She hadn't tried to call either of them.

Why?

Amy was being childish. She would either get over it or she wouldn't.

And Manuel?

He was hurt. Because she didn't remember what he had said he wanted for their lives all those years ago?

That seemed childish, too.

She had more important things to consider. How was she going to get enough money to make the changes they needed to turn this ranch into an ecological mecca, a research ranch, an education facility?

And was that what she wanted?

She wanted to live on the land in peace.

Why did everything in life come down to economics?

She rubbed the top of Jimmy's head.

No sense asking questions like that. It was like asking why the sky was blue.

"Why is the sky blue, Jimmy?" Connie said. "For that matter, why is Sky blue?"

The silent thrumming changed in pitch or tone. Something. Connie closed her eyes. How could silence change its tone?

Jimmy raised his head and looked toward the front door. Connie got up from the couch and switched off the light. She went to the door, slipped on her shoes, and then opened the door and stepped out onto the porch. Jimmy followed her.

The night air was chilly.

And something else.

She felt electricity in the air. As though a storm was coming.

She closed the door, then stepped off the porch.

The night seemed preternaturally light. Wasn't it near dark moon?

She saw a kind of glow coming from behind the house. As though a giant TV set was on in the back yard.

She and Jimmy walked toward the light. Her heart thumped in her chest.

She reached the end of the house. She hesitated and then made the turn around the corner.

Jimmy whimpered. Connie laughed.

Sky was running around the back yard. Her tail and mane flowed behind her. And she was glowing. It was nothing like a TV set. It was more like a gigantic firefly glowing blue. She lit up the sycamore as she ran by it. She whinnied, restlessly.

Connie knew in that instant there were more horses like Sky, and Sky was missing her herd.

Why did she stay?

"You can go," Connie whispered. "You don't need to stay for us."

Sky turned and trotted toward Connie. Connie had never seen anything look so thoroughly wild and ethereal all at the same time.

How could such a creature exist?

She was like one of those fluorescent fish from the Amazon, only this desert was her river.

Sky stopped two feet from Connie. Connie walked up to her and put her arms around her neck. She closed her eyes and breathed the horse's musky smell deeply. Could Sky cure her of all that ailed her?

Like her broken heart?

A minute later, Connie stepped away from the horse.

She didn't feel any different.

Not really.

She still missed Chuck. She still didn't want to think about Manuel or the life they might have had together.

"I guess there are some things a blue horse can't fix," she said. "Good night, Sky."

Connie turned away from the horse and went back into the house.

Chapter Twenty-Two

Connie dreamed that the siren went off, again and again. She kept riding out to answer the siren call, but she could never quite reach it. She heard the screech of the siren again and again, like an incessant alarm clock that kept going off every few seconds.

She tried to come awake from the dream, but she couldn't quite climb out of it.

And then someone was shaking her.

"Mom, wake up. Mom!"

Connie opened her eyes. Matt was standing over her.

"You sleep like you're dead."

Connie sat up.

"Thank you for that." She rubbed her eyes. "What's going on?"

"Get dressed and come see," he said.

He hurried out of the room.

"I don't like beginning the day with a mystery!" she called after him.

She pulled on her jeans and then got a shirt from her closet and put it on. She ran her fingers through her hair and then went to the living room.

"Matt?"

The front door was open.

"That's right," she said. "Let every rattlesnake and desert varmint in."

She went outside and closed the door behind her.

"Holy moly," she said.

A line of people snaked around part of her house and out to the barn. Her driveway near her truck was packed with parked cars. Beyond them, cars were kicking up dust as they drove slowly down the drive.

People stood in groups in line, laughing and talking. She recognized nearly everyone. Alice and Howard saw her and they got out of line and walked toward her. Dunnett and Joseph Williams followed.

"What's everyone doing here?" Connie asked. "It looks like the circus has come to town."

"Yep," Alice said, "and you are the circus. We've come to see the blue horse."

"Are you kidding me?" Connie stepped off the porch and walked around the house until she reached the back porch. Sky was under the sycamore tree. Near her, Nancy Blancher stood with her granddaughter, Susan. Everyone else stayed about fifteen feet back, to give them privacy, Connie guessed. Sky's ears twitched in Connie's direction.

Matt came and stood next to Connie.

"It's been like this all morning," he whispered. "Someone brought a jar and everyone's leaving donations. Sky doesn't seem to mind the people. I thought it would last maybe an hour, so I didn't wake you. But it's been like this since dawn."

Sky put her head down and began to graze.

Nancy and Susan turned away from the horse. They walked

by the porch and dropped something into the open ceramic jar. They nodded to Connie, then kept going. The next person in line walked up to the horse. Connie didn't know this man. Sky lifted her head and nuzzled the man's palm and ate the carrot on it.

Connie looked at Matt. He shrugged. They walked back around the house toward the front porch.

"Can this be good for the horse?" Connie asked.

"I don't know," he said. "No one is keeping her here. She could walk away at any point."

Alice, Howard, Dunnett, and Williams all watched her as she approached them.

"Dunnett, this is your doing, isn't it?" Connie asked.

He shook his head. "Not me."

"I heard it through the grapevine," Alice said, "from Marilyn and Phil."

"Of course," Connie said.

"You got yourself a little miracle here," Williams said. "Eh? Your own Virgin of Guadalupe. You'll have Mexicans up here for sure. They'll believe anything."

"Look around, Joseph," Connie said. "Seems like nearly everyone in this line is Anglo."

"A horse can't cure an ill," Williams said.

"I wouldn't think so," Connie said. "But she does seem to help."

"Helped me," Dunnett said. "And Bernice. She brought our granddaughter early this morning. Much better already."

"Is that why you're all here?" Connie asked.

"We wanted to see one of Delilah's horses," Alice said.

"And we heard you're thinking of taking all your cattle off the land," Howard said.

"Chuck is gone," Connie said. "As far as we can tell, he's not returning. He was the cattle guy."

"I thought he was an accountant," Alice said.

Connie looked at her.

Alice shrugged. "Sorry," she said. "Mob mentality is catchy."

"What I do with this ranch isn't really anyone else's business," Connie said. "We're neighbors and we're all a part of the association, but why do you care if I don't have cattle?"

"If you lose your ranch, some developer is gonna come in and buy your land," Williams said.

Connie laughed. "Hah! What developer would come out here? Especially with that shit road? Look, I'm just doing what some of you all have been doing for years. I want to restore the land."

"And you'll give the government ideas," Howard said. "If you succeed, they may decide it's better for cattle to be off all land. At least off our allotments."

"That's a pretty big 'if,'" Connie said.

"You won't be able to get a loan from the bank," Howard said. "Not without cattle."

"Hey, guys," Matt said. "First you bitched at us for having too many cattle and now you're griping because we may have too few cattle. Give us a break. Dad left us in the lurch and Mom's just trying to figure out what to do."

"Maybe one of us could buy your land," Williams said. "Or the association could buy it. You could take off and live *la vida loca,* if you know what I mean."

Connie's eyes narrowed. She looked at Dunnett.

"I didn't say a word," Dunnett said.

"A word about what?" Alice said.

"We've all got eyes," Williams said. "The cat's away and the mice will play."

Connie groaned. She rubbed her face. Then she said, "The cat is not away. He ran off with another pussy. I'm not a mouse and neither is anyone else here. Like all of you, I'm just trying to figure out how to get through the day. Why are you so hostile anyway, Williams? I think you need to spend some time with Sky and get your mind right. Now if you'll excuse me, I'm going to have breakfast. You can join me if you like or you can get the hell off my property."

Alice tried to reach for her hand, but Connie turned away quickly and went back into the house. She heard Williams say, "Who the hell is Sky?" And Alice said, "Shut the hell up. You have not helped."

Matt followed Connie into the house.

"What if the media gets a hold of this?" Connie asked. "We'll be overrun."

"It might be good publicity for the Sky Blue Horse Ranch," he said. "If only I had the brochures done."

Connie gave him a look. He laughed.

"I'm just kidding," he said. "I don't think any media's going to come down that road, at least not right away. We'll be okay. Besides, I think Sky can take care of herself."

"You weren't so sure yesterday," Connie said.

"Brand new day," he said.

Connie couldn't stomach much more than a piece of toast and tea. She hoped when she finished her shower, everyone would be gone.

They weren't.

The line seemed even longer.

It got warm. Connie and Matt took turns bringing out water and sandwiches to people in line. Every couple of hours, Connie stopped people from coming up to Sky. She walked around with her, made sure she was eating and drinking. Took her over to Bear and Loosey, who were now her best friends. Eventually Sky would trot back to the sycamore, as though that was where she belonged, and Connie's neighbors, people from town, and others she didn't know took turns visiting with Sky.

Sometimes the people talked quietly to the horse. Sometimes they just put a hand on her. Sometimes they wept.

Connie tried not to watch. Each interaction seemed so private. And each person was changed by the experience. Physically. Connie could see it. They stood straighter. Or their cheeks were pinker or browner or something. They appeared healthier. Each person looked like they were more present in the world.

Phil and Marilyn showed up with their girls. After they met Sky, the girls left with friends, talking excitedly about the blue sea horse.

Late afternoon, Connie had Matt tell any newcomers that they would have to come back another time. The horse needed her rest.

Reluctantly, people left.

The cloud of dust that had hung in the air nearly all day settled back to the ground.

Phil, Marilyn, Matt, and Connie ate sandwiches for dinner after they fed and watered the animals.

"I wish Amy were here," Matt said. "I miss her cooking."

Later Matt brought in the jar and turned it upside down on the couch. Dollar bill after dollar bill spilled onto the cushions. Matt kept shaking the jar and money continue to fall out.

"I didn't think anyone in our community had any money," Connie said. "This is amazing." She counted out some of the bills and then handed them to Phil and Marilyn. "Here, use this to go get that training in Texas, on using horses to facilitate healing. I think that's enough cash."

"I don't think we have to learn how to facilitate anything," Marilyn said. "People just like being in Sky's presence."

"This won't last forever," Connie said. "She's only one little horse."

"Aunt Delilah said there was a whole herd," Phil said. "Think what we could do with all of them."

Connie glanced at Matt. "Let's see what happens tomorrow."

After Phil and Marilyn left, Connie went out to check on the horses. Bear seemed completely relaxed and at peace—like a normal horse. That was the fastest horse doctoring she had ever done. She patted Bear. She knew she was not responsible for his recovery, at least not wholly. Sky stood on Connie's side of the fence, nose to nose with Loosey. Connie patted both horses. Sky nudged her in the chest.

"Ladies," Connie said, "I have no idea what is going on. Why are you here, Sky? Especially after all this time? And how are you helping these people? Is it hurting you being with all these people? Sometimes I feel overwhelmed being with four people, and you're with person after person. How can a wild thing endure that?" Connie sighed and stroked Sky Blue's forehead. "I wish you'd been there when Rosalia was trying to cross the desert. Or that boy. I wish you could have helped them. I keep having nightmares about them. Or about me." She laid her face against the horse's neck. "I miss Manuel." She sighed. "I miss my life. Make sure you take care of yourself. Don't let anyone suck the life out of you. Always stay wild."

Connie awakened before dawn. Greg had arrived in the middle of the night, and he and Matt made breakfast for the three of them. They fed and watered the animals. Matt put out the jar on the back porch.

He introduced Greg to Sky. Greg put his hand on her neck and began to weep. Matt put his arms around him. Connie watched them. How tender they were toward one another. How apparent their emotions and affection.

She didn't know how to do that. Be easy and affectionate. She had at one time, hadn't she?

Maybe when she was young, wandering the land with Manuel.

The line of people started just after dawn.

Matt and Greg helped make certain everyone had water and food. Most people brought their own. People picnicked all over the yard. Children ran around, chasing one another, and laughing. Connie watched them and wondered what Samantha was doing. Wondered how Gabriela was.

The ground was getting trampled around the house, looking like a herd of cattle had gone through.

A film of dust seemed to cover everything. Connie heard people coughing throughout the day.

But everyone appeared to be happy—and eventually healed.

No media showed up.

At the end of the day, the jar was filled with money again.

At dinner, Greg and Matt showed Connie plans for the permaculture garden. Someone else was working on the blueprint for the new "old" house, hacienda style. Greg and Matt seemed excited about their projects. Connie listened and nodded and smiled. After they left, she went out the back door and watched Sky, who glowed softly as she grazed. Every once in a while she lifted her head as if to listen to some faraway sound.

Was it her herd she was listening for?

Was it the siren? Had it gone off?

Connie went back into the house and checked the siren box. All lights were green.

She looked out the door again. Sky had raised her head and was staring at Connie. She reminded Connie of a deer, ready to leap away at any second. Then the horse began grazing again.

Connie had a difficult time falling to sleep that night.

She had a miracle in her backyard, but she didn't feel any different. Any better.

She still felt so lost.

Would everything be better if Chuck came home?

She heard a knock.

She got out of bed and went downstairs. Who could it be at this hour? Chuck? Manuel?

She looked out the window.

It was Julian, her daughter's husband.

She quickly opened the door.

"Julian, what is it? Is everything all right with Amy?"

He frowned. He was a tall thin man with dark curly hair, and he often frowned.

"I came here to get Amy," he said. "I thought she was with you."

"Oh. Well. Come on in. How did you get out here?"

Julian stepped into the house. He carried a small suitcase in one hand.

"I rented a car in Tucson," he said. "It took me forever to get down that road. It gets worse and worse, doesn't it?"

"Yes," Connie said. "Come on in. Put your suitcase down. There's some coffee left."

Julian followed her into the kitchen.

"Are they asleep?" Julian asked.

"No, Julian," she said. "They aren't here. They left a few days ago. We had a fight."

"What happened?"

Connie looked over at him. He looked completely panicked.

"No, they're fine," she said. "Matt has spoken with Amy. She's in Scottsdale or Phoenix, either with my parents or her dad."

Julian sighed and pulled out a chair from the kitchen table and sat in it.

"Oh man," he said. "I've really blown it. I should never have let it go this far."

Connie poured them each a cup of coffee and brought the cups over to the table. Then she sat at the table with Julian.

"What do you mean? Amy didn't talk to me about what was going on with you two. She doesn't talk with me about much."

"She hates it in Boston," he said. "She wants to open a restaurant. I thought it was too risky. She just seems to go from one interest to another, so I didn't know if she was serious or not. And I've got my teaching job. I got tired of fighting, so I left."

"Ah, so you really fought for the marriage."

"Well, you tell me," Julian said. "What do you do when one person has ties to one place and the other person hates that place? How have you and Chuck worked out these things over the years?"

Connie looked at her son-in-law. She didn't know him well, and she had never particularly liked him. But then, she hadn't really liked her daughter very much either. They both seemed like know-it-alls. But maybe all along it had been her problem: She had become so insular out here in the borderlands that she didn't know how to communicate with anyone who lived in a city, or with anyone who was exposed to culture all of the time.

Not that they didn't have culture out here.

Or did they?

Wasn't the wild the opposite of culture?

No. Tame was the opposite of culture. Good culture maintained the wild, somehow, in all its creations.

Didn't it?

"Amy didn't tell you that Chuck and I split?" Connie asked. "He left me for a much younger woman. And he embezzled money from the ranch and left us nearly broke with a loan due from the bank."

Julian's mouth fell open.

"Yep," Connie said.

"You always seemed so happy."

Connie laughed. "I guess you're not a very astute observer of human nature."

"Did you see it coming?"

"Nope."

"Then I guess you're not a very astute observer of human nature either."

Connie laughed. Julian smiled.

"You've got that right," Connie said.

"I haven't spent enough time with Amy's family to know much about you," Julian said. "The desert makes me nervous."

"It should," Connie said. "It is a dangerous place."

He nodded.

"So why did she leave?" Julian said. "I thought you were getting along well this trip."

"She told you that but not about her father leaving?" Connie asked. "She's an odd duck. Well, she found out Manuel and I were having an affair. Although I don't think you can actually call it that. Our spouses left us, so we were unattached. We had sex one night and your wife accused us of having an affair before Chuck left." Connie watched his face as she told him all this.

"She's always been devoted to her father," he said. "I've never really understood it. He seemed like a lump to me."

"Amy likes lumps," Connie said. "She doesn't like anyone disagreeing with her."

"That's the truth," Julian said.

"Anyway, she didn't believe Manuel and I hadn't been having an affair all along," she said.

"I remember Manuel, vaguely," he said. "You two seemed tight. Good friends. Or was I wrong about that?"

"I've known him since we were children," she said.

"And nothing was going on between you?" he asked.

"We loved each other when we were kids," she said.

"So you've loved each other from afar."

"No," she said. "I never wanted to come back here, you know. It was Chuck's idea after Aunt Delilah left the farm to me and Phil."

"Didn't you like it here?"

"It was too wild for me," Connie said. "And too agricultural. Something. I wanted to live a different life from this one."

"But you and Manuel are together again?"

"No," Connie said. "He's mad at me because I can't remember the promises we made to each other when we were kids."

"You do remember."

Connie laughed. "Why are we having this conversation? I've never had a conversation like this with you. I haven't had a conversation like this with my own daughter."

"Do you remember?"

"I remember we were going to be together," she said. "We wanted to see the world. We wanted to search for truth and beauty. We saw a bright shiny life in front of us."

"Did you stop loving him?"

"I went to college," she said. "This place seemed so far away. And unrealistic. Out here we hunted for sea horses and dodged scorpions and rattlesnakes. This was chaos. Chuck seemed stable. Normal. Plus—plus I didn't believe him."

"Didn't believe Manuel?"

"When we talked about our lives together, he said all he wanted to do was love me," Connie said. "That was his great ambition. I suppose that's all right when you're seventeen, but you can't make a life out of that. You have to work. You have to make a living."

"You didn't think he had any other ambitions?" Julian said. "What was your ambition?"

Connie laughed again. "My ambition was exactly the same! I wanted to live with him and be his love. We wanted to find land we could protect and watch over. We wanted to have babies and love each other. That would have been great, but life doesn't work that way."

"And Chuck had ambition?"

Connie shook her head. She felt so tired. She couldn't say any more of this out loud.

"No, but I thought he would have a job," she said. "And he didn't have passion. Not for me or anything else. That felt safe, you know? Because if you lose passion, that'll break you. Sometimes having passion breaks you, too. It's like a fire burning brighter and brighter and hotter and hotter and you think it'll burn you up. I was relieved when I met Chuck. I was glad I didn't have to choose that life with Manuel."

She rested her head on the table. She wanted to cry. She felt sobs welling up inside of her, but they didn't come out. They couldn't come out.

Why couldn't she cry any more?

She lifted her head and looked at Julian.

"You're not really here, are you, Julian? So I don't have to be embarrassed about all this later."

"You shouldn't be embarrassed," he said. "You're being honest. What do you think of your choices now?"

"I can't believe this is the life I have now. I'm such a cliché." She sat up straight. "But it ain't all bad. It's all strange, but it ain't all bad. Let me show you something."

She went to the back door, and Julian followed. They looked outside.

"What's wrong with that horse?" he asked. "Is he radioactive?"

"No," she said. "She's a she. Did Amy ever tell you about her great aunt Delilah?" He shook his head. "It's a long story, but the short of it is she always believed our relatives were part mermaid and they brought sea horses across the ocean to this place."

"Sea horses?"

"Whatever that means," Connie said. "Faery horses. Magic horses. Some strange breed of regular horses. I don't know. But I found one. Her name is Sky. Go out and say hello."

"Really?" he asked.

"Yep."

She watched Julian go outside. Sky lifted her head and walked toward him. His long thin arm shook as he reached out to the horse. He began petting her. Connie watched for a bit. Then she went back to the table and left him a note, "Pick any room except the middle one on the left. See you in the morning."

Then she went to her room with Jimmy and eventually fell to sleep.

She awakened early, near dawn. She quickly got dressed and went outside. Greg, Manuel, and Matt were working over where the trucks were parked.

She walked toward them. It looked as though they had created a kind of parking lot.

"Hi, Mom," Matt said. "This should help with some of the traffic congestion."

Manuel turned around. Connie felt her stomach lurch. She smiled at him. He grinned. She hurried up to him and put her hands on his cheeks and kissed him on the lips.

"I'm so glad you're back," she said. She put her arms around him. He held her tightly for a moment. Then he released her.

"He's only been gone a couple days," Matt said. "Geez, Mom, get a grip."

Greg slugged him in the arm. "Leave her alone."

"Now that's a good son," Connie said.

"Matt told me about all the traffic," Manuel said, "and the dust. This should help. I also borrowed a van so we can bring people back and forth once the parking lot fills. That'll cut down on the dust."

Connie stepped back. "Oh. Matt called you? I thought—" She stopped. She didn't know what she thought. She gazed at Manuel. He looked like he always looked. She didn't see any sign of affection or loathing. He was just Manuel, the man she had known since he was a boy.

"Well, thanks for your help," she said.

"We're partners, remember?" he said.

"Yep," she said. She had nearly forgotten. He had invested in the ranch. Of course he wasn't going to leave. He might leave her but not this place.

"Mom, are you okay?" Matt asked.

"I'm fine," she said. "Just tired. I keep dreaming the siren is going off and I can't get there in time."

"Putting up the siren was supposed to put your mind at ease," Greg said. "Can we do anything to make you feel better?"

"I don't know," Connie said. "Can you?" She smiled. She didn't want to look at Manuel. She was embarrassed she had kissed him. "Maybe it will fade over time. Or maybe we should put up sirens every hundred feet. That way if someone's in trouble they can just push the button."

She put her fingers out, as though she was pushing the black button on the siren pole.

Help.

The front door opened and closed. The three men looked at her and then at the house.

"I had a visitor last night," Connie said.

Julian walked toward them.

"Julian," Matt said when he was close enough to recognize him. "How are you?"

The men shook hands.

"Julian, this is Greg," Connie said, "Matt's boyfriend. And this is Manuel, an old family friend. I think you've met before."

The men all shook hands.

"What's going on?" Julian asked.

"You fill him in," Connie said. "I'll make us a quick breakfast."

The people began lining up after dawn again.

Connie watched Sky. She took breaks with her. At lunchtime, she put her face in the horse's neck. It smelled more like barn than desert.

Manuel directed traffic. He brought around water. He answered questions. He was gracious and kind. He was good with people. He always had been. He looked over at her once and caught her watching him. He smiled and waved.

He had left after saying he "couldn't do this again." Now he was back. Did that mean he could do it? Or were they only friends again?

Mid-afternoon, Connie looked up to see Samantha jump out of the van and run toward her. Amy got out a moment later.

Connie crouched down. Samantha ran into her arms and knocked the two of them to the ground.

"Hello, my darlin'!" Connie said, squeezing her granddaughter. "I'm so happy you're here."

"Where's Gabriela?" Samantha asked.

"I haven't seen her lately," Connie said, "but your dad is here. He just went into the house."

Samantha jumped up and ran toward the house. Connie stood and brushed the dust from her jeans. She smiled. Man, it felt good to have that little girl around again.

"Hi, Mom," Amy said as she walked up to Connie.

"Hi, yourself," Connie said. "What are you doing back here?"

"Great welcome, Mom."

"You know what, Amy? I'm tired of your constant criticism

of everything I say and do. It's a perfectly legitimate question. Why are you here?"

"Dad said I had to leave," she said. "They live in this tiny apartment above the bar. And Grandma and Grandpa don't have room for the two of us either. So I came back here."

"You could have gone home," Connie said. "I've spoken to Julian. He told me what's going on. He treats me more like a mother than you do."

"What?" Amy said. "You two have barely spoken in seven years."

"We had a nice long talk last night," she said. "He loves you. You should try to work it out. Unless you don't love him."

"Love isn't everything," Amy said. "You've taught us that."

"Why pay any attention to me?" Connie asked. "I know nothing. Maybe love is everything. Maybe love is all there is. The rest is just . . . oatmeal."

Amy looked at her mother. Then she started to laugh. "What?"

Connie shrugged. "I don't know. That's all I could think of. Oatmeal." She started to laugh. "I never professed to be a font of wisdom."

"Oatmeal. I'll remember that." Amy looked around. "What the hell is this all about? Manuel wouldn't tell me."

"Go get your husband and daughter and I'll show you," Connie said.

"Husband? He's here?"

"He's here," Connie said. "He's in the house."

Sometime later the three of them came out of the house. Connie said, "Go show your family Sky, Julian. They'll let you take cuts."

Julian waited until the person with Sky was finished, and then he walked with Amy and Samantha up to the blue horse. Samantha squealed. Amy cried.

Samantha came running up to Connie again. "This is the horse. This is the one in the dream. She's come for you. Are you all better now?"

"Well, all these people are getting better," Connie said. "And the ranch has some extra money. Lots of things are better."

"But are you better, Grandma?"

Connie looked down at Samantha.

She sighed, then shook her head.

"No, darlin', I'm not better."

"Don't worry, Grandma," Samantha said. "It'll get better."

"I hope so," she said.

Chapter Twenty-Three

After everyone left for the day, Amy made a big dinner. She used recipes from Aunt Delilah and told stories about each dish. Connie couldn't concentrate on what she was saying. She looked around the table and saw everyone happy, healthy, together again, laughing and talking, and she felt separate from it all. Manuel squeezed her hand once and she looked over at him, but she hardly felt anything.

What was happening to her?

It felt vaguely familiar and comfortable.

She excused herself from the table and went outside to check on the horses. She felt some sense of relief or release when her feet touched the ground, when she heard the horses snorting, when she smelled the dry desert air.

What did it smell like?

Dirt?

Not like the sea.

When she'd first met Sky, she kept smelling the sea.

Now she didn't.

Sky barely glowed in the darkness.

"Are you all right, girl?" she asked Sky, who looked over at her and then nudged her. She seemed fine. Her eyes were bright, her ears forward, her muzzle soft and warm. Connie put her face in Sky's neck.

She smelled like the barn again.

"How is that possible?" Connie asked. "Don't you sleep out here? Look at me, girl. Don't lose the wild. If that starts to happen, you need to leave. You need to run like hell."

Connie went back into the house and into her room. Jimmy tried to follow her, but she didn't let him. She closed the door, sat on her bed, and stared out into the darkness outside her window.

A few minutes later, someone knocked on the door. She wanted to tell whoever it was to go away. Instead, she said, "It's open."

Manuel came into the room and closed the door behind him. He sat on the bed next to her.

"Are you all right?"

She shook her head. "I feel like I'm disappearing," she said. "I'm not sure why."

"I'm sorry I got so upset," he said. "It was just hurt feelings."

"But you were right," she said. "I couldn't commit thirty-five years ago, and I can't commit now. I'm just starting to remember things as they were. I remember how much I loved you. My whole body ached. When I went away to college, I was sick for weeks. I'd throw up before and after class. I missed you so much. I missed this place, too. I couldn't stand that feeling of needing someone so much. Of loving someone or something so much. After a while I started whispering to myself, 'I feel nothing. I feel nothing.' And it got better."

Manuel moved a strand of hair off her forehead.

"I felt the same way," he said. "Only I cried and wrote you letters. Wrote you songs. Drank some."

Connie smiled. "You were braver than I was."

Manuel shook his head. "I don't blame you. If you hadn't made the decisions you did, you wouldn't have your children, and I wouldn't have Gabriela."

"I would rather have had happiness," she said.

"So you do remember what I wanted out of life?"

She smiled. "The same thing I did. We would love each other and live our lives together. And I worried we'd end up as bag people. Or in such poverty that happiness wasn't possible."

"That never occurred to me," he said. "I knew we'd always get by."

"People do live in poverty, you know," Connie said, "even those who are in love and think nothing bad will happen."

"I never said nothing bad would happen," he said. "I just wanted us to be together. I wanted to be with you."

"That felt like too much responsibility," she said. "You were so wonderful and beautiful and spontaneous. And I was me. I figured eventually you'd be sorry. I still think that."

"I don't know what to say to that," Manuel said. "You are still beautiful and the most interesting person I've ever known. I believed that then, and I believe it now."

"But I don't feel things," Connie said. "Not like you do. I think I turned that all off and it's too late to turn it back on. I've tried."

"You've had a rough few weeks," Manuel said.

She shook her head. "I've felt this way for a while. I thought once we found the sea horses I would feel better. But I don't. In fact, I think it's worse. The Borderlands Ranchers Association has offered to buy the ranch. I'd like us to think about it."

"But we've got all these plans," Manuel said. "We haven't even started implementing them."

"Well, then, maybe you all could buy me out," she said. "I just don't think I want to be here any more."

"What about the sea horses?" Manuel asked.

"I'm not sure what to do about them," Connie said. "I need to sleep on it."

"Let me stay with you," Manuel said.

She shook her head. "I want to be alone. In fact, I wish everyone would just leave."

"No," Manuel said. "I'm not leaving you alone again. I'll sit in the chair all night if you like, but I'm not leaving you. You sound too depressed."

"All right," Connie said. "But come to bed with me. If I've got some man meat in bed with me, I might as well take advantage."

Manuel laughed. "At least you haven't lost your sense of humor."

"Who's kidding?" she said.

Connie woke up in the middle of the night. She got out of bed and went into the kitchen.

Something felt off. Strange.

Maybe it was because she still had some of Chuck's belongings in the house.

She got a box from the laundry room and began walking through the house looking for things that reminded her of him. His phone. In the office she found a photo of him out hunting. A photo of him on his horse. An old key chain. Nail clippers in the bathroom. She went into the kitchen and opened the junk drawer.

That damn lock was still there. The one where the combination was Amy's birthday, Matt's birthday, and her own—only it wasn't hers. It was his birthday. Because they were soul mates.

Hah!

She dropped the lock into the box.

She opened the front door and put the box on the porch.

She stepped outside.

It was cold, but not as cold as yesterday or the night before. Summer was coming to the desert.

She walked around the house to go see Sky.

The horse wasn't there.

Connie looked around for the glow. She couldn't see it anywhere.

"Sky?" she called.

The horse nickered. Connie walked over to the corral. Sky was in the corral with Bear and Loosey.

"What are you doing in there?" Connie asked.

She went to the gate and opened it up. Bear and Loosey trotted out. Connie reached for their halters to stop them from going further. Sky came out, too.

Connie turned Bear and Loosey around, and they went back into the corral. Sky started to follow them.

"No," Connie said. "You don't belong there."

Sky looked at her and nudged her chest.

"You don't belong there," Connie said again, "and you don't belong here." The horse looked at her. "You've got to leave here. Go find your tribe. Your herd. I know Samantha believes you came here to help me, but it's not working. You've helped a lot of other people, but I think it's draining you. I think it's taming you. I want you to go back into the wild."

Connie walked away from the corral and out into the desert. She looked back. Sky followed her. When they were a ways from the house, Connie said, "Go on. Go find what you lost."

Then she slapped the horse on the rear. Sky galloped away. Connie stood for a while in the darkness, listening to the horse run. She listened to see if the hoof beats were coming back toward her, but she heard nothing.

The horse was gone.

After a while, Connie turned around and went back into the house.

In the morning, Connie got up early to see if Sky had returned. She had not. She went out and closed the gate to the ranch. She wrote out a sign that read: "Sky has gone back to her herd" and she hung it on the gate.

When she went back into the house, everyone was sitting around the kitchen table, except for Manuel who was just walking into the kitchen.

"Sky is gone," Connie said. "And I hope she stays away. She started smelling like the barn. She was losing her glow."

Her family stared at her.

"Come on," Connie said. "We couldn't have kept doing this forever. The media was bound to come out. That much publicity wouldn't be good for anyone's quality of life."

"Sky is a wild thing," Manuel said. "It is good she's gone back to the wild."

"Where is Gabriela?" Samantha asked.

"She is with her mother," Manuel said.

Connie looked at him. "I hadn't even asked about her," she said. "I'm so sorry. My mind is so preoccupied. Is she staying with her mother for good? Or have you two gotten back together?"

Everyone at the breakfast table looked at her.

"What?" she asked.

"You two just spent the night together and now you're asking that question?" Amy asked.

"What your mom does or doesn't do is her business," Julian said.

"Speaking of what's my business," Connie said. "Are you two back together?"

"We're working on it," Amy said. "Manuel, are you back with your wife?"

"No," Manuel said. "Gabriela is with her mother, and she'll be returning today. All is good."

"You seem so sanguine about it," Matt said. "She left you for another man."

Manuel went to the stove and got a plate for himself and one for Connie. He scooped scrambled eggs from the pan and put some on each plate. Then he carried the plates to the table. The others moved over to make room.

"I never really loved her," Manuel said as he sat down at the table. "It wasn't fair to her. I have loved your mother since we were children. I couldn't help it."

"And you, Mom?" Amy asked.

"Are you going to stomp out of here if I tell you the truth?" Connie asked. She sat at the table next to Manuel.

"I'll try not to," Amy said.

"I loved Manuel when we were kids," she said. "But I wasn't able to commit to him. I was afraid of our life together. Your mother is not a very brave woman. Your father was safe. He never loved me too much, and I never loved him too much."

"That's awful," Amy said.

Connie shrugged.

"I still can't commit to Manuel," she said, "or to any part of my life. I really don't know what I want. But I think I want to leave this place. I think I'd like to take the Borderlands Ranchers up on their offer to buy this place. Or you all can buy me out. I didn't want to be here thirty years ago, and I don't want to be here now. Running this ranch was your dad's idea, not mine."

"You didn't want to come back to the ranch because you still loved Manuel," Amy said. "You didn't want to face him or the life you'd given up."

"That's probably true," Connie said. "But it's all water under the bridge. I just don't think I can make this transition. I don't know where I fit in. So maybe I should take some money and wander the world for a while."

"We couldn't afford to buy the ranch," Matt said. "If you go, everything we've planned on doing goes away."

Connie pushed the plate away from her.

"That's too much responsibility," Connie said. "It's so much land. It's been damaged by the cattle. It's our responsibility to bring it back. To protect the wildlife. To keep people from dying. To be here for one another. And I don't know if I can do any of that."

"Can you think about it?" Matt asked. "We've got so much riding on this."

"Of course," Connie said. She wanted to sound reasonable, but she felt so sad that she could barely stand being in the room with any of them.

"The people are going to start coming looking for Sky this morning," Connie said. "So Matt and Amy, could you call people and ask them to spread the word? Tell them that Sky has left. I closed the gate and put up a sign."

"And then I'm going into town," Amy said. "We have absolutely no food."

"You're staying?" Connie asked. "Don't you have to get back to school, Julian?"

"We're on break," he said. "Besides, I want to be with my family."

"We're not leaving you, Mom," Matt said. "If you feel bad or depressed or whatever, that's all right. We're here with you. Whatever you need."

"What if I need you to go away?" Connie asked.

"Except that," Matt said. "Although Greg and I need to go into town, too. And if you're serious about getting rid of the ranch, you're going to have to break it to Uncle Phil and Aunt

Marilyn. They're all excited about starting that training in a couple weeks."

"Yeah, and the permaculture gang is supposed to come out next weekend," Greg said. "And the architect."

"I get it," Connie said. "I'll disappoint a lot of people. I can't think about that right now."

"Grandma, are you sad because Sky left?" Samantha asked. "Haven't you been looking for her your whole life?"

Connie sighed. "I'm glad I found her," she said. "Or she found me. But it was time for her to go. I told her to go."

"And she did what you said?" Samantha's eyes opened wide.

"It's in Connie's blood," Manuel said. He stood and began picking up dishes. "It's in your blood, too, Samantha, and Amy's as well. Your grandma Consuelo is a siren. She sings to the wild things, she wrangles sea horses and dust storms. She directs coyote choruses and bargains with ravens. She does not hear the call of the wild. She is the call of the wild."

Connie felt a chill go up her spine. Everyone stopped and looked at Manuel.

"Where did you hear that?" Connie asked.

"I didn't hear it," Manuel said. "I know it. I've always known it. Your aunt Delilah knew it, too."

"Hmm," Amy said. "She doesn't seem wild. She seems tame."

"Don't talk about me like I'm not here," Connie said.

"Sorry, Mom," Amy said. "We better get going. Anyone have money for food?"

"I've got plenty," Julian said. "Any requests?"

Connie's children and their loved ones walked to the front door and out into the morning. Jimmy followed them.

Manuel stood next to Connie.

She looked at him.

"Is that how you see me?" she asked.

"Yes, because it's the truth," he said.

She shook her head. "No, it's not."

"It's how you finally brought Sky to you," he said. "It is how you will find your way again." He took her hand. "I need to go home for a short time. Isabella is bringing Gabriela back. I won't be long."

Manuel kissed her forehead.

"I love you deeply with my one wild heart," he said. "And all I want is to be with you for the rest of my life."

Connie nodded.

"That's what I said back then," he said.

"I know," she said. "I remember."

"It's still true," he said.

Then he left.

Connie finished picking up the kitchen. She did the dishes. She liked the quiet now after days of chaos. She took a shower and got dressed. Then she went outside. She looked down and saw the box of Chuck's stuff. She should have had Matt take it to the dump. Or somewhere else.

It was strange to be outside, alone, after days of having so many people coming and going. Whoever had left last had forgotten to close the gate and someone was coming down the drive. Dust billowed up around a turquoise-colored vintage car.

How had they ever gotten a car like that down that road?

Connie squinted. It was a Thunderbird.

The car came through the open gates. Jimmy ran out of the house and toward the vehicle, barking, his tail wagging.

The car did a U-turn so that the driver's side was closest to Connie.

She stood on the porch watching. She could hear her heart in her ears.

The passenger door opened, and Isabella stepped out. Connie

had forgotten how beautiful she was. How young she was. Was it any wonder that Chuck preferred her?

Gabriela must have gotten out of the car, too, because she was running toward Connie. When she reached Connie, she wrapped her arms around her.

"Hi, Consuelo," Gabriela said. "I'm back. Have you missed me? Where's Samantha? Hi, Jimmy. Is Sky still here?"

"No, honey," Connie said. "Sky is gone for now. Yes, I missed you. Samantha will be back. Why don't you and Jimmy go inside. I'll be there in a minute."

"I thought Manuel would be here," Isabella said. She stayed on her side of the car.

"He said he was meeting you at the house," Connie said.

Why wasn't Chuck getting out of the car? Was he too much of a coward to face her?

"Oh," Isabella said. "We got it wrong. We heard about the blue horse."

"You want to see the blue horse?" Connie said. "Chuck will have to get out of the car to see it."

"He won't get out," Isabella said. "Should we take Gabriela to the house?"

"I'll call Manuel," Connie said.

Connie kept staring at the window on the driver's side. She saw a shadow inside, nothing else.

Her heart was beating so fast.

She looked at Isabella.

Then at the car.

This was what he had left her for. This woman and this car?

This was what he had destroyed their family for?

Connie suddenly felt so angry she could barely see.

She bent over and picked up the box and started to walk toward the car.

"Hey, asshole," Connie said. "You left some of your crap

here. It's bad enough you stole from me, but you left your junk here."

Isabella disappeared from view. Chuck must have told her to get in the car. He started the car.

"Don't run away from me, you coward," Connie said. She had no idea what she was saying or what she was doing. She just couldn't stand the idea that he wouldn't face her.

He couldn't even look at her?

The car started moving forward.

Connie reached into the box. She wrapped her fingers around the combination lock and took it out of the box. She let the box drop. Its contents spilled out on the desert floor. She ran toward the car as Chuck tried to race away.

"Here's your stupid lock with its stupid combination," she said. "I am not your soul mate or any kind of mate!" She screamed this as she threw the closed combination lock at his window. The lock hit the window. The glass shattered.

When Connie heard the glass break, she suddenly felt like herself again.

The car jerked to a stop. Isabella screamed.

Oh crap. It was an old car. No shatterproof glass.

Connie ran to the car.

Blood was streaming down Chuck's face.

"Can you see?" she asked. "Did it get in your eyes?"

"Not that I can tell," he said. "But there's a lot of blood."

"I looks like a piece got near your eye," she said. She pulled a shard of glass from just above his left eyebrow. She got a handkerchief from her jean pocket and pressed it against the cut. "Hold this against your face. Get out of the car. I'll bandage you up."

"She's crazy," Isabella said. "Don't let her touch you!"

"Isabel," Chuck said. "She won't hurt me. Is it bad?"

He had never liked blood.

"You might need stitches."

She heard a truck and looked up.

Manuel.

Thank goodness.

He stopped the truck next to the Thunderbird.

"What happened?" he asked as he got out of the truck.

"I lost my temper," she said. "And Chuck got hurt. I think he needs stitches."

"Doesn't look like he can drive," Manuel said. "I'll take them into town. Come on, Chuck. Isabella. Where's Gabriela? Can you take care of her, Connie?"

"Sure," she said.

She heard her phone ringing.

She listened.

It wasn't the phone. It was the siren.

She and Manuel ran toward the house.

"Come take us from this place!" Isabella called. "She's gone loco! He's going to bleed to death."

"Oh shut up," Connie said. "He'll be fine."

Connie and Manuel went into the house. Gabriela and Jimmy stood in the kitchen looking at the siren box. Connie pressed the button, to let whoever it was know she was on her way.

"You better take Gabriela with you," Connie said.

"You gonna take the horse or truck?"

"I think the horse will be faster," Connie said.

Manuel kissed her. "Be careful, my desert siren. I'll come out as soon as I'm through."

They ran out of the house again. Connie went to the barn and called to Loosey. Manuel drove away with Chuck, Isabella, and Gabriela. Connie put a couple bottles of water into her saddle bags, next to a bag of trail mix that was already there.

Then she and Loosey headed out in to the warm day.

They hurried toward Box Canyon, toward the siren call. Jimmy ran ahead some and then doubled back. From habit, Connie watched for the blue shoe. She watched for wild horse tracks that disappeared into thin desert air, too.

The mountains looked like slouching giants, waiting for someone to pass them a beer, a remote, a wild life.

A hawk flew overhead for a while.

Then a vulture.

She saw the siren in the distance.

Then the sand bar.

Then a figure of a woman slouched over, near the siren pole.

Connie reined in Loosey and then dismounted. She got the water and trail mix and walked toward the woman.

Connie glanced around.

The trunk was gone. She didn't see it anywhere.

Had someone actually stolen the trunk?

They had picked up the entire thing and hauled it away? Where to?

She couldn't think about that now.

"Hola," Connie said. "Are you all right?"

The woman raised her head. She looked about eighteen years old. She was wearing black shorts and a purple short sleeve top. Sandals. Her eye makeup had left smears of black beneath her eyes. Connie remembered when she was in high school they used to call those raccoon eyes.

What a strange thing to remember.

Someone needed to tell those who walked betwixt and between that they needed to dress for it.

"Did you need water?" Connie asked. She held the bottle out to the girl. The girl took it, unscrewed the top, threw the top on the ground, and then began gulping the water.

Connie picked up the plastic top and put it in her pocket.

"I've got food, too," Connie said. She held out the bag of trail mix.

The girl snatched the bag from Connie and then emptied most of the bag into her hand and began eating it from her palm.

"You're all right now," Connie said. "I'll call Border Patrol and they can come take you home."

The girl looked around and saw Connie's horse. Her eyes narrowed and she looked up at Connie. Connie wondered if the girl was reevaluating every decision she had ever made.

Did people do that at her age? They probably figured they had forever to make up for whatever mistakes they had made.

"No truck?" the girl asked. Her accent was thick. English was not her first language.

"No," Connie said. It hadn't occurred to her that she might have to take the person in trouble somewhere.

That had been stupid of her.

They didn't usually transport any of the migrants who crossed their ranches. They called Border Patrol.

The girl pushed herself up. She staggered slightly. Connie reached out to help her, but the woman backed away. She drank the rest of the water, then threw the bottle on the ground. She grabbed the other bottle of water from Connie and then started to walk away.

"Wait," Connie said. "You need help. It's too hot to keep going on your own."

Connie touched her arm.

"Don't touch," she said.

"Wait."

Connie put her hand on her arm again.

"Let go," the young woman said.

Connie held on tighter.

The young woman turned around and punched Connie in the face.

The punch was so hard, it knocked Connie onto the ground.

The woman walked away into the desert.

Jimmy began barking. Loosey trotted away. Was she going after the woman? Going back to the barn?

Loosey never ran away.

Maybe she had spotted Sky and wanted to join her in the wild.

Connie put her hand up to her nose.

It was bleeding.

"Christ on a crutch," Connie said. "She better not have broken my nose. I was trying to help, you little asshole!" she screamed. "Loosey! Get back here."

She'd given her handkerchief to Chuck.

She leaned her head back while she unbuttoned her shirt. She took the shirt off and pressed it against her nose.

"Talk about instant fucking karma," she said.

She started to laugh.

It hurt.

She looked around.

She was all alone on this little sand bar in the desert, next to a pole with a siren on it.

Jimmy and Loosey had deserted her.

Stupid girl she was trying to help punched her freaking lights out.

"Let go," the girl had said.

Let go.

Connie closed her eyes.

Let go.

She was never going to change the past.

She had made her decision.

She had shut down.

For thirty years, she had lived with a man who didn't love her.

Maybe he loved her.

Did it matter?

What about now?

Let go.

Let go.

Let go.

She felt sadness welling up inside of her again.

Sadness for what she had lost.

All those years.

All that passion.

All that wildness.

It was gone. She was white-haired. She was a grandmother. She was a dried up old hag.

She heard Manuel's voice in her head, *"Consuelo is a siren. She sings to the wild things, she wrangles sea horses and dust storms. She directs coyote choruses and bargains with ravens. She does not hear the call of the wild. She is the call of the wild."*

"No, I'm not."

The sun beat down on her. The sand beneath her fingers was hot.

I'm not wild.

She could see Manuel in her mind's eye. She could see herself. The two of them. Standing on the banks of the sometimes river. She stood on a huge old rock, her arms extended to the sky, and she was howling as the sun went down. Manuel laughed as he watched her, and then he joined her.

She could see herself running. Running through the desert. She was a coyote, jaguar, bobcat, gazelle.

No one could catch her.

Sometimes when she was near the water, she felt as though she was remembering something. An old song. A chant? A memory of another time.

How had she ended up in this place, all alone, punched in the face?

Let go.

Sadness spilled over. Out. She began to cry.

Tears streamed down her cheeks. Her tears fell on the sand and mixed with the blood from her nose.

Her body began to shake. She began to wail.

She couldn't breathe she cried so hard.

How could she have let Manuel go? How could she have left him behind?

And the sea horses: How could she have ever forgotten them? How could she have left them, even when she returned?

They were magic, and she had lost them—had never found them. Her entire family had lost them.

Had she and her family forgotten how to protect? How to love? How to feel in their wild hearts?

She opened her mouth and sobbed.

How could she have shut herself off from the passion she felt for the world?

Because it was too difficult to be in love with the world when everyone around her wasn't.

Except for Manuel.

They could have been in love with the world together.

She hadn't been brave enough. She hadn't been able to make the leap.

Take the leap.

Sing the song.

Her siren song.

Her wail turned into a wordless song, just like the one she had sung before when she had been in this place.

She stood and opened her arms wide. Her shirt fell to the ground. She hoped the bleeding had stopped. She sang and sang. The sound vibrated through her whole body, down her legs and into her feet.

The desert vibrated with her song.

The song of herself.

The world?

She cried and laughed and sang.

She saw a girl at the edge of her vision.

It was Rosalia. "Hello, *Señora,*" the girl said. "Thank you for all you have done. I run with the sea horses now." She wore a blue dress, just like Connie had imagined. Another girl stood next to Rosalia. She was older. They held hands. The other girl smiled at Connie. Was she eighteen? Her hair was long and kinky, just as Connie's had been at her age.

"You'll do all right," the girl said.

"Are you off to run with the horses now?" Connie asked.

"I guess so," the girl said.

"Doesn't that mean you're dead?" Connie asked. "Doesn't that mean I'm dead?"

The girl laughed. Rosalia and the girl squeezed hands.

"Look, I could never do what you're doing," the girl said. "I never had a siren song."

They turned and ran. Disappeared. Like wisps of smoke.

Connie's feet felt wet. She looked down.

Water was bubbling up from the ground near her.

"What?"

Was this part of the hallucination, too?

She leaned over and put her hand in the water.

It was a pretty realistic hallucination.

She smelled the sea.

Heard hoof beats.

Felt an ocean breeze.

She stepped back, away from the water which was several inches deep now, and stood on the high part of the sand berm.

And suddenly she was surrounded by water—and a herd of colored horses, their hooves sounding like thunder on the desert floor. The horses ran together, in a circle around Connie, their colors flowing together like paint on an abstract art piece, only this art piece was moving—beautiful streaks of blue, turquoise, orange, yellow, black, white, red.

The horses whinnied. They snorted. They slowed until they each stopped at the edge of the new pond and sipped the new water. Connie watched them and sang softly. Sky broke from the herd and walked through the shallow water toward Connie. When she reached her, the horse bumped her in the chest.

"Hello, Sky," Connie said. She put her arms around the horse's neck. Sky whinnied.

"I'm glad to see you're back with your tribe," Connie said. "I called you with my song again, didn't I? And now what do I do with you?"

She gazed at the herd of sea horses. They looked so solid and real, yet she felt certain they could disappear any moment.

"I don't need to do anything with you," Connie said. "I can just protect your existence. Your right to your wild life." Connie kissed the horse's muzzle.

Other horses began coming up to her. They walked closely to her, sometimes bumping her, like fish in a pond. She had never seen a horse so black. Anything so yellow—like the sun. Any animal so turquoise.

And they walked in and out of the water, and Connie wasn't quite sure but it seemed like each time they walked in or near the water they became part fish—their legs shapeshifting into tails—and when she let the water touch her feet, she felt herself shifting, changing, too. She laughed and kept one hand on the back of a horse—whichever horse was near her—to steady herself.

Then she realized Loosey had returned, only she wasn't wearing her saddle or bridle. And her black was the blackest black, except for the spots beneath. When she neared the water, she changed.

Or maybe the whole world had changed.

Connie was hallucinating on this hot day. Or she wasn't.

Loosey's fetlock hair was orange. How had Connie never noticed that before?

Loosey nudged her.

"So you're one of them," Connie said.

"Wow," someone said.

Connie turned around.

Manuel was standing on the other side of the herd, on the other side of the new pond. Connie felt her heart in her throat. She remembered how she had felt every time she had seen Manuel when she was a girl. She remembered how she had felt every time she had seen him since then—and how she had stuffed it down.

Ah, he was beautiful.

Connie stepped down into the ankle-deep water.

"I love you with my one wild heart," she called to him. "For always. I want to live with you and be your love."

He smiled. "What happened to your nose?" he asked.

"The woman I came to help punched me in the face," she said. "That's what I get for being a pretentious asshole thinking I could save the world with a desert siren. She punched me and then she walked into the desert. We should probably go looking for her."

"Why?" Manuel said. "I don't want to get punched in the face."

Connie laughed.

Matt walked up and stood next to Manuel. Connie's love for her son welled up inside of her. And there was Greg. She loved him, too, for loving her son. And Samantha. Man, she adored her. And Amy. Amy smiled and waved.

"I love you with my one wild heart, daughter of mine," Connie said.

Amy put her hand over her mouth in surprise. Her eyes watered.

"It's all right, darlin'," Connie said. "This pond is made from all my tears and a bit of my blood. Tears help us remember our siren songs."

Julian and Gabriela were there, too.

"I love you all," Connie said. "How is Chuck?"

"He'll live," Manuel said.

Connie threw back her head and laughed.

Her family and Manuel, Gabriela, and Greg began walking toward her, through the water and the herd of sea horses. The horses didn't seem to mind.

"What are we going to do with them?" Amy asked.

"Nothing," Connie said. "But I wonder what they're going to do with us."

"I guess this means we're keeping the ranch," Matt said.

"I guess so," Connie said.

"Have you figured out your job?" Matt asked. "You said you didn't know what your place was in all of this."

"Hmm," Connie said. "I don't know that you'd call it a job, but I'll be the Desert Siren, resident wild woman. One of at least three. Maybe four, if Gabriela wants to join us."

"Yes," Gabriela said. "Can we ride the horses sometimes across the great old sea desert?"

"If they let us."

"What about you, Manuel?" Connie asked.

Manuel finally reached Connie and took her in his arms. "You know the answer to that," he said. He kissed her on the mouth. She held him tight.

"Grandma," Samantha said. "Look what I found."

Manuel and Connie let go of one another. Connie looked down at her granddaughter, who had waded into the water to be next to her.

Samantha held out a small blue cotton shoe to her grandmother.

"It was floating in the water," Samantha said.

Connie looked at Manuel and then back at Samantha. Connie took the shoe from Samantha. It felt light as a feather in her hand, even though it was damp.

"Is this the blue shoe you've been looking for?" Samantha asked. "The one the girl lost?"

"I believe it is," Connie said.

"Do you want to save it and give it back to her?" Samantha asked.

"We could take it up to the grotto," Manuel said.

Connie shook her head. "No, she doesn't need it any more," she said. "And neither do I."

She reached back, as far as she could, and then she flung the blue shoe up into the air. It went so high up it became part of the blue blue sky.

About the Author

Kim Antieau has written many novels, short stories, poems, and essays. Her work has appeared in numerous publications, both in print and online, including *The Magazine of Fantasy and Science Fiction, Asimov's SF, The Clinton Street Quarterly, The Journal of Mythic Arts, EarthFirst!, Alternet, Sage Woman,* and *Alfred Hitchcock's Mystery Magazine.* She was the founder, editor, and publisher of *Daughters of Nyx: A Magazine of Goddess Stories, Mythmaking, and Fairy Tales.* Her work has twice been short-listed for the Tiptree Award, and has appeared in many Best of the Year anthologies. Critics have admired her "literary fearlessness" and her vivid language and imagination. Her first novel *The Jigsaw Woman* is a modern classic of feminist literature. She has also written *The Gaia Websters, The Fish Wife,* and *Church of the Old Mermaids.* Kim lives in the Pacific Northwest with her husband, writer Mario Milosevic. Learn more about Kim and her writing at www.kimantieau.com.